MW00883135

on the *line*

JACKIE NASTRI BARDENWERPER

For more information:

www.jnbwrite.com

On The Line

ISBN 978-1470120191

To my mom, for teaching me to write. To my dad, for teaching me to fish. And to my husband, for never letting me give up.

.

CHAPTER ONE

Benny tells me about Marina just as a bonefish takes my line.

"So Piper, she said yes last night," he says, as my rod bends downward.

I breathe in deep and grip the rod tight as the fish dashes toward the weeds. "Uh, that's great," I say through gritted teeth.

He beams. "Isn't it? I took your advice and asked last night, when we were hanging out at Rosalie's. And she didn't even blink. Apparently she already thought she was my girlfriend."

"See, I told you," I say between huffs and I think I mean it too, at least in an if-Benny's-happy-then-I'm-happy sort of way, but as I struggle to bring in one of the strongest fish in the Florida Keys, it's too hard to string together the words to tell him.

"I'm taking her to dinner tonight, but I don't know where to go. I want to stay on Islamorada, but I want it to be special too. Not just another night at Rosalie's, you know," Benny says, as he leans back in the captain's seat bolted down in the center of my 12' Boston Whaler.

He starts listing restaurants rapid fire as if I'm listening, but all I hear is his rising voice. And see a whole lot of dollar signs that we're supposed to be saving.

"I thought we were saving our money for the Bonefish Scramble entry fee?" I say, reminding him of the fishing tournament that's supposed to make us $25,000 richer.

If we win, anyway.

But Benny doesn't respond. He just keeps blabbing about how Marina is so cool. She wears the best perfume. Tells the funniest jokes. Throws the coolest parties at her mom's hotel, the Becco Lodge.

I sigh, remembering how up until last month Marina didn't even know Benny's name. But this I don't bring up. Because no matter how many times I tell him that dating Marina is strange, that golden haired beach bum Marina will never be part of our catch-it-or-lose-it fishing culture, he just doesn't listen.

Which is why I told him to ask her out in the first place. For whatever reason, she has been showing him interest. And at least if they're dating, well that's one less annoying conversation Benny can dwell on. Or, so I thought. Right now his gushing might be even more annoying.

So I try to tune him out and focus on reeling in my line. But as the fish nears the boat, I start to panic. Because Benny is still sitting there in the captain's chair, instead of hovering over me with a net.

"Hey, a little help?" I ask as he flings his flip flops off his feet with his toes.

"Yeah, some help. That's what I was asking for. You're a girl, Pipes, where would you like to go..."

Ugh, there he goes. Back to the dinner reservation. "No. I need help. Now. Don't you see the fish?"

Benny sits up, blinks, then rubs his eyes before walking toward the aft of the boat to grab the net.

By now the fish is fighting again, cutting through the water like a torpedo racing away from the boat at full speed.

"Forget this," I say as I let my rod bend for just long enough to stop the burning in my arms. Then with Benny still fiddling for the net and going on about Marina — which is really testing my nerves seeing as Marina still has made no effort to be nice even though she's dating my best friend - I lower myself off the bow and into a bed of grassy weeds submerged in chest-deep water.

"Piper, what are you doing? I said I was getting the net," Benny says, walking toward the bow.

"The fish was running. I couldn't wait," I say, though we both know that landing a bonefish in the water is no easier than netting it from a boat.

The only benefit to being in the water right now is it gets me away from Benny. And all this talk about his new girlfriend.

With more freedom to follow the fish, I reel in my line and walk in his direction until his shimmering body glides by, his stroke looking effortless as he sends ripples through the sparkling, purplish water. I admire his slender body before taking in the slack and reaching for the spot where the line disappears into the water.

Wrapping my hand around the line, I bring it, and the fish hooked to the end of it, toward me, wishing with every splash that I'd remembered to wear gloves. But of course, my hands are bare and the line slices them like a knife cutting into a ripe tomato.

"Ah, that hurts," I say, as every nerve in my palm fires hot against my skin. Yet despite the pain, I don't let go. Because there's nothing worse than losing a fish. Especially over a little burn.

"Hang on, Pipes, I got it," Benny says from the boat. He's leaning over the edge now, net in hand.

"You'll never get him that way. You have to jump in

the water," I say.

"No way. The water's full of weeds."

I sigh. Benny has never been one for swimming in the weeds.

"Well we're going to lose the fish," I say as my hand gives out, letting the line fly free.

"Not a chance, watch this." Benny creeps off the bow another inch then swoops down toward the water, netting my bonefish in one motion.

It's the move of an expert, but then seeing as Benny's spent almost every minute of his life on the water with me since we were six years old, it makes sense. When it comes to catching bonefish, Benny is a lot like me. A pro.

"So, you thought you could land him on your own, huh?" he says, grabbing my rod from my hands.

"I would've had him," I say, pulling my cracked palms down to my waist. The salt water burns the chafed skin, but as usual I don't cry out. Instead I let Benny place my rod down on the bow and wait to feel his arms around me, hoisting me out of the water.

They're Marina's arms now, I think, as he locks his fingers behind me and pulls. Not that I really care whose arms they are. As long as next time he's quicker with the net.

The bonefish thrashes in the bottom of the boat as I inch toward him, then work the hook out of his mouth. Benny waits with the scale behind me, ready to record what is easily the biggest catch of the day. Maybe week.

"Ten point two pounds," he says, and for a moment the gleam in his eyes tells me he's immersed in nothing but the fish. "Geez Pipes, you catch one of these during the Scramble and we just might win that prize."

"That's the plan."

"What did Wyatt win with last year anyway? A twelve pounder?"

"Something like that," I say, knowing full well that Wyatt Jacoby, superstar fisherman extraordinaire and host of the Expedition Channel *Fishernational* series, beat out us locals with a bonefish weighing in at 12.8 pounds. Not a monster, but no baby either. "And I bet this year he gets one even bigger. Rumor has it he spent some time fishing for bonefish this spring in the Bahamas."

"Yeah, I remember," Benny says, and just as fast as the gleam appeared it's gone. And this time he doesn't even mention Marina.

For a moment I wish he would, but I know that by mentioning the Bahamas, I've broken the spell. Because we both know that the only reason Wyatt Jacoby's off practicing in the Bahamas instead of Islamorada, the Sport Fishing Capital of the World, is because of last winter's oil spill. The one that's still got tourists scared six months later. Even though the scientists keep preaching that it had no lasting effects. Which is pretty much true, minus the disappearance of my beloved sea turtles that is, and even then their population numbers were weak before the spill. At least that's what the marine biologists said at Turtle Save just before shuttering their doors and boarding a plane to another coastline full of turtles that still needed them.

But knowing that the fish are swimming and anemones swaying does little to calm those of us living above water. People like Benny's parents, who run a restaurant in town. Or my mom and dad, who have lived off teaching tourists how to catch bonefish since before I could even swim.

"So do you think we can get in a swim at the ledge now?" Benny asks, eying the tips of the sea grasses breaking through the waves. "The water's so much cleaner there, you know."

I smile, happy he's changed the subject. "Not cleaner. Just less weeds, which are vital to the ecosystem."

"Yeah, yeah, whatever. Right now I don't care what they're good for. I just want to swim."

With the sun bringing us what's got to be another 100-degree day, it's hard not to agree with the idea of swimming in cool, deep water. But with the tide almost low, our swim will have to wait. Because low tide means reconnaissance, which is probably the most important part of my entire fishing practice.

It's more like fish research really, but I started calling it that back when I was a kid, and it kind of stuck. It started out as a way I could help Dad with his fishing charter business, by learning about the changing coastline. After storms and before fishing seasons started, I'd scope out new coves and weedy areas where fish might congregate. After a few years, I found that I could tell what kind of fish would frequent what kind of area, not just based on the weeds or bottom, but on the other creatures living there. And that's how me and Benny took to scoping out different coves each low tide we could, diving right into the weeds when the water was low and the fishing bad – most fish follow the tide out to deeper water – looking for remnants of shrimp. Crabs. Tiny fish. Anything bigger fish might eat.

"Maybe we can go swimming after I check out this cove," I say, hoping to appease Benny. "I think we still have some time before we need to help my dad with his 1:00 charter."

But Benny frowns. "You just caught a fish here. Doesn't that prove this is a good spot?"

"One fish in three hours doesn't mean anything except that more research is needed."

"Come on, Pipes, do you think the tourists are going to care if they don't catch the world's biggest bonefish?"

"Maybe not, but my dad's paying us to help him and we need to do a good job. Not to mention that this data is the only thing we'll have going into the Scramble that Wyatt Jacoby and the others won't."

"I guess," Benny says, "though I still wish we could go swimming."

"We will, after we finish work," I say, then dive into the shallows, finding my footing on a smooth bed of rocks.

"So if you're not gonna come in, can you throw me my mask?" I say after catching my breath.

"Sure," he says, tossing my goggles to the left of my open hands. A breaking swell coats each lens in a thin layer of salt and seaweed.

"And you say you're going out for football this year. Not with that aim," I say, letting my words burn just a little less than the salt trickling off my mask and into my eyes.

"Not everyone in football throws the ball," he says.

"Right, well, I still think you should stick with swimming. You almost made varsity last year, as a freshman."

"I already told you. No one watches swimming. Football is the sport." He says this matter-of-factly, sounding a lot like me when I'm talking about the shrimp carcasses in the grasses.

"I'm diving under now, okay? Keep an eye out."

Benny nods as I take a deep breath and start

swimming. With no snorkel chaining me to the surface, I fan my arms and kick my legs until my face is flush with the bottom. Bits of coral, broken loose from a recent storm, sway gently in the waning current. A flounder, covered in sand and crushed shells, leaps from the bottom as my hand floats over his hiding place. Besides the coral and the rocks and the flounder, there is little else. Despite the tall grasses, there are no shrimp or crabs.

Before surfacing for air, I force myself to look around one last time. To focus on what I'm doing now. Not on Benny or Marina or the tournament. But the truth is that these days all I can think about is the Scramble and that $25,000 prize. Sure, Dad says not to worry about money, that he and Mom will always have enough for fresh fish on our dinner plates and even that marine biology degree I'm banking on, as long as I go in-state and keep my grades up enough to get a partial scholarship. But it's hard not to see that there's been a change. One that's evident in every shuttered store window. On every vacancy sign. Deserted restaurant. And empty charter trip.

Full out of air, I dart to the surface, take six deep breaths, and then hold in the last one. Before Benny can make out my tangled web of hair, I'm back under, moving deeper into the grasses.

As I swim over a patch of loose sand, I begin to relax. Searching for bonefish always lifts my mood.

Probably because the bonefish is so much like me. He doesn't like the deep waters or choppy waves or big prey. He's a homebody, weaving in and out of the muddy flats surrounding the island. He lives for the weedy shallows and prides himself on intelligence, on his ability to swoop into the shallows and round up a whole school of brine shrimp for dinner. It figures we share the same taste in food, too.

A little farther from the boat, I come across a colony of banded coral shrimp, small tiny creatures with long alien antennas that tend to inhabit areas full of fire coral and other pain-inflicting animals. Knowing coral shrimp are not a bonefish's favorite dinner — technically, they're not even shrimp, but crustaceans — I back away slowly so as not to disturb them. After last week's encounter with a sea anemone, the last thing I need is another run-in with a stinging bottom dweller. But as usual, I've ventured too close.

As I back out of the grasses, my hand hits a hydroid, a slender, seaweed-looking thing, with a punch even stronger than the anemone. It shoots a stream of poison into my hand, sending a numbing pain down my arm.

I burst through the water and gulp down a breath of air. "Stupid hydroids," I yell, shaking my hand.

"Get you again?" asks Benny from the boat.

I paddle back toward the Whaler as Benny jumps off the bench seat and starts fumbling for my spray bottle of vinegar. His shirt is off now and his brown stomach muscles are glistening with a layer of sweat. Not that I'm trying to look with him dating Marina and all, but what can I say? It's impossible to miss.

"Want me to throw the bottle?" Benny asks as I grab the side of the boat.

"Nah, help me in. This spot still looks dead. Just a bunch of those stinking coral shrimp."

"It's weird that last year this spot was so hot." Benny offers his hands and I grab on, then jump off the bottom as he pulls me back into the boat. Again, his muscles tense. I try not to look.

"These fish are smart," I say once I'm back in the boat. "They know when they're being stalked. It's why they change it up so many times. Why the fish finders just don't work."

Benny hands me the vinegar and I spray it onto my hand, waiting for the pain to dull. As my nerves relax, so does my brain. Benny's reaching for his shirt now, so I grab mine, although I have little to cover up. No well-oiled muscles or anything else that boys like Benny would ever find interesting. Not that I should be worried, according to Mom. These things just take time and my time just hasn't come yet. Even if it has come for Marina, at least according to Benny and the rest of the male population. Lately Benny spends almost as much time with Marina as he does me. Making his attendance on reconnaissance missions spotty at best. And now that she's his girlfriend, it's only going to get worse.

"So are we swimming at the ledge or heading back in to Rosalie's?" Benny asks as he grabs an oar from the bottom of the boat and starts pushing us away from shore. As the ocean bottom starts to blur, he drops the motor down into the deeper water.

"Swimming I thought. Unless you'd rather go back to the harbor," I say, craving the fried grouper special that's made the Rosalie Harbor Restaurant famous.

"No, let's swim. As long as your hand's okay."

"It's fine." I try to hide behind the steering console so he can't see that my shirt is sticking to my ribcage and making me look like a washed up sea cucumber. Benny would not be surprised though, even if he saw. Because Benny knows everything there is to know about me, from my favorite animals to the way I refuse to wear dresses, will only cut my toenails out in the grass and once got a fishing hook stuck in my eyelid. Used to be I knew everything about him too. But this year, it's different. And it's not just Marina. We've been on summer break for two weeks now and I can't shake the feeling that something has changed. Hanging out with Benny looks the same, but feels different. Like the island after a storm's churned up the water. Even though the muck and rocks and crabs eventually find the bottom, they never settle in the same place.

The ledge is crowded today with skiffs drifting nearby, filled with tourists in bright Hawaiian print shirts that for some reason everyone that visits the Keys thinks are necessary, along with Jimmy Buffet music, conch fritters, key lime pies, swim with the dolphins excursions and roadside stands of cold beer. Funny though, in all my years on this island, I've never listened to a Jimmy Buffet song from beginning to end. At least not voluntarily.

Benny and I wave at the boats and throw out a dive buoy as a sign that we're heading into the water. The guides wave back, along with a string of tourists who've got their lines all crossed. A sure way to start a pretty tangle.

"Geez, poor Rick, looks like he's got a bunch of amateurs," Benny says, watching the boat closest to us. The tourists are jerking their lines back and forth now, as if they are deep sea fishing for grunts instead of sport fishing in the backcountry for bonefish.

"Yeah, let's hope we don't get some of the same," I say, peeling off my shirt before leaping in.

Benny nods, but doesn't respond. He knows as well as I do that the caliber of clients has dropped off recently, almost as sharply as this ledge. Instead of getting the mid-level fishermen out for a day of beer and sun, we're getting a splattering of the usual experts and novices from landlocked states up north who've probably never caught anything except a stream trout. They're all about the experience, trying something new. Apparently that's the only thing worth investing in these days. Which is why we're witnessing the catastrophe happening on Rick's boat. People with no sense of fishing at all. Suntanned tourists who can't tell a sand flea from a fishing fly.

I take another dunk under the water and start swimming back to the boat. On my way back, I pray to God that today we've got some experts.

Nothing I hate more than sharing my secrets with those that don't understand they've got a secret to keep.

CHAPTER TWO

"Piper, are you ready? You have to get going now," says Mom over the whir of our dying air conditioner.

"One more sec," I say, yelling toward the half-open door separating my room from the kitchen down the hall. I'm plopped down on the duct-taped bean bag chair slumped in the corner of my room, laptop and hand-held GPS balanced between my knees. A list of fishing locations sorted by GPS coordinates greets me, along with a string of dates running across the top of the spreadsheet. I turn back to my GPS and pull up the coordinates marking today's cove, then after typing out a quick note about catching only one fish, I enter a glaring NOT into the final column marked "Hot or

Not." I ignore the column marked "Turtle Sightings." Seeing all those blank rows hurts almost as much as that hydroid sting.

With only three fishing spots in the past two weeks returning any signs of bonefish, I load them into my GPS so they're first in my list of favorites. As I finish, Mom starts yelling again. This time she's louder.

"Hurry up! Benny's been here for ten minutes now and it's almost 1:00!" she says.

"I told you, I'm coming." I turn off the computer without shutting it down, then head for the door.

"Sorry, had to update the GPS," I say, entering the kitchen in a flurry. I grab Benny's arm and bolt for the door, before Mom can lecture me about my tardiness and the importance of every charter trip now that we're getting less and less calls about appointments.

"Have a good time," Mom mutters as I bust through the screen door. "And don't forget to fill Lignum's water dish on your way out."

The door slams shut as a wave of thick, salt-heavy air clogs my lungs. "Geez, how does Liggy take it out here? This heat is suffocating."

"She's an animal, she's used to it," says Benny. "Now let's get this done quick. It's already 12:50. Had I known you'd be this late, I would've stopped to get lunch with Marina."

"Well knowing you, it's probably better you have

an empty stomach. Maybe you won't be so sleepy now."

Benny laughs as he follows me to the backyard, where Liggy is lying under a small scrub pine no taller than my shins. Her fur feels wet like she's already sweated out the water I poured her an hour earlier, so I take the hose and fill up her dish. I never did know key deer could sweat until Liggy. Somehow it seemed unnatural, especially since she's supposed to be used to the heat, seeing as key deer only live in the Florida Keys. But then Liggy, well, she's always been different. Hence the sweat. Though sometimes I wonder if that's just because she only has three legs, on account of the car accident that won her a permanent residence in our backyard. Not that four legs would stop the sweating, but it would let her travel somewhere with more shade than our one scrub pine and spindly orange tree that hasn't bore anything resembling a real citrus fruit since we've lived here.

Liggy looks up and blinks her big coal eyes. I smile before leaving her to dive into the water, her only real treat until I can get home and sneak her into my room for some late-night girl talk and bean-bag ripping. Two of our favorite activities.

The walk down to Rosalie's, the restaurant overlooking the harbor where we dock our boats, takes less than five minutes as we cut in back of a deserted beach house and onto the main road. It used to be the walk took ten, back when we had to walk on the streets instead of stampeding through people's lawns. But now that the twenty-room beach houses behind us are empty, the inhabitants forced out from unpaid bills and foreclosures, the walk is much shorter.

We reach the boat just in time to see Dad revving the engine and preparing for the trip. Our guests haven't arrived yet, so I hand over the GPS and instruct Dad on the hot fishing locations, while Benny runs to the bar to stock our cooler.

"Founder's Inlet looked good yesterday, especially when you get deep into the grasses. I saw a bunch of crab shells that weren't even underwater at low tide, so we might need to get into some pretty shallow water," I say as Dad checks the fuel gauge.

"I saw Rick earlier, he said they had some interest near the ledge today," Dad says.

"Oh yeah, Benny and I saw him out earlier. Believe me, the only interest those people had was in tying up their lines. Did Rick say he actually saw any fish?"

Dad shrugs.

"I'd start with Founder's Inlet. If that doesn't work, I'd drive over to Lignumvitae. Benny and I saw a pretty big school of them a couple weeks ago. No boats around either. It's really the only spot that's still undiscovered."

"Was anyone else at Founders?"

"Not when we were there. Lately, most of the

boats I've seen have been either at the ledge or in the grasses to our east, where we were catching those bonefish last fall."

Dad turns back to his gauges. He isn't one for talking much before a big charter, saying that his clients usually eat up all his words. It takes a lot of energy to make people feel happy, especially when they're amateurs prone to tangling up fishing lines and asking questions about the types of seaweed or fish swimming in the shallows. Like we're nothing more than a tour guide you'd get at Sea World or out on some glass bottomed boat.

"Pipes, catch," Benny says from the dock before throwing a sack full of waters and Gatorades straight at my head. "Rosie says she just put them in the fridge so they're still a little warm. Better get them in the cooler before we get going."

I grab the plastic bag and spill the contents into the bait well, the large plastic compartment built into the floor of the boat. "Anything else we need to do before we head off?" I ask Dad.

"Just retrieve our guests. You mind looking for them, honey?"

"Sure," I say, tucking in my green polo with the giant sailfish logo emblazoned over my entire backside.

The outdoor deck at Rosalie's is in full swing today, even though there are no fishing events on the agenda. Kids are swarming the tables, laughing over fried fish sandwiches and pitchers of Coke as a flock of charter guides swap stories over pints at the bar. Most of the patrons look like vacationers.

In the far corner a group of tenth graders from my school – the sprawling public school that is two islands and one hellish bus ride away – is just finishing lunch, but with Dad and Benny waiting, I decide not to say hello. They aren't close friends, though they're not strangers either. In fact, Sardi is probably the only girl from Coral High that knows my name and house. She even met Liggy back when we had to work on a group science project. But even so, she knows little about my fishing life or Dad's charter. Besides for the guys down the docks, not many people do. Not that I try to hide it, but at school sometimes it's just easier to blend in. To not be that girl who spends every afternoon fishing for bonefish instead of tanning and gossiping on the beach.

So I try to walk by Rosalie's quickly, hoping Sardi doesn't catch a glimpse of my shirt. The one with my last name and that big sailfish jumping over the "e." But of course, the shirt proves to be a perfect target.

"Hey Piper, is that you?" Sardi yells, just as a group of tourists looking very much like guys ready for a fishing charter, walk across the small footbridge near the entrance of Rosalie's.

"Oh Sardi, good to see you," I say, as the tourists inch closer. They're looking over the edge of the footbridge now, pointing at something in the water.

"I didn't know you came to this place. But I guess it makes sense. You live around here, right?" Sardi is smiling from ear to ear, her voice rising higher on every word.

"Yeah, my Dad runs a charter boat. I'm actually helping him out and really need to get going. I'm supposed to grab that group over there." I point to the tourists who've turned off the bridge and are standing next to the ditch, gawking at the tide pool and poor sea creature that was unlucky enough to get stuck. Two hours to go, baby, and the current will take you out, I think, as Sardi inspects the crowd.

"Whoa, lucky you, I wish I could spend the day on the water, but of course Mom volunteered me to be a camp counselor over at the Blessed Sea Church camp. Thank God it's only half days though. Don't think I could stand it much longer than half a day."

"Yeah, sounds rough," I say, trying again to end the conversation.

Sardi's still smiling though, even as my face grows more strained. "Hey, what are you doing tomorrow night?" she asks.

I shrug, looking away.

"If you're free, a group of us are hanging out at the Becco. Marina's planning a bonfire. You should come by."

I stop walking as Sardi mentions the party,

thinking of Benny and how he's failed to mention it. Not that I'd expect him to, seeing as I have never fit in with Marina's crowd. But still. A mention would've been nice. Yet with Sardi twirling her hair and smiling right at me, I know it's no time to lose my temper. So instead I focus on all the reasons why I'd never go to the party in the first place. How the bonfire will be filled with girls from school that wear makeup and clothes from trendy stores in Miami. Girls I know well enough, but have never considered friends. And then there's Marina herself, who just last week walked right by me on the docks to get to Benny. No hello or anything, like I was just some weird tourist that was in her way instead of the girl that spent the past year sitting next to her in English class. Benny claims she didn't see me, but still. Even if that was true, what kind of girl is she if she can't recognize a classmate that sat across the aisle?

After a minute of grinding my teeth, I respond. "Oh, I don't know. I think I have to stay home tomorrow."

The tourists are losing interest in the ditch. It's time for me to walk over.

"Oh come on, can't you get out of it? Benny'll be there and Marina's friends are awesome. It'll be a good time. Maybe we can even go together," Sardi says.

"How about I call you later and let you know," I say, hoping my words will stop Sardi from trying to convince me further.

"Cool, call my cell. You have it, don't you?" she asks, reaching into her pocket.

"Yeah, I got it."

"Great. Hopefully I'll see you later then. Call me when you figure it out."

I give Sardi a final wave and watch her skip back over to her table. I wonder why she doesn't drag someone else to Marina's but then remember that she's the only one of her friends that actually lives on Islamorada. And in the Keys, it's rare to travel far at night. Not that it's difficult to do – in fact it is usually quite easy on account of there being less traffic – but because each island is like its own community, with its own events like group cookouts and parties at Rosalie's. Apparently there are bonfires too, not that I've ever attended one. Most of my nights are spent eating a pint of Cherry Garcia ice cream in my docked Whaler with Benny. Back when Benny had time to hang out with me, anyway.

As I picture another night home with just Liggy, my anger at Benny fades and the bonfire starts to sound more appealing. Maybe I will tag along with Sardi tomorrow. Smooth over my friendship with Benny. Try to befriend Marina. The idea sounds intriguing and ludicrous at the same time, though right now I don't have time to sort it out. So instead I take a deep breath and head for the footbridge, ready to meet my guests.

"Hi guys, are you the Cook group?" I ask, plastering on a smile.

A thick man wearing a massive collage of orange blossoms looks over his shoulders, then walks away from the ditch, leaving the other two to gaze into the tepid water. "Yes, that's us. Are you with Wesley Charters?"

"Yup, I'm Piper Wesley, and I'll be your crew today. We're all ready to go whenever you are. The boat's right there on the dock." I point back to the skiff where Dad and Benny are double-checking the lines, inspecting the flies and making sure none of the imitation shrimp is missing a head or body.

"Great, I'm Nick Cook. Let me round up the rest of the guys. Charlie, Logan, let's go," he says, but only one of the guys is ready to leave the ditch. The other just stays and stares, as if he's seeing a pool of water for the first time.

The new guy saunters over, unbuttoning the collar on his pink seashell shirt as he walks. "Hi, I'm Charlie," he says, going in for a high five.

"Nice to meet you," I say, trying not laugh. The guy has got to be pushing forty and he's still hooked on a hand gesture that's so dead even ten year-olds won't use it in public. But of course, I overlook this and keep smiling. So much for a day with some experts. These guys scream amateur.

Charlie and Nick seem pleased with the introductions and after a few more pats on my back and a trip back to the outdoor bar for a to-go cooler of beers, they start ambling down the ramp leading to the docks and our boat.

"Uh, don't you have one more?" I ask as they turn away, leaving the third member of their party behind to stare in the ditch.

"Oh yeah, where's Logan? Don't tell me he's still staring at that stingray. Piper, you will never believe it, but there is a stingray this wide down there in that pool of water. It's the whole width of the stream. I didn't know they made them that big," says Charlie, growing animated enough for me to wonder if the to-go cooler isn't the first alcohol he's procured today.

"Yeah it's crazy big, I'm so mad I forgot my camera. Usually never leave home without it," says Nick with a laugh.

"Lucky us," says Charlie. "Nick here is a professional photographer. Be glad he forgot the camera. His shooting can be quite annoying."

"Hey it's photojournalist to you. And I do still have my cell phone." Nick takes it out and starts walking over to the ditch, now convinced he can get an award-winning shot with the grainy no-flash camera built into the phone.

I fold my hands across my body as Nick stumbles over the crushed shells lining the path, then joins the third member of their group. He points the phone, admires his work, then whispers something into the guy's ear. A minute later he's back with Charlie, still one man short.

Nick lets out a long breath then tightens his fists. "Logan, come on down here! It's time to go," he says. "God, here I try to take him out for some father-son bonding time and all he wants to do is stare at that ditch. Unbelievable."

"Looks like he's turning. He'll catch up," I say, directing Nick and Charlie back toward the dock.

"Thank God, I tell you, ever since we moved down here, that kid's been nothing but trouble. If it wasn't for Charlie coming down for a week, well let's just say we wouldn't be going fishing."

"Aw, come on Nick, give him a break. He's homesick. But don't worry, he'll loosen up." Charlie reaches into his to-go cooler and pulls out a can. "Have another beer. Relax."

As we reach the boat, I jump aboard, ready to start untying the lines from the dock. But when I look back, I'm startled by the third member of the group. Logan. He's younger than I expected, maybe even my age, and seems preoccupied by Dad's set of twin Mercury engines.

"Come on, it's time to go," Nick says, almost shouting the words until Logan looks up and acknowledges him.

"I'm here aren't I," he says, with a look that reminds me a lot of Marina in English class. Narrowed eyes, tousled hair and a scowl of indifference that would probably make my own dad fire me if I ever tried one on.

He jumps on board then pauses to adjust his jeans before walking by his father to join me and Benny on the bow.

Well this should be interesting, I think, trying not to stare at Logan's slim black t-shirt and slimmer jeans that make his pale skin white in the gleaming sun. I wonder how he's not slick with sweat before remembering he's only been outside a few minutes. Give him an hour, and he'll probably be soaked. I can tell Benny's thinking the same thing as he snickers under his breath.

Logan pretends not to notice and instead introduces himself to Benny, saying it's nice to meet a guy his age. It's then that I remember Nick and Charlie's conversation when we were walking down the dock. Something Charlie said about Nick and Logan moving down here. I cringe, wondering if this new guy will soon be another face ignoring me in the Coral High hallways. I try to shake off the thought as he turns to me and smiles.

"And you must be the famous Piper," he says and the way he extends his hand makes me wonder if he's actually a lot older.

I crinkle my nose and stare before shaking his hand. "And how do you know my name?"

He laughs. "My dad told me. Said he picked this charter because it was the best. He came down the docks last week and everyone here said you knew where to find the fish."

I frown, not buying his story. Sure, a lot of charter captains have heard Dad bragging about my special gift of finding fish. But none of them would ever tell a prospective customer that Dad's boat was any better than theirs. Or that I was the reason for his success.

But, having had enough scuffles with customers over the years to know when to keep my mouth shut, I just smile. "Sounds like you've done your homework," I say.

Logan laughs. "Guess we're about to find out."

CHAPTER THREE

When we arrive at Founder's Inlet, the spot is deserted, just like when Benny and I scoped it out. I help Benny with the anchor as Dad kills the engine and reaches for the fishing rods. It's time for his demonstration, where he shows the guys the proper bonefish fly fishing technique. Teaches them how to jig the line, so the imitation shrimp tied onto the hook glides through the water as if it were real. And how to look for the fish in the water and then cast on top of them, tempting them with a tasty prize.

Once the guys are comfortable with their rods, I fall into my normal routine of untangling lines, replacing torn plastic shrimp, and teaching Nick and

Charlie – who claim to be real freshwater pros up on Lake Michigan – how to cast and reel without letting the line go slack.

The men are slow learners, their progress stunted by an ever growing number of empty drinks in the to-go cooler. Surprisingly, Logan catches on much quicker. Not that I'm watching or anything. But it's a relief to have one less guy calling me over to fix his line.

That is, until he yells out that he has a fish. I drop the Swiss Army Knife from my hand and fall over a rat's nest of fishing line as I race towards him. When I get there, the fish is gone. And Benny's taken my place by his side. He seems unfazed by Logan's earlier attitude, which isn't surprising seeing as it's rare we have a charter boat with a kid our age. Especially one that could be a potential classmate.

"Good try man," Benny says, patting Logan on the back. "You'll get the next one. These fish are hard to hook."

Logan nods, then grabs his t-shirt and lifts it off his skin, creating a fan. "Yeah, hard to concentrate on anything in this heat."

Benny nods, then starts rummaging through a bucket, emerging a minute later with a pair of khaki shorts.

"These should help," he says, throwing them at Logan.

The first hint of a genuine smile crosses Logan's lips as he hands Benny his rod and goes to the back to change. When he returns, he rolls back his shoulders and retrieves his fishing pole before diving into conversation with Benny.

I try not to listen as I return to helping Dad bait hooks in the back, but with the wind carrying their words across the boat it's hard not to pick up on a few facts. Like how Logan's dad got sent here on a one-year assignment to work on a documentary about the infamous Labor Day Hurricane that decimated the Florida Keys in 1935, a pretty popular topic down here that attracts a fair number of writers and photographers every year, each set on uncovering a new twist in the storm that killed over 400 Keys residents. My mind drifts to the last journalist to visit about the story a few years back. He'd been more interested in the human interest side than the storm itself and spent weeks tracking down the families of survivors. I wonder if Nick is here to do the same, and start to imagine who he'll interview, just as Logan dives further into his past. About how most recently he was living in Michigan where he was some kind of big football star.

Now that's all Benny has to hear to get going good.

As soon as the word football leaves Logan's mouth, Benny attacks with more questions than I can count.

"So how many years have you been playing for

now?" he asks between breaths. He takes a big swig of Gatorade and spills half of it on his shirt. Right now Benny looks more flustered than when he is hanging out with Marina, which is typical seeing as he has got this new theory that he's going to be some football pro.

"It's been over ten years now, started when I was five," says Logan, casting out his line. Logan yawns as the line goes slack, then he wipes the sweat off his face with the back of his hand.

"There aren't any good programs around here until high school. And last year I got sick during tryouts so I couldn't play," says Benny. "You must be real good if you've been playing since you were five."

Logan shrugs. "I started last year as a sophomore running back, but I wasn't one of the best. I still can't get my 40 yard dash under five seconds."

I hold my breath on the "sophomore." He's a year older than us. Around sixteen. At least he won't be in our grade, I think, returning to my baiting duties.

"Under five seconds, wow, that sounds fast," says Benny. "Maybe we can get together this summer and practice. Squeeze in some drills before summer sessions start." Benny is salivating now, drops of bright blue Gatorade staining his lips and tongue.

"Yeah, maybe." Logan grabs the drifting fishing line in his left hand just like Dad demonstrated and tries to make his imitation shrimp swim.

I can't help staring at his perfect rhythm until

Nick screams from the aft. From the looks of his rod, he's got a fish.

"I got one! Oh Jesus, this is big," Nick yells, jerking the rod up into the air.

"Great, reel it in slowly now," says Dad, jumping over to help.

"This fish is monstrous, he's fighting! This ain't no trout," he says, again shaking the rod instead of reeling in the line.

"Here, steady the rod," Dad says, patting him on the back. He takes the beer can plastered in Nick's left hand and sets it on the center console.

"Now bringing him in isn't much different than what you'd do with a trout. This guy's just a lot stronger," Dad says. "Let out a little line while you lift the rod slowly and let him swim. Then start bringing the rod down until it's parallel with the water and reel real hard on the descent."

Nick listens to the instructions but doesn't seem to process them. His rod lunges toward the sky before he can loosen the line. A second later, Logan's hollering as well.

"Uh, guys? I think I got one too." He stands there motionless, his rod bending like a tree in a tornado. He doesn't loosen the line or reel in the slack or anything. He's just shaking and panicking, like he's forgotten what to do.

"Piper, go help Logan," Dad says as he struggles to

help Nick.

"Sure, I got it." I run over to the other side of the boat, skimming by Benny as I move into position. I reach Logan's side just as the tip of the rod dips into the glassy water. "Logan, let out some line, you're going to lose him!"

"Yeah, okay." He looks down at his reel and fumbles with the lever responsible for releasing the line. Before he can open it, his rod dips deeper into the water and the clutch starts moaning. The fish is running and Logan's doing nothing to stop it.

"Get the rod up, you can't keep it in the water. And let out the line. Flip the lever away from you real quick. It's probably just stuck because of the salt." I continue to shout commands as Logan stares at me, his rod dunking so far into the water that it's mere inches from hitting the muddy bottom.

"I can't get it open," Logan says, frowning. "Damn rod's broken! Stupid piece of shit."

As Logan starts a very unproductive rant filled with more four-letter words than I knew existed, Dad starts screaming from the other side of the boat. "Benny, grab the net, we're going to land this one!"

Benny retrieves the net, then runs over to Dad as I try to encourage Logan. Because right now the rod's bending down so far that if he doesn't loosen the line soon, we're going to lose the entire rod, along with whatever's got the end of his imitation shrimp.

Logan makes another feeble effort to let out some line, but his trembling hands can't grip the metal lever. "Piper, please, take the rod. I don't know what the hell I'm doing," he says.

"Just calm down," I say. "You need to flip the metal switch…"

"I can't!" he yells.

I hesitate, then take the rod. I mean, he's in trouble and needs my help. No matter that he's some football player from Michigan with a mouth so dirty it would've won me a night sleeping out in the backyard with Liggy. Logan Cook can't reel in a bonefish. And I'm pretty much convinced that I can.

With the rod secured in my right hand, I pop open the line feeder with my left. The line starts flying out and the clutch goes quiet, though the rod is so hot, it's burning my hands. I turn back to Logan, who's still standing there, lips cursing and hands shaking.

"Grab a bottle of water from the bait well and throw it on the reel," I say. "This thing's overheating."

"Uh, okay," he says, then walks to the back of the boat. He doesn't run or leap or even walk quickly the way Benny and me and Dad always do when a fish is on the line. Nope, he walks, as if we have all the time in the world and my hands aren't getting burned to death every time I touch the reel.

"Wait, what's a bait well?" asks Logan.

I sigh. "The container built into the floor. You

should see a metal handle."

"Oh yeah, sure."

I turn back to the fish as Logan fumbles with the bait well. The rod is out of the water now and straight, having recovered from the horseshoe Logan bent it into before. After letting the fish take some line, I flip the lever back and start reeling in the slack, jerking the line from side to side every time the fish tries to bolt into the weeds. I repeat the process about five times before seeing the bonefish glide by the boat. He's about 20 inches long and silvery, his body glistening in the crystal clear water as he swims by. It's one of the biggest we've seen this season, which seems to have the rest of the guests excited, even if Logan misses it on account of not being able to find the bottled water in the bait well.

"Holy moly, that's ten times the size of mine," says Nick, clinking Bud Light cans with Charlie.

"Hey Logan, you hooked a monster, no wonder you couldn't bring him in," says Charlie.

Knowing that Charlie's looking for an excuse as to why his friend's son had to give his rod to a girl, I make one up for him and tell them the fish took a run under the boat and tangled himself in the weeds. Logan did a great job, but what can you do with the fish is in the weeds? Only thing left is to let him run and hope he gets out, and that's a pretty complicated maneuver. I keep embellishing the story until Nick and Charlie are patting Logan on the back and offering him a sip of beer, telling him he's quite the angler to hook such a monster fish.

I fight my catch for another ten minutes and by the time Benny nets it, I'm as tired as the fish. Lucky for both of us though it is now time to relax. After measuring the bonefish and snapping some pictures with Logan holding him, Dad throws it back into the water, since most of our charters are catch and release, given that the bonefish isn't good eating and lately the entire population, like everything else here, has been under distress. I smile as the bonefish scurries off, free again to swim through the weeds and feast on the crabs and shrimp that have moved in for the summer.

With everyone's lines out of the water, Dad revs up the motor and starts the trip back to Rosalie's. I grab a seat back in the aft with Benny and Logan, who has been looking at me kind of funny ever since I told Nick and Charlie that story about his bonefish taking a dive under the boat. I hope he's not angry at the lie, or that I took his rod. Maybe I should have given it back before his dad could see I even had it? Alternate scenarios race through my head, but I end up defeating each one. Truth is, Logan was in trouble. He needed help before he lost that fish and our rod. And on the water, fishing has to come first, even if it does mean I might have made a new enemy at Coral High.

When the pier marking Rosalie's comes into focus,

I jump from my seat and help Dad guide in the boat. Once we are docked, Nick and Charlie pick up their empty cooler and stumble over the side of the boat.

"That was some trip, thanks so much," says Charlie.

"Yeah, those bonefish are beautiful. Put up quite a fight too." Nick reaches into his pocket and grabs a few soggy bills, transferring them into Dad's fist with a handshake.

"You're welcome guys, glad you had a fun time," Dad says. "Nick, you and Logan should feel free to stop by any time, just for fun. Piper and I would be happy to teach you the ropes, maybe even take you deep sea fishing. Now that you're neighbors and all, it's time you learn how to fish like the locals."

Nick nods and waves, but his eyes are already looking down at his cooler. "No doubt, now that I've got a taste, I'll definitely be back. Who knows, maybe after a few trips I'll even be good enough for one of those tournaments they're always advertising around here," he says.

Dad nods, but doesn't say much back. A good idea seeing as the only tournament Nick is ready for is one that takes place at a bar. And even Dad won't stoop that low for a few extra bucks. Our schedule may be slow, but making a few hundred in the scorching heat teaching someone how to hold a rod and not act like an idiot, well that'll never be worth it.

"So we'll see you around then," Nick says just as he begins steering Charlie toward the outside bar at Rosalie's. The two disappear into the crowd in seconds. But Logan doesn't follow. Instead he follows Benny and me back over to the dock ramp, kicking crumbs of cracked oyster shells with every step. His lingering makes me jittery as I stand with one foot on the ramp and the other on the pavement.

"Well, it was nice to meet you, Logan," I say after a moment, breaking the silence. I give a short wave and start to turn back toward the docks just as Logan stops me.

"Thanks," he says, bringing his eyes up to my own. "For earlier. You know, with the fish. That was pretty cool of you, the way you brought it in." He stutters and looks down at the shells, and in the moment his eyes look sad instead of strong and I wonder if I've misjudged him. If really Logan Cook has been sad all along.

"Oh, that was nothing," I say, trying to lighten the mood. "If you go out a few more times, you'll get the hang of it. The technique's a little tricky, that's all. It's the shallow water that really adds an element. All those grasses and rocks and corals, makes them harder to land than other fish."

"Yeah, sounds like Rosie was right. You really are the expert fisherman."

Rosie. The owner of Rosalie's.

My cheeks burn as I hear an explanation that fits. Of course Rosie would recommend me over the other guys down the docks. She's been friends with Mom and Dad forever. Used to babysit me as a kid.

"Yeah, Piper here's a pro," says Benny, patting my back.

And all of a sudden Benny's singing my praises and I wonder if it has more to do with Logan's football pedigree than my actual skills. Either way, I can't help but get excited by the way Benny's talking. There's something about that booming voice that makes everything sound so special and serious.

"She's got her own boat and everything," Benny says, "and we're entered into this massive bonefish tournament this August with a $25,000 prize. You might have even heard of it – it's the tournament Wyatt Jacoby won last year, you know the guy with that crazy fishing show on the Expedition Channel?"

Logan nods, now all smiles. "That's the show where the host arm wrestles the fish!"

Benny laughs. "Yup, that's Wyatt Jacoby for you. He's insane, but always the best. Rumor is he's coming back this year too."

"Yeah, it should be pretty cool," I say, not in the mood to discuss the tournament's that got my stomach all in knots.

But Benny's never been shy. "If anyone has a chance at beating him it's me and Piper. But anyway, you should come out on the skiff some time with us for some real fishing. We could give you some private lessons or something," he says.

Logan's eyes dart up again, some of the sadness softening. "That would be really cool. We've been living here a month now and I haven't done anything but hang out inside."

Benny stands up straighter, rolling back his shoulders and making his arm muscles pop. "Well in that case, we definitely should chill. You know tomorrow there's a big bonfire happening over at one of the hotels. A lot of kids from school will be going. You should come check it out."

Ah, Marina's bonfire. Figures he'd mention it to Logan, I think, biting my lip.

"Will Wyatt Jacoby be there?" Logan asks, laughing.

"Nah, he has other engagements. But it should still be fun."

"Cool," says Logan. "What time does it start? Where should I meet you guys?"

Benny pauses, gives me a glance, then keeps talking. "You can meet me at my house, over on Gimpy Gulch Drive." He shoves me aside as he starts spitting out directions. "You know, you can come too, Pipes, if you're free."

"Oh, you aren't going?" Logan asks.

I open my mouth to speak but Benny's already

filling it for me. "Nah, Piper's usually too tired to stay out too late. You know, all that fishing can be pretty exhausting, and..."

I grind down on my teeth, furious at Benny's dismissal. "Actually, I'm going with Sardi. She invited me earlier."

Benny snaps his mouth shut, then wrinkles his nose.

Logan smiles. "Cool. In that case, I guess I'll see you both there tomorrow."

"Sounds good man, see ya later," Benny says.

Once Logan is out of hearing distance, Benny turns to me, whether to scowl or explain himself for not inviting me earlier to the bonfire, I can't tell. And I don't wait around long enough to find out. By the time he turns around, I'm already on the dock, racing back to Dad's boat to help clean up.

"Come on, Benny, my dad's waiting," I call over my shoulder.

He sighs, then starts to follow. "I know, Pipes, I know. I'm right behind you."

My mouth turns up into a smirk as I hear his feet clomp against the docks. Benny's always been right behind me for as long as he's been my best friend. Only this time, I'm not so sure I believe him.

CHAPTER FOUR

"Can you slow down?" I ask, as my ankle starts to roll off the top of the shoe. "I can barely walk in these things."

Sardi sighs loud enough for me to hear her twenty feet away. "Come on, they're not too bad. No different than flip flops."

"Right. Because everyone knows flip flops and high heels are interchangeable." I hide my scowl as Sardi skips down the street. She's got me dressed up in the only skirt I own and most likely the only tank top in my closet without some sort of stain on it. It's not my usual fare, but Sardi is convinced that all the girls at the bonfire will be dressed in skirts. And if there's one thing I know about Sardi, it's not to argue. Especially when it comes to girly stuff.

"You couldn't wear flip flops, not with a dress. Flats would make you look stubby."

Yup. There she goes. Sardi the fashion queen. "So what's the rush anyway?" I ask as we round the corner of my street. We only left my house three minutes ago and already we're ten houses away.

"I'm just excited to see everyone, that's all," she says. "I haven't seen anyone really since school ended and that was, what? Two weeks ago now? Can you believe it, Piper, it's been two weeks!"

I nod, still unsure what, or who, she's after. Two weeks and I'm still recovering from the trauma of eight months of missed low tides.

"Uh, aren't you a counselor with your friends at camp?" I ask, thinking back to her group yesterday at lunch.

Sardi stops jumping. Her steps fall in line with my own. "Uh, yeah, but they're not my good friends. And it's been two weeks since I even looked at Travis."

Sardi whispers the name, as if someone will hear. I turn my head to both sides, but all I see are two empty sides of street, and a row of unkempt houses with overgrown lawns and scrub pines that sprouted up last spring.

"So you like Travis," I say, thinking to the freckle-faced kid from math class, the one that Benny says is going out for football with him. Geez, Travis. The most likely to get squashed like a bug. Probably during the first practice.

"Huh? Oh no, we're just friends. Like you and Benny."

I debate whether to point out that Benny and I have been friends since almost birth while Travis and Sardi just met last year. But I keep my mouth shut. Tonight I could use a friend, especially since seeing Benny with Marina never puts me in a good mood. It's not that I like him, or at least not in the way that Sardi seems to like Travis. But there is a part of me that has always thought of Benny as more than just another friend. Probably because we've known each other for so long. Sometimes he feels like an extension of me. My sarcastic, muscly counterpart. And while it's not like I want to be his girlfriend, I do wish that he picked a girl to date that was more fun to hang out with. Or who was at least nice enough to say hi sometimes.

I sigh, wishing that things could be more like they were last summer. Back when Benny still had time to catch hermit crabs in the salt ponds and count the stars out on the dock. Which is probably why until now I've avoided seeing him and Marina together. Because whenever he's with Marina, I don't even exist. And knowing tonight that Benny's going to be fawning over Marina and Logan, well that just makes the situation even worse.

I start to second guess my decision to even go to the bonfire just as the Becco Lodge Vacancy sign comes into focus. But there's something about the way Benny dismissed me to Logan, as if the idea of me going was just so crazy, that makes me keep going.

"So who else do you think will be here?" I ask as we walk by the entrance. Two geckos skitter across the sandy road and take refuge in the lush palm garden lining the drive.

Sardi shrugs. "Oh, I don't know." She runs ahead without really answering the question, as if she's best friends with everyone there and can't wait another second to say hello.

I arrive at the party a minute after Sardi. The bonfire is loud and smoky, with about ten kids gathered around the fire. Closest to the ocean are Benny and Travis, with Logan hanging behind. To our left exiting the closest guest house are Marina and her girlfriends Ella and Kali, who I've never talked to and probably wouldn't know at all if not for their yearbook pictures being on the same page as mine. Two guys wearing gray shorts and tie-dyed t-shirts are lounging in the sand. Their faces look even more remote than the girls.

"Sardi, I'm so glad you could make it," says Marina as she approaches the fire. She looks even more perfect than I remember, in a pink mini skirt with a tiny black halter that ends two inches before her skirt begins.

"It's so great to see you too!" says Sardi. "I've been meaning to call ever since school got out. We just need to hang out again soon!"

"Yes, def," Marina says, clutching Sardi's hand.

She then turns to me and smiles, her voice rising higher. "Oh Piper, I didn't know you were stopping by. I heard you've really been putting my Benny to work lately."

Right. Her Benny. Is that why she avoided me on the docks last week? Just thinking about it makes me want to scream. But instead I plaster on a smile. "Yeah, we've been working hard."

"Hah, good. Always the optimist, huh? I don't know how you stand being so close to those fish guts all day. But then Benny says you're good at it, so I guess that's cool you've found your thing. Anyway, I should go mingle, but I'm sure we'll catch up later."

Marina leaves us with a cool wave before running over to Benny. As soon as she reaches his arms, Benny kisses her forehead, then introduces her to Logan, turning his back to the fire, and everyone else. Even from the other side of the fire, it's easy to tell that Benny's group is closed to company. So I turn away and direct Sardi to the cooler where we grab a couple Cokes.

We linger on the side of the benches until our

sodas turn warm. Then we head over to the girl cluster and drum up some conversation with Ella and Kali. We ask about their summers – both of them are helping out Marina at the hotel, working as receptionists – and learn that the two hippies in the sand are their boyfriends. They're a year older, going into eleventh grade in the fall, they explain, as if that would excuse their appearance.

Sardi starts to say something about how she works with some older guys at her camp, but before she can spit out the words, Marina runs over shrieking.

"OhmiGod girls, we have to go get our project. Benny and Logan want to see them! We need to set everything up! They think our idea is completely brilliant," says Marina.

"Really? I don't know if they're ready for prime time..." says Ella.

"Don't worry, I told them these are prototypes, and they're totally cool with it."

"If you say so," says Kali.

Marina locks arms with her clones and disappears into the guest house she's claimed as her own.

"What was that all about?" I ask Sardi. Of course Benny's never mentioned anything about a secret project. Even if we have spent every day together since school ended.

"Who knows? I haven't talked to Marina in two weeks, remember? I am completely out of the loop!"

"In that case, let's go see Benny," I say, dragging her toward the guys who've plopped themselves down right where the waves meet the sand.

"Oh, I don't know if I'm ready to go over there yet," says Sardi, staring at the group.

I look back at Benny, now talking with Logan and Travis. I know Sardi's scared to see Travis, and I'd rather not see Logan again as well, but the whole reason I'm here is to show Benny I'm not afraid of a party, or his girlfriend. Meaning I need to make my presence known.

So I shrug off Sardi's comment and start walking. "Okay, if you don't want to see the guys, you can stay here then and talk to um, Ella's boyfriend," I say.

Sardi turns to the tie-died couple playing footsie in the sand. "All right, let's go."

"Hey Benny, have we missed anything exciting?" I ask as we reach the group. I kick off my horrid wedge sandals and dip my feet in the gentle surf.

"Besides Marina screaming? Not so much," Benny says, grinning. "Just trying to show our boy Logan here a good time."

My eyes dart towards Logan's as he curls his lips into a smirk.

"Oh yeah, Sardi, I forgot. This is Logan. He just moved down here a few weeks ago. We took him fishing on my dad's charter yesterday," I say.

Sardi nods and I can see her cheeks flush as she

grows more animated.

"I remember you," she says. "You're the one in that black shirt, right? Geez and here I thought you were a tourist, but this is so much better. It is so nice to meet you, Logan, you are going to love it here. Just love it!"

For a moment, Sardi seems more excited by Logan than Travis so I sneak another look, hoping to figure out why. But once again, all I see is the same Logan from the charter. He's in another black t-shirt, this time with jean shorts that still look out of place next to Benny's board shorts and Travis' khakis. And his hair is messy with bangs so long they skim the tops of his eyebrows. It's a sharp contrast next to Benny's buzz cut and I wonder if that is part of the appeal. That or his blue eyes, the only part of Logan that seems to sparkle, to hint that there might be something more hiding under all that hair.

"Well at least it sounds like things are off to a great start, with you meeting Benny and Piper," says Sardi, her eyes still locked on Logan's.

"Looks like it," he says. "They've been doing a good job showing me the ropes."

"That's great. And here Piper didn't tell me a thing about it," says Sardi, her face glistening from too much glitter body gel.

"We haven't shown him much..." I say.

"Well you did land that monster fish and invite me to a party," says Logan.

"Hey man, I believe I told you about the party," says Benny.

Logan laughs. "You're right, but without Piper would it really be a party?" He points at me and laughs and I feel my cheeks grow warm. Once again I think back to the Logan on the boat. The one with the cool, indifferent stare. Who Benny was quick to tell that I hate parties.

Figures. The new guy is making fun of me already.

But before I can call him out on it, Marina is out of the guest house. Yelling. Again.

"Benny, Logan, we're ready for you!" she says.

"Don't want to keep your woman waiting," says Travis, patting Benny on the back.

"Pushy, isn't she?" Benny says.

The guys get up and head back toward the guest house.

Travis pauses, then looks back at Sardi. "Coming Ladies?" he asks.

This time Sardi's cheeks turn bright red and I can see that whatever effect Logan may have had, it wasn't lasting.

"Yes, wait up!" Sardi says.

"Then hurry up," says Benny.

Sardi nods, then turns to me. "Piper, you coming?"

I shrug, looking back at Travis and Logan. As if sensing my gaze, Logan looks back and opens his mouth as if to speak. But before he can, Marina's there, wrapping her arm around his back and pushing him toward the door. So much for her being in love with Benny, I think, gritting my teeth. I wish I could see Logan's face, or Benny's, to know what the gesture means. But the way Logan just saunters inside tells me enough. Looks like even Marina's quite taken with his spell.

"So is that a yes?" asks Sardi.

I reach for my shoes but my hands are shaking too much to fasten the buckles. "Go on without me, I'll catch up in a second."

"You sure? Because I will totally wait."

"Nah, go before you lose Travis. He was looking at you before, you know."

"OhmiGod, really? You think?"

"Yeah, definitely," I say, even though I'm not sure that it's true. But hey, it is Travis after all. Sardi would actually be a good catch. In fact, she'd probably be the only thing he's ever caught.

Squeals of laughter escape the guest house as Sardi and the guys pile inside. Sardi's high-pitched voice carries the farthest, her giggles proof that she belongs. As my hands relax, the shoe buckles unclasp easily and I slide my feet between the straps of smooth leather. With everyone in the guest house, the beach is still except for the crackling of the fire and a flock of sand pipers running on top of the sand.

Toward the left of the guest house, an iguana

emerges, then skitters off toward the row of tiki torches that lines the resort. The music from the main dining room, a steel drum duo that sometimes plays at Rosalie's, melds together with the hum of the voices and crashing of the waves to create a low, mesmerizing sound. The sound of a secret passing between friends. The sound of the ocean telling me to go home.

Deciding that the ocean is always right – and that no one will even miss me here anyway – I decide that like the iguana, it's time to skitter home. Yet the sound of a nearby gull stops me just as I turn away, ready to find the road. The sound is sharp and hurried, an unusual call for a gull, especially at night. So I turn back and follow the noise into the dark, through a garden of palm fronds and onto a hidden beach. But as soon as my feet hit the sand, the noise dies. There is no injured bird, no animal in need of help. Just cool sand and lapping water and a few tiki torches burning in the distance. I start retracing my steps, hoping the crowd is still in the guest house, that no one has noticed me slip out. And it's then, as I cross over a small strip of sand between a mass of tall weeds that I see it. A glistening, barnacle-covered face rising from the water. For a moment I can do nothing but stare. The animal I've been searching for is back. On Marina's beach. My knees shake as I fall back into the sand and take cover in the grasses. Just in time to watch the island's lost friend return home.

CHAPTER FIVE

"So why did you leave last night?" Benny asks as we walk down my street toward Rosalie's. He picks up a conch shell on the side of the road, examines it for holes, then throws it back on the ground.

"Because I was tired," I say, wiping an already substantial film of sweat from my forehead.

"You disappeared at like 9:00, Pipes. The party was just getting started."

"I know, but after I saw her I was too excited to stay. I had to come home and tell my parents. Not to mention we have a busy day of practice today. I wanted to be rested."

Benny sighs. "Saw her? Are you talking about that

dumb turtle again?"

"That dumb turtle?" I stare back at Benny. Here I've spent an hour telling him about the first turtle I've seen in months and all he's done is act like it isn't important. As if he doesn't know that turtles are my favorite animal – after Liggy of course – and that I've been searching for new nests ever since the turtles disappeared last fall.

"Look, I know you have a thing for turtles, but sometimes there's more important stuff going on," Benny says, his voice taking an accusing tone.

I bite my lip, deciding this is not the best time to tell him I was planning to bail on Marina's long before I saw the turtle. Or that Marina's new project, whatever it is, will never be the most important thing going on. In my life, anyway.

"Sometimes you really have to just chill out. Spend a little less time in the grasses," he says.

"Uh, Benny, did you even hear what I said? It was a loggerhead! The first I've seen since the oil spill probably, and it was nesting on Marina's beach!"

"I know, it's exciting and all, but you were a guest at Marina's party. Leaving like that was rude."

"What are you talking about? You all were in the guest house so I figured I'd just slip out. No harm done."

Benny shakes his head. "You didn't say goodbye. It was weird. Where were your manners?"

My mouth drops at his accusation. Leave it to Benny to hit below the belt. In Benny's family, everything revolves around manners. Well, and food. In fact, the two pretty much go hand in hand. Those fried plantains look good? Interested in a fresh pork sandwich with homemade pickles? Then you better show Mrs. Benitez that you know your manners or you'll be going hungry.

And I'm not just talking about the normal things, like saying please and thank you. No, in Benny's house, it's all about the little things. Mrs. Benitez always says it's because of how things were in Cuba when she was a little girl, before she left in one of the few Red Cross planes that made it out when the country's borders were pretty much closed.

Today the sanctions still are pretty limiting, but back then, it was worse. People couldn't choose their jobs, schools, or anything. Which was why the little things mattered. I've always really been in awe of Benny's mom because of that, not to mention the way she's taught Benny to fold every napkin diagonally when setting the table, to always hold the door for an elder, to never go to a friend's house empty-handed.

In fact, Benny is so polite that a lot of his skills have rubbed off on me, something I'm usually proud of. But, in this situation with Marina, Benny's right. I never said goodbye. A major breach of etiquette.

I take a deep breath and decide to forgive his

disinterest in the loggerhead just this one time. "You're right. I should have said goodbye. It was rude not to."

His upper lip twitches as the victory sinks in.

"Why don't we run by her place before today's reconnaissance mission so I can apologize?"

Benny lifts an eyebrow. It's the first time I've ever shown any interest in Marina. "Really? I mean, that's really nice of you, but there's no need. We're almost halfway to Rosalie's..."

"No, no, you were right. It was rude of me to leave, and the last thing I want to do is start any trouble."

"Well, actually then, I was going to tell you. We may not need to go all the way over to Becco Lodge after all."

"You sure? I do need to stop by anyway and check on the turtle nest. I was thinking of getting some netting to protect the eggs from raccoons and lizards..."

"Cut!" Benny snaps his hands together like a director and scowls. "This is still about the turtle! You aren't even listening! We don't need to go to Marina's today because we're already meeting her in an hour. I asked her and Logan to go fishing with us."

"Wait. What?" My mouth hangs open as Benny shifts his weight from side to side. "You invited people on my boat without asking? During low tide? You know we need to do reconnaissance now. I can't share that with them."

Benny shrugs. "What are they going to do? Sell your findings to the highest bidder?"

"Maybe, how do I know," I say, my cheeks growing warmer. "Logan's been here for like two seconds. He's not exactly a known quantity. And Marina, has she ever even been out on the water? I thought she hated fishing!"

"Well maybe if you'd stuck around the party a little longer, you could've suggested a better time. But you weren't there and Logan seemed really interested in fishing with us. He was talking about it almost all night. And once Marina heard that we were taking out Logan, I had to ask her too. She is my girlfriend, and she's wanted to see what we do out there for a long time. I just never asked her before because I knew you'd freak."

"Then why did you ask either of them?" I yell.

"Because I thought it would be fun!"

"Right, well it sounds like a lost day of practice to me."

"Come on, Pipes, I know Marina's not your favorite, but she's trying. And Logan was an All-State football player last year. I need him to give me some pointers."

I grind my teeth to keep myself from cursing. Benny knows he's supposed to be helping me survey fishing spots today, not teach novices how to cast a line, especially when those novices are Logan and Marina. I debate making him call them both and cancel, but the thought of further angering Benny makes my stomach shake. With less than two months to go until the tournament, I need him on my side.

So instead I unclench my hands and think of my manners. "How about next time I don't leave a party early without saying goodbye and you don't invite peeps on my boat without my permission. Deal?"

"Definitely. Thanks Pipes." Benny pats my back as I look down at my watch. There's not enough time for a full reconnaissance mission, but with a little luck and some calm seas I figure we can still check some of the coastline near Rosalie's before meeting Logan and Marina.

Except that waiting for us in front of the Whaler is Marina. A half hour early. And covered in tears.

"Whoa, honey, are you okay?" asks Benny, running over to her.

Marina's sprawled out on the deck, her whole body heaving. She doesn't say a word for a minute. No, make that two. Three. Finally, a sigh.

"Come on, baby, talk to me," says Benny.

She lets out a piercing cry, then rises to her knees. "Okay...I'm sorry... it's just so terrible..." she says, falling back into Benny's shoulders.

"What happened?" he asks.

"It's Ella and Kali," Marina says between sobs.

"They left me this morning. For...for...for the whole freaking summer!"

God. Is that it? Her friends leave and she throws a fit? I bite my lip and look away, hoping Benny can't see how close I am to kicking them both into the water.

"Oh honey, that's horrible," Benny says. "What about your project? Weren't they supposed to work for your mom this summer?"

Marina nods. "Yeah, until those two hippie freak boyfriends of theirs planned some stupid road trip."

"So where did they go? I bet they'll be back soon," Benny says.

Marina shakes her head. "No, I doubt they'll ever be back. They made a pact to see all fifty states in fifty days or something, though I don't know how they plan to get to Hawaii or Alaska, especially since my mom was only paying them minimum wage."

Benny laughs. "I bet they don't even get out of Florida."

"I don't know, you should've seen the van they packed. It was stuffed with tents and camping bags and a grill, and Ella even brought her retainer. I mean, you don't bring your retainer unless it's a necessity. Teeth don't move in just a week, you know."

"Well consider yourself lucky," says Benny, standing up. "Who wants to spend all summer driving in a van? It sounds lame. And this way you can keep all the profits from your purse project for yourself."

As soon as Benny mentions the word "purse," Marina falls to pieces. Again. Benny turns to me, his eyes pleading me to do something. But I'm about as good with girl talk as I am with high heels. Yet given that Benny looks like he's about to pop a blood vessel and Marina's crying so loud that the entire harbor is staring, I need to do something. So I plop myself down onto the dock and replay the conversation in my head.

"Come on Marina, it's going to be all right," I say.

She looks up at me. Frowns. Scowls actually. "How can you say that? You don't even know what's wrong."

"True. But I'm guessing it has to do with purses, right? Is that your new project?" I try to sound caring, sincere.

Her eyes widen. "Yeah. We were designing a collection of them, for the hotel. It's for a promotion my mom and I came up with. If you book a girl's weekend in the fall, everyone in your party gets a bag. They're supposed to be unique, one-of-a-kind designs from local designers. Who were supposed to be me and Ella and Kali."

"Oh I'm sure you'll find someone else to help," I say. "And if not, your mom will understand. Maybe you can just do the promotion another time."

Another torrent of tears falls to the dock. "No, it needs to be now. I promised Mom I'd help..."

Benny grabs her hand and squeezes tight. "Don't worry. We're going to figure that all out," he says.

"Promise."

She stares back into his eyes and smiles.

I look toward the ocean as Benny talks with Marina until she starts laughing. Their words blur together as I stand there, evaluating the waves. The water is as smooth as glass, except for a single whitecap breaking over the sandbar on the horizon. In another ten minutes, the sandy patch will be fully exposed. The tide will be dead low. The reconnaissance conditions will be perfect. But now that Marina's here, there's no longer any time for even a quick mission. Another day of practice lost. Another afternoon spent teaching novices. And this time, I'm not even getting paid.

A few minutes later, Logan ambles down the dock and smiles as he reaches the Whaler. His enthusiasm surprises me, especially given his last experience when he had to give up his line. But knowing his dad has already booked another charter trip for next week, I try to be polite and charming, just like Dad would want. I don't even stare at his stained jean shorts or the faded red t-shirt that's frayed at the seams. At least it's not black, I think, as Benny yells out a greeting.

"Hey man, ready to fish?" Benny asks, motioning for him to join us.

"Definitely, just picked up a real rod and everything," says Logan, pointing to the shiny fishing pole in his hand as he jumps aboard.

A minute later, Benny starts the motor and guides the Whaler toward the ledge. Seeing as I have a small boat and only a handful of rods rigged up for bonefish, I decide to teach Marina and Logan to catch pompano instead. Pompano are easier to catch, requiring nothing more than a regular old rod and a baited hook. No special flies or jigging the line required. Only after two hours pass without a hit, I start to wonder if maybe we should have just gone after the prizewinners feeding in the grasses.

"So are we really using fleas for bait?" asks Marina as she reels in her line to find yet another empty hook.

"No, they're crustaceans," I say for the fifth time. "Sand flea is just their nickname."

"I still can't believe you're touching them," she says as I reach into the bucket and grab one for her hook.

"Yeah, well, someone has to bait the lines," I say.

"Hey, I never said I couldn't help," says Logan, reaching for the bait bucket. But when he grabs the rim of the pail, he pulls too hard. The bucket tips and the sand fleas, along with about a gallon of water and sand, go flying.

"Ewww, they're everywhere!" Marina jumps up and stands on top of the bench seat. "Benny, get them away, quick before they bite me!"

"Sand fleas don't bite. They're harmless really," I say, reaching for the mess.

"Yeah, calm down, baby. They won't bite. Promise," Benny says.

As he comforts Marina, I pick through the globs of sand and sift out the squirming crustaceans, placing them back into the bucket one by one.

Logan watches me corral the bait, and for a moment I think he's going to help, but in the end he decides to keep his hands clean.

"Sorry about that," Logan says, more to Benny than to me.

"Don't worry about it," I say back, hoping he can't tell that I'm ready to strangle him. Turning away, I grab an empty soda can and dunk it into the ocean, then empty the fresh sea water back into the bucket.

"Are we safe yet?" Marina asks, staring at Logan.

"Yeah, I think we got them all," he says.

I almost choke on the "we."

Benny laughs. "Pipes, the look on your face when those fleas started scattering was priceless."

"Yeah, I bet," I say, thinking it probably doesn't look too different now.

"And after that excitement, I'm giving up," Marina says. She passes her rod to Benny and climbs onto the bow. "Anyone up for sunbathing?"

Benny looks back at me and shrugs. "Sure, baby, I'm on my way."

So much for our fishing trip.

I flick two sand fleas out of the bucket and bait Logan's hook, then mine.   "All right, cast away."

"Here it goes." Logan drops his line into the water, then reels in the slack. "Thanks so much for taking me out again today. This is great."

"Yeah, no problem," I say, wishing I could relax and just enjoy the day. But with Logan sitting just three feet away from me, my feet won't stop twitching. There's something about Logan that just feels different, strange. That combined with Marina's complaining and Benny's teasing does little to help my concentration.

"Am I doing something wrong?" asks Logan, catching my face.

"Oh no, you're cool," I say, looking away. "I was just thinking."

"Let me guess, it's about that tournament of yours."

I turn and stare. "No, it's nothing. Just wondering if we should try another fishing spot."

"Given my track record with fish, I'd hardly say it's worth it."

His comment makes me laugh and I look up, letting my eyes meet his straight on for the first time.

"You really weren't that bad," I say.

He grins. "Yeah, and you aren't thinking about the tournament."

At this, Benny snickers from the bow. "She's always thinking about the Scramble," he says.

"Seems like a big deal," Logan says. "What was the prize? $25,000? My dad hasn't stopped talking about it since your dad mentioned it yesterday. He says he's going to register himself. I think he's going to ask your dad to train him."

I whip my head around so fast that I almost hit Logan in the head with the fishing pole. "Wait. Nick wants to compete?" I ask. "But he doesn't have any experience. Or a boat!"

Logan shrugs. "I think he was hoping to go out with your dad during the tournament, but I'm not sure. I left before he called him."

"Uh, right," I say, unable to believe that Dad would ever let an amateur out on his boat during the Bonefish Scramble.

Logan smiles. "Might not have looked it yesterday, but my dad's actually a quick learner."

I nod, but right now the last thing I want to be doing is thinking about Nick or the Bonefish Scramble. The beating sun's got me dizzy and all that flirting in the bow between Benny and Marina has my stomach in knots. "Hey, maybe we should head in," I say. "Let's pull up the lines. Nothing's biting."

No one fights me as I reel in my line and start pulling up the anchor. Marina stands up and stretches as she and Benny laugh about some jellyfish passing by the bow. Apparently it's the grossest thing she's ever seen. Even worse than that clump of seaweed she saw earlier. She tries to point it out to me and Logan, but before she can find it again her feet start to wobble.

"Whoa, careful," says Benny, grabbing her arm.

"Crap!" she screams, reaching for the side of the boat.

"You okay?" I ask.

"Yeah, I'm fine, but, oh god, my bracelet! I felt it slip off my hand. The coral one my mom bought for me last year. That thing cost like $200! She's going to kill me." Marina's face begins to crumble, just like it did earlier on the dock.

"Did it fall into the water?" asks Logan, scanning the surface.

Marina nods. "I'm positive."

"Shoot, well maybe we can get another one? I'm sure your mom won't notice if it's a little different," says Benny, his hand reaching for Marina's back.

"No, she will. This one was gold, with little flowers carved out of the coral. It was super special and expensive. I'll never be able to replace it."

"All right then, let's get it," I say, peeling off the tank top covering my bathing suit.

"Get it?" asks Logan. "How? Isn't the water here really deep?"

I glance over at the depth finder. Thirteen feet.

"We're near the ledge but right now we're actually before the drop off. As long as the current didn't get it, there's a good chance it's right below us."

Before waiting for an objection, I curl my toes over the side of the boat and leap, excited for the chance to escape into the water. As soon as the water hits my skin, my muscles relax, the tension evaporating along with the air bubbles fleeing my mouth. I take a few strokes underwater, then paddle up to the surface. Breaking free of the water, I spin around until I'm facing the Whaler. Only with the anchor up, it's drifting. Fast. Meaning Marina's bracelet is probably drifting too. So much for a leisurely swim. A few more minutes and it'll be over the ledge in sixty feet of water. Gone forever. Or until some lucky fisherman hooks it from the bottom.

Not wanting Benny to see me fail, I dive down to the bottom and resume my search. The sand here is a mixture of crushed coral and sea anemones, their tentacles swaying in the current. A school of grunts swims beneath me, their yellow tails glistening in the bright morning sunlight. They look ready for their lunch now, and make me wonder if we should keep fishing so I can hook a few and show off my skills. But then, these are only common grunts. Not as exciting as pompano or bonefish.

As the grunts clear out, I descend closer to the ledge, scanning each rock and crater for the bracelet.

Besides a few rock crabs and starfish and brains of mustard yellow coral, the bottom is barren. There's no gold bracelet with coral flowers anywhere nearby. With my air supply getting low, I push off the bottom and surface for a quick breath of air. But this time I find the boat even farther. In the center of the ledge.

I throw up my arm and wave, hopeful that Benny will see me and circle back with the boat, but all three of their heads are looking down near where I coiled the anchor. So much for getting a ride in, I think, as I debate whether to return to the bottom or head for the boat. Overtaken by a wave of dizziness, probably from too much time underwater, I decide to let exhaustion win and start swimming back.

Yet every time I think I'm making progress, the boat drifts another few feet. It's almost over the other side of ledge now, back where the water gets shallow near the shelf that's usually teeming with eels and corals and a whole colony of life that only grows on a ledge where deep water meets shallow layers warmed by the sun. It's usually one of my favorite areas to explore, but right now I'm too tired to care. So I kick my legs harder and venture out over the deep part of the ledge. The water grows colder, and the bottom more distant, with every stroke.

About halfway over the ledge, my arms start to cramp. "Benny, over here," I say, using a full breath of air.

No response.

I fill my lungs again and let out another call.

Still no one turns.

And the boat's slipping farther away.

"Guys, over here!" I choke on a mouthful of sea water just as Benny pops up his head and waves back.

"Hey Pipes, come on back. We found the bracelet in the boat," he says.

So much for being sure it fell into the water. "You're drifting too fast," I say. "Can you drive over and pick me up?"

"Yeah, no problem." Benny runs to the steering wheel and fumbles with the throttle, but the motor never clicks. "Pipes, where are keys?"

Shoot. The keys. They're on my shorts of course, where they always are, hooked onto my belt loop and shoved into my pocket so I won't lose them.

"They're with me, just forget it," I say. "Can you throw me a line?"

Logan runs to the bow. "How about the anchor rope?"

"Just untie it from the anchor first," I say.

I'm closing the gap now and figure if I can just grab onto a rope, Benny can pull me the rest of the way. Not ideal, but given the power of the current and unlikelihood that anyone is going to learn how to hotwire the engine anytime soon, it's the best I'm going to do.

But when I look up again, Logan's still trying to untie the anchor. And Benny is doing nothing to help. In fact, he isn't doing anything. He's just standing there, frozen, his face a whitish green.

"Hey, what's wrong?" I manage.

Benny frowns. "Piper, you have to get out of there now. Just keep swimming," he says.

"What's going on?" I ask, my throat tightening.

"Just swim, Pipes," he says, his eyes fixed on mine.

Logan frees the line and joins Benny, his eyes narrowing. "Oh God Piper, swim faster! And don't turn around!"

With that, I glance over my shoulder, already knowing what's waiting for me. A sharp dorsal fin, not rounded like a porpoise. The fin of a shark. One that's not very far away.

Now, seeing as I swim in these waters every day and have since I pretty much learned to breathe, this is not my first encounter with a shark. I've swum among reef sharks hundreds of times, helped Dad land huge Makos on more than one shark fishing excursion, and I've studied just about every species in the marine center a few blocks from my house. But right away I can tell that this encounter is different. First, the dorsal fin is gray and jagged, instead of the dark spotted beige common with reef sharks. And there are no waves this shark could be riding, no schools of fish he could be stalking for food. No, the grunts left ten minutes ago for the shallows, leaving me as the shark's only target. In sixty feet of water. About twenty-five yards from the boat.

"Benny, throw out that line," I say, trying not to cry. All the facts and training on shark attacks from the marine center come flooding back, but right now I'm too paralyzed to use any of them. Don't splash. Keep calm. Try not to look like a manatee or turtle. As if I have any choice in what I look like right now. I switch my freestyle to a breast stroke to cut down on the splashing and push harder, forcing my oxygen-deprived muscles to forge ahead toward the boat.

"Shit Piper, keep going, faster, faster," screams Benny.

"Oh my God, I can't look," says Marina, burying her face in her hands.

Logan grabs the anchor line and throws it toward me. They've tied a lifejacket to the end of it, which bobs just ten feet from my outstretched hands. But the water's churning around me, and I'm scared. Almost too scared to keep swimming.

"Piper, don't stop," Logan screams.

This time I listen. Three more strokes and I've got the lifejacket. Ten more seconds and Benny and Logan have me up against the side of the boat. And out of the jaws of a massive bull shark.

CHAPTER SIX

"Benny, get the keys! Now!" I roll over the side of the boat and reach for my pocket, pulling the lump of keys out of my pocket until they're dangling from my belt loop. Benny unhooks them as I lay there, gasping for air on the hot fiberglass floor.

No one says a word as Benny races toward the steering console. The gray fin is circling us, and I know if we don't get out of here soon, our new friend is going to start rocking the boat Jaws-style. Because at 12' long, my Whaler looks a lot like a hefty manatee or porpoise. Not too intimidating for a 500 pound bull shark.

And then before I can think another thought, it's

like the shark has read my mind. The boat is rocking and Marina is crying. Logan is screaming for everyone to lie down on the floor so we don't fall out. But the side closest to the shark is tipping almost into the water, making the bottom no safer than the bench seats up top.

"Benny, what the hell is wrong? Start the motor now!" I yell as the shark retreats back. His first charge has been unsuccessful – we're still right side up and there are no leaks taking in water – but he hasn't given up. The fin is moving faster now, churning the water all around us.

"I dropped the keys!" says Benny. "I think they're under the front bench seat."

Despite the throbbing pain in my legs, I force myself onto all fours and crawl over to the seat. I stick my hand underneath the bench until my fingers feel a clump of metal. The keys. My fingers wrap around the keychain as I pull myself to my feet.

"I've got them! Here!" I throw them to Benny, who catches them just as the dorsal fin skims by the bow. It's almost close enough for us to touch now, meaning his razor-sharp skin and rows of jagged teeth are not too far behind.

"Benny, we gotta get out of here now!" Marina screams. "This thing is looking at me! He wants to eat me!"

The motor roars to life before Benny can answer.

"Hang on everyone," he screams, then slams down the throttle.

"Holy shit!" says Logan as we all tumble back from the sudden start, a tangle of arms and legs and screams.

Benny pulls back on the gas, then starts steering us in to shore.

"Is it gone?" asks Marina.

"I don't know. I don't see it," says Benny.

"Then it's gone," I say. "Bull sharks are pretty fierce, but it's rare they'd chase us at this speed."

Logan nods, then crawls up onto the seat. Marina follows his lead.

"Hey, it's okay. It's gone now," Logan says, his voice a whisper. I look over to see Marina shivering, her eyes wet, her shirt soaked from the dirty water sloshing in the bottom of the boat.

"Thanks, yeah. That...was...insane. I didn't know there were sharks like that around here. I'm never going swimming again." Marina's lips are quivering, the words coming out in small spurts.

"Tell me about it. Piper, you are crazy, jumping into shark infested waters," says Logan, his eyes glassy.

I drag myself off the bottom of the boat and walk over to Benny. "I can drive now if you want."

Benny shakes his head. "Sit down before your legs give out. You aren't doing another thing."

"How are you going to get it into the slip? I know you, you'll crash it into the dock."

"Piper, sit down. I'll manage."

"But I'm fine, honest."

"Piper," Benny's voice is deeper now, more forceful. "You were six inches away from ending up in that shark's mouth. Now sit down!"

My legs give out as Benny stares me down. I knew the shark was near me, I felt the churning water and rocking boat. But six inches. That's even shorter than the length of my hand. I take a deep breath as my butt collides with the bench seat. "I didn't know it was so close."

"Its mouth was open, Pipes. I saw its teeth."

"We all did," said Logan.

"I...I'm...sorry?" I say.

Benny sighs. "Don't be. Just chill. I've got the boat."

And he does, docking the baby a few minutes later without so much as a bump to the dock, which is probably a good thing given that we're all more than a little on edge. Especially when we get out on the dock and take a good look at the damage. The Whaler's hull is all scratched and there's a huge dent in the center of the side. A patch of fiberglass is missing from the bow, just above the water line. An inch lower and we would've had a much different ride back.

"So, when's the next fishing lesson?" asks Logan as

we walk up the dock.

"Umm, how about never?" says Marina.

"Sounds good to me," says Benny.

But Logan just shakes his head. "I don't think I've ever wanted to fish more."

"You might want to reconsider that," says Marina.

"Well either way, looks like the boat's gonna be out of commission for a while," I say. "It's definitely going to need a patch. And we should probably report this to the Coast Guard. Make sure they tell all the lifeguards and swimmers to be on high alert."

Benny pulls out his cell phone. "You want me to call?"

"No, I can do it. But maybe not right now. I think I need a break."

"Why don't we head over to my parent's restaurant then? I can use some lunch and it might be good to get away from the docks for a bit."

"Yeah, I'm starved," says Logan, meeting my eyes.

I look away, uncomfortable with the attention, as we start walking to the Overseas Highway, the main road bisecting the island. Only after a block do I return my gaze to the group, hoping to find Logan's stare gone. But it's still there, following me with every move. His eyes are tracking my feet, and then when I turn back they shoot up, pausing on my hair before settling on Benny's t-shirt, then moving on to the road. I try to walk faster, hoping his glance will fade but it never does.

"Everything all right?" I ask him, wondering if the shark's still on his mind. As if it's possible it's not.

"Yeah, I'm fine," he says, "I just can't get over how close that shark came to all of us. And how well you handled it back there, Piper. If it was me, I would have frozen dead in the water as soon as I saw that thing. But you, you just kept swimming." His voice cracks on the last words and it's then that I remember he's from Michigan, a world away from the ocean.

"Believe me, if there was a shark behind you, I can guarantee you would find a way to swim," I say.

"Maybe," says Logan, "But maybe not. Either way, I think I'm going to need some swimming lessons too."

At this Benny laughs. "You really want to go back on the water still, huh?"

Logan shrugs. "Guess I sort of like a challenge."

"Well in that case, I am sure Pipes has a lot of other stuff she can show ya. You know, sharks aren't the only predator in these waters..."

I punch Benny in the side, annoyed he'd bring up yet another expedition without asking me, just as Marina lets out a scream, echoing her sentiments from earlier about the shark.

Marina calms down just as we reach Oswardo's. It's rare Benny and I visit the restaurant, mostly because it's usually crammed tight with loud groups of tourists. But right now I'd rather deal with picture-snapping visitors than the locals, who'll ask questions about our day. Pump us for information until we crack and spill about the shark.

As we enter the restaurant, a wave of air conditioning envelops us, making my teeth chatter as Benny guides us toward the kitchen. The smells of cilantro and roast pork grow stronger as we navigate by a family of six and a group of old men that look like they've just gotten back from a fishing trip.

"Should we sit down?" asks Marina as we pass by a group of empty tables. It's one o'clock, the peak of lunch hour, but already the restaurant is clearing out. It's not uncommon for June since there's no fishing tournaments coming up, but it's unsettling nonetheless. I can tell Marina thinks so too, as we weave through two rows of polished tables set for groups of four, two and six. Something tells me it's a similar scene back at the Becco Lodge.

"Let's eat outside," Benny says, pointing to a thick wood door next to the kitchen. He seems oblivious to the empty tables or the young hostess sitting in the back, rolling together a mound of silverware and napkins. But then, Benny's never been one to worry, probably because his parents have weathered hard times before. There's something about growing up with nothing that makes the slow times here not seem as bad.

Once outside, Benny plops down at a red picnic

table surrounded by lime trees. "It's much better out here, no?"

"Yeah, this is awesome. Do your parents really run this place?" asks Logan.

"Uh-huh, they opened it when I was a baby. It's an institution. Best Key Lime pie ever made."

"Yeah, and it's named for him too," says Marina.

"What is? The pie?" asks Logan.

"No, the restaurant," I say. "Oswardo."

Marina laughs. "You should see his face every year on the first day of school. The teachers always get it wrong."

"Thanks guys," says Benny, his cheeks turning red. "Let me tell my parents we're here. Pipes, maybe you can put in a call to the Coast Guard?"

"Oh, yeah, good idea." I excuse myself from the table and walk to the edge of the lime trees. Then I hit speed dial number three on my phone.

"Islamorada Coast Guard, how can I help you," says a familiar voice.

"Hey Kip, is that you?" I ask.

"Sure is, Piper. What's up?"

"Well, it's nothing too big, but we just had a shark sighting," I say, trying to keep my voice steady.

"Let me guess, you were near the ledge."

"How'd you know?"

"I got cut off a few minutes back from someone who thought he saw a shark getting real close to some boaters down there. Was that you trying to radio it in?"

"No, wasn't me. We've been off the water for about thirty minutes now. We just saw the dorsal fin."

"Only saw the dorsal, huh? Could you tell what kind of shark it was? Any ideas?"

"It was a gray fin, pretty big, and we weren't in much water. If I had to guess, I'd say it was a bull shark."

"Sounds like a good assessment. I'll let everyone know. And be careful out there, Piper. Bull sharks are nothing to sneeze at. Only shark scarier is the great white."

"Yeah, I know. Luckily no one was in the water."

"Good thing. Might want to keep it that way for the next few days too. You know those suckers like the shallows. They'll come right up on ya, almost follow you straight onto the beach!"

"Yup, we'll be careful," I say before walking back to the table.

"So why'd you tell them no one was in the water?" asks Logan.

I shrug. "My dad's pretty connected. He talks to Kip at the Coast Guard office all the time. Last thing I need is him knowing how close I just came to that shark."

"But shouldn't they know that he almost killed us? That he attacked the boat? Doesn't that make him more dangerous?"

"Not really. Everyone knows bull sharks are dangerous. As long they know that's what they're dealing with, they'll take it seriously."

"Are you sure that's what it was?" asks Marina.

I nod, happy that for once, she's interested in something I have to say. "Its body was stocky and its nose looked all pushed in. Typical bull shark."

"Impressive," says Logan. He gives me a weak smile just as Benny reappears, a tray of glasses and lemonade balanced on his arm.

"My mom's on her way with menus, and you better watch out," he says. "She is in one helluva mood."

"Oh shoot. It's because we didn't call, isn't it?" I ask.

Benny grins as the door swings open.

"Piper, hello Doll!" Mrs. Benitez runs over and grabs my neck, then plants a huge kiss on my cheek. "I am so happy you came, but my Benny, he didn't call! I had a beautiful suckling pig out back just waiting to be roasted, but he didn't call, so now you need to order something off the menu. Or maybe not the menu, no we'll cook you something special, but I'm afraid we can't make the pig. Unless you have a few hours?"

Ms. Benitez whizzes by, spitting out sentences rapid fire, until she reaches Logan and Marina. "Now Benny, introduce me to your friends. Where are your manners? Oh and where are mine? Here I am talking about food before I've even met either of you. I don't even know if you like pig. But you do, right? Everyone loves a good suckling pig!"

Benny sighs. "Mom, this is Logan and Marina, just like I told you inside."

"It's so nice to meet you both. Benny's told me lots about you, Marina and you are even more beautiful than I imagined."

Marina blushes as Mrs. Benitez leans in for a kiss. "It's nice to meet you too," she says, flashing a smile.

Mrs. Benitez runs around the table to shake Logan's hand, then disappears into the kitchen to make us something special. Seeing as it is close to 100 degrees in the shade, I'm hoping it's something lighter than a pig. Like maybe a gallon of water. With a side of key lime pie.

It seems that Mrs. Benitez is reading my mind when she appears with a plate of fresh tomato salad drenched in lime juice, along with a platter of grilled snapper filets with my favorite bean and mango salsa. One whiff and my appetite is back in full force. There is nothing like a meal at Oswardo's to reenergize my body and make me crave more food.

I debate asking Benny if we can come back tomorrow and take his mom up on that suckling pig when Mrs. Benitez comes out with four to-go bags, stuffed with pulled pork sandwiches.

Again, she apologizes that it's not fresh suckling

pig, and tells us she'll make one for us next time. I swear, the woman really does know exactly what I'm thinking. Or at least what my stomach is.

"So I should probably get back to the hotel," says Marina as we each grab a brown bag. "I've got a lot of work ahead with these purses now, but this was fun. Really."

Seeing as her knees have only stopped shaking a few minutes ago, I'm not really sure the trip was what she'd call fun, but at least it was a distraction. Or bonding experience of sorts, if you can call almost dying together an experience.

"Do you want some company?" Benny asks Marina, as we walk out to the parking lot. "I can help critique the purses for you."

She nods. "Company would be good. Logan and Piper, you interested?"

It's the first time Marina's invited me to anything and part of me knows that if I want to keep Benny happy, I should go. But with a dented boat in serious need of repair, I shake my head. "I've gotta patch that fiberglass before my dad gets in from his charter tonight, or he'll know something's up."

Benny frowns. "You know it might not kill you to actually just tell him what happened."

"Right," I say. "If he finds out, he'll keep me out of the water for weeks. As it is, I'll probably have to stay on land for a few days just for reporting that shark."

"Good. The water's not safe. And this way Logan can teach me some of his football drills."

"In this heat?" says Logan. "Man, first you try to feed me to the sharks, now you're talking about sweating me to death. If I didn't know better, I'd say you guys were trying to get rid of me."

"Not at all," says Marina. "Why don't you come with Benny and me? The hotel's air conditioned. We've got satellite TV too. You guys can watch sports or whatever while I paint. It'll be fun."

Logan smiles, then turns to me. "Thanks, but I kind of want to see this patch mission. And you know, make sure Piper stays out of trouble."

The second the words come out, I stare at him, speechless.

"You sure?" I say a moment later, folding my arms across my chest. "You know I'm pretty good with patching, it's really not necessary."

"Well if I'm going to be an expert fisherman, isn't patching a boat part of the job?"

"Uh, I guess," I say, wondering when he decided being a fisherman was so important. Probably around the same time his dad decided to enter the Scramble.

"Great, then we'll catch up with you guys later," Logan says to Marina and Benny. "Piper and I have some work to do."

I nod, still not really comprehending anything that's happened in the past three hours, except that

I've almost been eaten by a shark, nearly sunk my boat, and probably eaten more than 10 pounds of food. And now Logan, the odd boy with long hair and an unnerving smile, wants to hang out with me. It's a strange turn of events, made even stranger by his sudden interest in fishing. But with a big patch job ahead, I decide not to dwell on Logan's motives.

"We'll swing by the hotel in a couple hours," I say to Benny. "We still have to cover that turtle nest before it gets dark."

"I forgot about that," says Benny, for once not giving me any trouble about the nest. "I guess we'll see you later then."

The last thing I hear is Marina's soft laugh as they disappear down the street. I turn back to Logan and wonder what to say next, but nothing comes to mind.

"So you really want to learn more about fishing?" I ask, feeling stupid as soon as the words slip out.

"Yup. And what's this talk about a turtle? You've got me intrigued."

"Oh, it's nothing. I just found a turtle nest near Marina's hotel that I want to protect. They've become pretty rare around here."

Logan pauses before shaking his head. "I can't believe I've been here a month and haven't learned anything," he says.

At that, I smile. "Well, the island's a complicated place. She only shares her secrets with those who listen."

"Good thing I found you then to help me learn how."

Logan smiles as a chill runs down my spine. His interest in the turtles and island excites and surprises me at the same time.

Leaving me to wonder once again if maybe I've misjudged the strange boy with the weird smile, who I don't quite know, and don't quite understand.

CHAPTER SEVEN

"So that will be $25.48," says Mr. Owens as he bags my fourth fiberglass repair kit of the year.

I hand over two crumbled bills from my Scramble entrance fee savings and pray that Mr. Owens doesn't ask what I crashed into this time. But of course, he always asks.

"So was it you or Benny?" he says as he reaches for my change. "Or maybe the new kid?"

"Benny," I say, not wanting to answer any more questions. "The new kid isn't allowed to drive."

Mr. Owens chuckles, then hands over the bag along with a stack of ones and coins. "I'm sure you'll have him trained soon enough."

"Of course," I say, then start walking toward the door. Logan follows behind me as Mr. Owens shouts goodbye.

"So I'm the new kid now, huh?" Logan asks once we're on the street.

"Guess so." I pick up the pace and start walking the two blocks between the Bass Pro Shop and the docks, hoping that maybe Logan will change his mind and decide to go home. But instead, he presses on.

"So is Benny really that bad docking the boat?" he asks.

"Nah, Benny's great. He hasn't crashed into the dock in months now. But he used to all the time, before he really learned how to maneuver in neutral. Once he mastered that though, he's been good. Not that I'd ever tell that to Mr. Owens. Especially since most of our crashes come from, let's just say less acceptable practices."

"Like running away from a bull shark?"

"Potentially."

Logan laughs as we walk down the dock to the Whaler. It looks the same as it did a few hours earlier, banged up and beaten, but no worse than if we'd bashed the side of a dock. So I get to work, cleaning the side with fresh water, then buffing it dry so the patch will stick. Logan watches in silence as I prepare the mixture, then slather it on with a wooden paddle. As the fiberglass dries, he takes off his sneakers and drops his feet in the water, dangling them over the side of the dock.

He jumps as a school of shiner fish circles them, then starts pecking at his skin.

"Ow, that hurts!" he says, reminding me of Benny.

I laugh. "Come on, those fish are smaller than my fingernail! It might tickle, but it most definitely doesn't hurt."

"But they're trying to eat me," he says.

"Just the dead skins cells."

Logan gags. "Now that is disgusting."

"Well, everyone's gotta eat."

"I guess so," he says, flashing me a smile.

This time, I don't look away. Instead, I smile back and find myself swimming in his swirling blue eyes. As much as I want to look away, to go back to staring at the Whaler or docks, I can't break my stare. Because Logan's eyes are different than expected. Completely different than Benny's inky brown. Sadder, too. Not quite as sure, or confident as I first thought.

I try to keep my hands busy, moving around the tools and canisters of fiberglass, so Logan can't tell how much they're shaking as I look away. Because besides Benny, I've never really hung out with a guy my age. Especially one that chose to hang out with me, especially after he saw the reactions of Sardi and Marina at last night's bonfire.

"Is the fiberglass ready for sanding yet?" Logan

asks as I put down my paddle.

"Few more minutes. It's still a little sticky," I say.

He nods. "So how long have you lived on the island?"

I roll back my shoulders and stare out into the distance, still avoiding Logan's eyes. "My whole life, give or take a few days. I was actually born in the hospital in Key West. My mom went into labor three weeks early, while they were at a big fishing tournament out there. Though way she tells it, the whole thing actually worked out better that way. Key West has a real hospital, unlike here."

"So you've never lived anywhere else?"

"Just the island."

"What about during the hurricanes?"

I laugh. "We board up the windows and hunker down inside. Why? Your dad want to interview me for his documentary? Or are you already bored with island life?"

Logan's eyes turn serious. "No. Just the opposite. I mean, I was bored until I met you and Benny. But now, look at me. Braving shark encounters, patching boats, eating key lime pie. How could I be bored?"

"Glad we could help," I say, and for the first time, I think I mean it.

"Seriously, you have no idea."

Logan's voice drifts as I turn back to the boat. "This seems pretty dry now," I say, running my fingers over the patch.

"Here, let me help." Logan reaches for the sandpaper, entwining his fingers with mine in the process. I jump back, his warm touch stinging almost as much as that hydroid.

"No, it's cool...I got it." I continue sanding as my mind wanders.

Hanging out with Logan is almost as tiring as swimming in a riptide. Just thinking of what to say is exhausting. It's not like with Benny, where words just kind of pour out unfiltered. But then, maybe pouring out everything isn't always the best thing. Seems these days with Benny all it leads to is a lot of whining. And so far with Logan, there's been none of that. Except when he's with his dad, anyway. But then, Logan is also an unknown, lonely in a new place. How hard is it to be nice to someone for a few days? Especially if it's between being nice to the weird girl or hanging out with the parents that made him move in the first place? Thinking about the possibilities makes my head spin.

"Okay, I think we're done here," I say, crumpling up the worn sandpaper. "And I should really get going. Still need to run by my house and grab that dragnet for the turtle nest."

"Well then, let's go," says Logan, taking my statement as an invitation.

I bite my lip, unsure if I'm ready to show him my

house. But then I look at his face, and think of boorish Nick and how if that was my dad, I'd want to escape too.

"Okay, sure," I say as Logan grabs the remnants of the fiberglass repair kit and starts walking down the dock.

As we reach the Rosalie's deck, I spot Sardi at the corner table on the back deck. Not in the mood to relive my abrupt exit at last night's party, I pick up the pace. But it's too late. She's already waving.

"Piper, hey! Wait up," she says. "Where'd you go last night? I was looking all over! You totally missed the s'mores! Did Logan tell you? They were fantastic, absolutely perfect. We had the best time. Really. And ohmiGod, Travis and I really hit it off. Like we have so much in common! Did you know he's working as a camp counselor too this summer? We are both counselors but at different camps. Isn't that crazy?"

"Uh, yeah, totally crazy," I say, still walking.

"We're hanging out tonight, can you believe it? I mean, it's not really a date or anything, it's more like a group. I wanted to see if you were interested. We planned it last night. I think Marina and Benny are going and maybe you guys can come too. Are you free? Please say yes, it would be so much fun!" Sardi is bouncing off the pavement as she claps her hands together.

"Oh, that sounds so awesome. Too bad I'm busy

tonight. You guys have fun though," I say.

"Aw that stinks! What are you doing? Something fun I hope, maybe fishing in the dark? I've heard some really cool things about those night trips, they're supposed to be super cool. You know you can even catch sharks?"

I force myself to smile. "Yeah, I've been on a few. Never caught a shark but it sounds really neat. I'm not doing anything too exciting tonight, though. I'm actually helping out my dad. We need to repair one of our boats."

"Oh. Okay then. Good luck. Logan, are you in?"

He shakes his head. "Actually I just promised Piper here I'd help her dad out with repairs. Seems they're having some engine problems, which are my specialty."

"Aww well you should come by if you finish early. We're meeting here at Rosalie's after dinner. They're going to have a band."

"They get one every Friday," I say. "For the tourists."

"Hey, they'll be locals too," says Sardi, crossing her arms.

"Of course. Well I better get going now. Maybe I'll see you later."

"Sure, call me if your plans change. It would be so great if you could come along, especially since Ella and Kali have gone AWOL, us girls have got to stick together, you know!" The way she mentions "us girls" makes me cringe.

"So looks like we're busy tonight," Logan says as we reach the edge of Rosalie's parking lot. "And here I thought your dad's boat was running perfectly."

"It is," I say, turning onto the main road. "That was just an excuse. Friday nights at Rosalie's are painful. It's the one night of the week where I try to avoid the place. But please, you should go. I'm really going to just hang home, and something tells me you don't want to spend another night with Nick."

"Oh, so Rosalie's isn't good enough for you, but it's okay for me?"

I sigh. "Rosalie's is fine, I mean, it's my favorite place usually. I'm just not a fan of their Friday nights. Trust me, after you go a few times, you'll realize it's all the same. Island music. Jimmy Buffet and steel drums. Not really original. But, since you're new, you'd probably like it."

"Well I don't like island music. And seems to me if I go, I'll be more of a fifth wheel."

"Sardi and Travis aren't even dating."

"I'd still rather hang out with you if you're available. Why don't I fiddle with your outboard? We could check the sparkplugs or something. I noticed the boat seemed a little slow when Benny gunned it today."

I turn to him and stare. "So you really are good

with motors?"

He shrugs. "More like car engines but how different can a boat be?"

I laugh. "Well it sounds appealing but I just had the spark plugs changed a month back. If the boat was slow it probably had more to do with seaweed caught in the prop."

"Shoot. Well what are we supposed to do now that we turned down Sardi?"

"Go to bed early?" I ask.

"You are not getting out of this that easy. If you tell me that Rosalie's on Friday is lame, you need to give me a replacement."

"I didn't say it was lame. In fact, I told you you should go. Just call Sardi and tell her your plans got cancelled. Or just go over with Benny and Marina."

"I told you, I'd be the fifth wheel."

"I don't think they'd mind."

"True," Logan says, winking. "But I'd prefer not to alienate my first friends just yet."

"Sounds like you've done it before."

Logan smiles. "Let's leave that discussion for another day."

"Why? I think it sounds pretty relevant," I say as we turn onto my street.

"So what we are going to do tonight?"

"Sure." I cross over to the left-hand side of the street as Liggy comes into view. "Why would I hang out with someone who would alienate a friend?"

"Hmm. Good point. How about I promise to do nothing to hurt our friendship. Will you hang out with me then?"

My toes start to burn. "Fine. What do you want to do?"

"How about night fishing, like Sardi mentioned?"

Right. Like I haven't seen enough sharks today. "Maybe we should just oil up the motor."

"In the dark? Hmm. Now that I think about it, that sounds dangerous. Night fishing is a way better idea."

"Only we'd need to take out the Blackfin and Dad only lets me go out on that boat during the day."

"Any reason he needs to know?"

"Logan, that thing costs like $200,000! I can't just patch it up with fiberglass if something goes wrong."

"Aw, you're a pro, I've seen you. And besides, we don't have to go out far. I just want to see the harbor at night."

Right. Sure he does. Really he's just looking for a story. Or to potentially get me grounded. For life. Yet strangely, sneaking out Dad's boat sounds kind of appealing.

As I roll the options over in my head, I open up the backyard fence and lead Logan inside. "Well, this is home," I say, closing the gate behind him. "And this is Liggy."

"Whoa, it's a deer!" Logan says.

"Yeah, she's a key deer."

"What happened to her leg?"

"Car accident."

"She's your pet?"

"And friend. My mom and I found her on the side of the street bleeding to death and brought her in. After she healed up, we tried to bring her back into the wild, but she kept coming back home. So we built this fence a couple years back, and she's been with us ever since."

"Wow, if I told the guys back in Michigan that you keep deer as pets, they'd be down with their guns so fast..."

"Stop! Key deer are not open for hunting. They're endangered."

Logan smirks. "Like your turtle."

"No, she's threatened. Though given the rate the loggerheads have been disappearing at, they'll probably be back on the endangered list soon enough."

"Unless you save them."

I grab the hose and fill Liggy's water dish, then head toward the open garage door. "Saving one loggerhead is not going to save the species."

"Neither is saving one deer."

"You're right. It won't."

"But you still gotta try," he says.

I stop walking and pause. "If you don't try, then

there's no hope."

"I couldn't agree more."

I shake my head, surprised by how much he gets me. How he understands the island mindset of working hard even when survival depends on things that can't be controlled. Like tourists. Storms. Cold snaps and heat waves and water damage to the Seven Mile Bridge. Around here, everyone deals with setbacks, but we all get up and keep going whether the restaurant is half empty, the charter's full of novices or the hotel has only five guests.

Out in the real world where roads and businesses cover the ground like a wide net just brimming with opportunities, people usually aren't so aware. Logan is an exception.

"So where's this net of yours?" Logan asks as I head for the garage.

"It's time to find out." I pull open the garage door and lead Logan by an entire museum of junk. In the center, an old boat that hasn't run in years sits up on blocks, taking up the room usually reserved for cars.

On the right lies a collection of diving buoys, fishing rods and half-filled tool boxes. We tiptoe around the mess until we reach a pile of nets and fishing line. The dragnet is on the bottom of the pile, tangled up with half a fishing rod I saved after some kid snapped it in half. At the time, I thought I could rebuild it, but that was two years ago and I still haven't done a thing with it. Except get it tangled in the old dragnet.

Luckily, the tangle isn't bad and we get the net free with a couple pulls. After collecting a few metal poles and cords to create a fence around the nest, I run inside, say hi to Mom who is on her computer working on the Wesley Charters website, and grab my cell phone, wallet, and purse. I meet Logan out front and punch in Benny's number as we start walking. The phone rings ten times before he answers.

"Hey, you still at Marina's?" I ask.

"Yeah, we're just getting ready to put on a movie. You guys coming over?"

"We're on our way now."

"Want us to wait for you?"

"Nah, you go ahead. It's getting pretty late and I need to be back for dinner at 6:00. We'll probably just cover the turtle nest and go," I say.

"Stop by after you're all done and say hello. And tell Logan he's more than welcome to chill here if he'd rather not fight through the weeds guarding that nest."

Leave it to Benny to worry about the weeds. "Will do." I close the phone and turn to Logan. "Benny and Marina are putting on a movie, said you should stop by if you're interested."

"Are they going to help secure the nest?"

"I don't think so. Benny sounded pretty tired."

Logan laughs. "He really doesn't like turtles, does he?"

"That might be my fault. I used to make him inspect hundreds of nests a day when we were kids."

"Mind if I still help?"

I start to nod, then notice the flip flops on his feet. "Actually you might want to sit it out. There's a lot of low-growing cacti around the nest that could do a number on your feet."

"They don't scare me."

"They should."

"You really think I should pass?"

"Go watch the movie, I've got the nest," I say.

"Okay then, but only because I want to see you tonight."

My cheeks grow warm. "Fine, though if you change your mind and just want to go to Rosalie's that's fine too. I won't be offended."

"And I won't be canceling. When should I meet you at the dock?"

My stomach rumbles as Logan folds up the dragnet and places it in my arms. "If we're really going to do this, we need to take the boat out late, when no one's around."

"Like 8:00?"

I shake my head. "More like 10:00. The dock office is open until 9:00."

"Okay then, I'll meet you on the dock at 9:00."

I nod, then keep walking into the grasses. A moment later, I'm in front of the turtle nest, but my hands are shaking so badly I can't even spread out the net. So I plop down into the sand and bring my knees up into my chest. Maybe I should've said yes to Sardi after all and just gone to Rosalie's with the crew. Would've at least been safer than plotting a takeover of Dad's prized fishing boat, the lifeline of our entire company. Though maybe it's not too late, after all. I can still back out and go to bed early. Just not show up on the docks. Pretend it's a normal Friday night.

Feeling a little better, I lift myself out of the sand and get to work securing the turtle nest. But as I craft the fence around the hidden eggs, a shiver runs down my spine. Because even if going to bed early is the smart option, my mind is already made up.

Logan said he wanted a challenge, and night fishing is definitely a challenge. Even if it does mean breaking a few tiny rules.

I mean, when have I ever let a few technicalities get in my way anyway? Never. And I'm not about to let them block me now.

CHAPTER EIGHT

The clouds decide to burst just as I turn onto my street, on my way home from the turtle nest. My feet slosh through the growing puddles as buckets of water drench my hair and clothes. The crackles of thunder in the distance make me jump, and then run faster. It's just an afternoon thunderstorm, nothing unique. But this one feels like it's just for me. Another reason to chill with Liggy tonight at home.

I walk into the kitchen and find Mom hard at work frying fish. My favorite dinner. Throwing down my purse, I pick up a raw filet of fish, submerging it in flour, then egg. And before I know it, I'm telling Mom that I'm busy for the night. Going out with friends. To

Rosalie's. I flinch as the lies come out and thank God that tonight we're eating fresh fish. Anything else and I'd be sure to lose my appetite.

"So you're hanging out with Sardi again?" Mom asks, taking my bait as willingly as a fish.

"Yeah, and Benny and some other friends," I say.

"That's nice. Is that new boy Logan going too?"

The raw fish slides out of my hand at her comment. "Oh, I don't know. I think so," I say, picking it up off the counter.

"Well I think that's great that you're hanging out with some new people. Not that I don't love Benny, but it's always good to cast a wider net. Life's more colorful when you have different types of people in it," she says.

"Yeah, right, I know, having friends is good. And Sardi does seem nice," I say, trying to steer clear from more talk of Logan.

"I'm glad you're adding some girls to the mix. Who knows, maybe one of them will like fishing too?"

"I highly doubt it."

"Well then, you should try to figure out what they're into. Maybe spend a little time trying something new. Not that you should give up fishing, but just take some time to see if you like anything else, too."

I smile as I move another piece of fish through the assembly line. Because that's Mom, always worried that by living on an island, she's somehow deprived me of all these experiences. Like going to the mall, seeing more friends. Joining girl scouts or the track team or school band. As if those activities would make me happier.

And no matter how many times I tell her that I'd never be interested in any of those things, and that actually Coral High offers most of them now, she just shakes her head and says she wonders what it would've be like if we'd moved to Panama City or Ft. Lauderdale or even up north somewhere like Raleigh, North Carolina, back when I was a kid. Maybe we'd have more money, and I'd have more friends.

Which is when I tell her that life would be exactly the same no matter where we lived, with me hanging down by the docks, not a planned activity on the calendar except for my next fishing charter. And that's when she smiles. Because thing is, back when she was my age growing up a couple mile markers away, she was a lot like me.

Okay, maybe she wasn't as into fishing, and judging from her pictures she definitely dressed more like a girl, but she, too, was in love with the island, spending her own lazy summers skipping around town with her pet parakeet Kiki and working double shifts for her summer job at the wildlife park Theater of the Sea, just so she could spend more time with the dolphins.

Not to mention the cute fisherman that always

stopped by to drop off buckets of fish for them to eat. Better known as my dad, the one and only Buck Wesley.

And that's why neither of my parents ever really considered moving away. Because how could Dad leave behind the bonefish? And how could Mom say goodbye to her dolphins? The same ones that still swim at Theater of the Sea, and that she goes down to feed every week?

Sure, going somewhere else may have brought more money, but we would've lost more than we gained. Because right now we have our community. A life. And as much as Mom wants me to be successful, to get a good job and not have her worries about money, she also knows that the things we have you just can't throw away.

We dunk the rest of the fish in flour and egg, then add it to the pan, sifting out the older pieces as soon as their crust turns golden brown.

"Mind if I eat the egg?" I ask once the fish is done.

Mom cringes as she washes off her hands. "If you must. Just be quick about it."

I wait for her to start setting the table before pouring the leftover egg into the pan. As soon as it hits the oil it rises up into a big fluffy pancake of fried egg and fish bites. Most people just throw away the leftover egg after breading their fish, but ever since I caught Dad frying up the remnants back when I was a kid, I've been hooked. There's nothing like scrambled eggs with the taste of fresh fish and a thick coating of fried garlic and salt.

The egg floats to the surface of the frying pan in seconds. I scoop it out and blot it with a paper towel, bringing the entire piece to my mouth in an instant before Mom sees me. Somehow it doesn't bother her as much, this eating what she considers to be scraps, if it happens when she's not looking.

On my last bite of egg, the door swings open and Dad comes in, his nose bringing him right to the pan. "No extra egg?" he asks.

"Just finished it.'"

"You didn't save any?"

"Mom was giving me the look."

"You should've hidden me a piece."

"You know it's no good unless it's hot!"

Dad tousles my hair, then helps Mom with the table. Three paper plates and glasses of fresh orange juice later, we are ready to eat. But even though fried grouper is our favorite meal and a Friday tradition, the conversation taints it, like an errant bone stuck in the middle of a white filet. Because as soon as I take a bite of fish, Dad is talking about the bull shark. And my conversation with the Coast Guard.

"Kip tells me it was a big one! That right after you called another fisherman came in saying it was at least fourteen feet long. Fourteen feet! Do you know what that can do to a small rig? I mean, that's longer than your whole boat," Dad says, popping a skinny finger of fish into his mouth.

"Not longer, about the same," I say. "And the shark really didn't look that big to me."

"Kip says you told him it was a bull shark. You must've been pretty close to have that kind of information."

I shrug. "It was swimming over near the Ledge, not too far from where that stream drains in. I just figured it had to be a bull shark since it was so close to the fresh water."

"Either way, I don't like it," Dad says. Mom runs her hand down his back, trying to relax his tensed shoulders.

"Don't worry, it's not the first shark I've seen."

"I'm not worried because it's a shark. I'm worried because there have been reports flying all afternoon that this thing was circling a small craft. That's some aggressive behavior for a shark. We haven't had to deal with anything like that since before you were born."

"Better hope the papers don't get wind of that," Mom says. "News of a killer shark will scare away the few tourists we have left."

"I know, Catherine," Dad says, his voice dropping lower.

"Sounds to me like people are just freaking out.

Would a shark honestly hurt a boat?" I ask, savoring a bite of fresh grouper. "It seems unlikely. I bet that was reported by some tourist who's watched too many episodes of Shark Week."

"I hope you're right."

"Did Kip say what they were going to do about it?" Mom asks.

Dad shrugs, then repeats the facts. "The Coast Guard is on high alert, and they're shutting down the beaches on the Bay side of the island, at least until Monday. If they find it, they'll shoot it, but odds of that are slim. Besides, even if they do find a shark, there's no way of knowing if it's the same one."

Mom opens her mouth, then sighs, and I know what's coming out of her mouth before she even says it. "Do these sharks go into shallow water?"

Of course. All she has to hear is beach closings and her mind turns to me. As if she doesn't know that bull sharks like shallow waters. And that there are sightings every year.

Only thing different is that this time there's this report about it circling a boat. Which said out in the open, does sound pretty bogus. But Dad plays right into her game, not that he needed prompting. I knew where he was headed as soon as he opened his mouth at the table.

So when he confirms that yes, bull sharks love shallow water, and of course Piper shouldn't be out boating or swimming until this whole thing blows over, I don't even scream. Instead I focus on the upcoming tournament. How I'm looking for patterns, hoping to track not only where the shrimp go, but also why, and when, the bonefish follow them. Data that's vital not only to Dad's charters, but to me winning the Scramble. A few days off means less data points. And more room for errors.

Knowing full well that without my reconnaissance, he'll have to run his weekend charters with days-old data – a lifetime for the bonefish who always mix it up – his brow softens. "How about this," he says. "You can go out on the Whaler, but no swimming. It'll at least give you an idea of whether the fish are there or not."

"That would work," I say.

But Mom's not buying it. "Didn't you say that shark was longer than her boat?"

"Mom, that's just hearsay. I'm sure it wasn't really that big."

Dad sighs. "No, your Mom's right. The Whaler won't work. I'd tell you to take out my Hellsbay, but I need to get it ready for my afternoon charter."

My mind races, settling on the image of the old skiff on blocks in our garage. "Well what if I take the old sixteen footer?"

"Geez, Pipes, that thing is a mess. That motor hasn't run in years," Dad says.

"What if we fixed it?"

He laughs. "Who, you and Benny? That thing needs a lot of work. More than just a new set of spark plugs."

And that's when I remember Logan and all his talk about cars.

"Actually I thought maybe Logan could help. He's real good with engines," I say.

"Has he ever worked on an outboard?" Dad asks, reaching for the last piece of fish on the plate.

"Uh, well nothing as powerful as this really, but he rebuilt a small outboard for his friend. They used to take it out on some lake." Now, I have no idea whether Logan has actually ever seen a lake, let alone worked on an outboard, but I know that if I have any chance of getting in my reconnaissance, I need the old skiff. And Dad doesn't let just anybody near his engines.

"Well, I did say that if you could get that thing running again it was yours. So if you trust Logan to do the job, then go for it. Though if it was me, I might keep on saving until I could get a mechanic down at the harbor to take a look."

"Thanks Dad!" I say, jumping up from the table to kiss his cheek. "I'm sure we'll have it up and running by tomorrow afternoon!"

"Oh Buck, do you think it's safe for her to be out there at all?" Mom asks.

"As long as she stays out of the water," he says,

more like a warning than a statement.

"Of course, you know me. Safety first." I'm clearing the table now, my socks sliding across the tile floor as I rinse the plates in the sink.

Dad smirks, then rises from his seat. "I must be crazy letting my fifteen-year-old daughter take apart an engine. Or go out in shark-infested waters for that matter."

"Well, the waters are always shark infested. And I am not a normal fifteen-year-old."

"Nope. Never have been."

With that, the conversation ends and Mom and Dad move into the small box of a room off the kitchen that we use as our family room. A chill runs down my spine as the voice of Wyatt Jacoby, fisherman extraordinaire, fills the house and I wonder how long Mom will let Dad stay tuned into the Expedition Channel before demanding they watch something different. Not that she hates fishing, or even watching Wyatt's show. In fact, Mom used to love it because of all the different wildlife they'd feature, along with these panoramic slices of life from places a world away, filled with people just as in love with their waters as we are with ours.

For a while I used to watch it too, thinking if I studied Wyatt long enough, I'd learn his tricks and figure out how to beat him in the Scramble. Only after a few months, I lost interest. Because with Wyatt, the only thing that changes is the scenery.

Every week, he travels somewhere exotic in search of the most difficult to catch fish. So far he's captured everything from piranhas to giant catfish and great white sharks.

Rumor has it next season he's planning to take on a giant squid. He wants to be the first fishermen to get one live on the line. That would be an episode I'd like to see. But the others? All he does is manhandle the fish. Use knowledge from the locals he meets to jump into an ecosystem he's not familiar with and wrestle out a giant fish. He's never demonstrated any skills that I've noticed. Except maybe some pretty outrageous upper arm strength.

I try to tune out the show as I finish up with the dishes and wipe down the table, but Wyatt's voice is hard to miss. Our house isn't big by anyone's standards – it's certainly nothing like the mansions dotting the coastline– but it's no tin can either.

If it wasn't for the fact that every word anyone says echoes off the walls, the place would be fine. But of course, Mom's never been one for decorating so the house has no rugs or curtains or anything else to drown out the noise. Just tile and stucco, which around here, carry sounds better than most cell phones and require me to keep my stereo blasting anytime I want some privacy.

Which, finishing with the kitchen, is exactly what

I do when I head back to my room. The TV is blaring with some movie now, Mom finally putting her foot down on no more Expedition Channel, so I rinse off about a shaker's worth of salt in the shower, then turn to my closet.

Ah, my closet. It's usually my friend, the way it's stuffed with a rainbow of nylon board shorts, ribbed tanks and racing back bikinis that stay in place even when I'm diving off the Blackfin. But tonight, none of these things feels right. A night at Rosalie's really isn't a special occasion. But sneaking out on Dad's boat with Logan is. Well okay, maybe hoisting Dad's boat isn't exactly special. But hanging out with Logan somehow feels different than a normal night with Benny, especially now that I need to convince him to help me fix the old skiff's motor.

For probably the first time ever, I wish Sardi was here to guide me through the selection. Luckily, the thought fades as I find my favorite shorts crumpled in the corner. Black nylon with a stripe of pink circling the waistband. Perfect.

I throw them on with a pink tank top and slide my feet into my flip flops. Not exactly boating shoes, but even I know wearing boat shoes on a Friday night is weird. And besides, I do better on large boats barefoot, since there's less equipment and tools underfoot than on the Whaler.

For the next fifteen minutes I fight with my hair,

first blow drying it straight, then giving up and throwing it into a ponytail when the flyaways spring back up a moment later.

At 8:00, I say goodbye to Mom and Dad, who wave without breaking their gaze from the screen, and run out the backdoor. In the yard, Liggy seems to smell my tension, padding over and placing her small deer head right against my thigh, as if she was marking a tree or scratching an itch behind her ear.

"Aw Liggy, I'll be home soon. I promise," I say, petting the back of her neck. Her water bowl is full and she's already eaten so I walk her back over to the orange tree where I've laid out a nest of blankets. "It's no beanbag, but it'll have to do for now. As soon as I'm back, I'll sneak you in the house. Deal?"

"Deal," says Logan from behind.

My hand drops from Liggy's back.

Logan brings his hand over my mouth before I can scream.

"What are you doing here?" I ask, once I've recovered.

He shrugs. "I was on my way to the docks when I saw Sardi and company walking to Rosalie's. I didn't want them to see me, and figured you might know a back way to go."

I laugh. "We live on an island. There's no back roads anywhere!"

"So what do we do, then? I don't know if I can take

another conversation with Sardi."

"Hmm, well I guess we can wait here with Liggy for a bit." I glance at the window to my right, relieved to see Mom and Dad still glued to their movie. Then, I plop down in the worn grass near the orange tree.

Logan hesitates before joining me. For a moment, we sit there in silence, not knowing what to say.

"So, uh, do you still want to take out my dad's boat?" I say, turning my hands over in my lap just as Liggy ambles over. She rests her dripping wet snout on my shorts, turning the pink nylon a shade darker.

Logan laughs as we scoot about, trying to get comfortable. "I thought that was the plan. Unless you're not up for it."

From the tone of Logan's voice I can tell he wants me to say yes. That of course we're still on for sneaking out of the harbor. Cruising right by our friends at Rosalie's and the closed dock office and the always buzzing Coast Guard Station.

But at the same time he's given me an out. And as much as I want don't want Logan to pick up and go home, I don't want to risk Dad's boat either. Especially for a guy that's technically still a stranger.

"You know, I'm really sorry, but you think maybe we can do something else?" I say as I rub the back of Liggy's neck.

Logan pauses before responding.

"Yeah, that's cool. I didn't think you'd go through

with it anyway."

"Huh, guess I'm pretty predictable."

"Nah, it just sounded like the boat was important." He looks up into my eyes as he says the words, not breaking the stare until Liggy sneezes, creating yet another stain on my now sopping shorts.

"You want to go in and change?" Logan asks, eying the mess.

I shake my head. "No, let's just go do something. Don't want to rile my parents. They probably think I'm at Rosalie's by now."

Logan nods, then brushes off his shorts as he stands up.

I push Liggy's head back toward the grass and start to get up. Only to find Logan's outstretched hand waiting for me.

"Here, let me help," he says.

I look at him for a moment, not sure what to do. After making him wait a second, I grab on.

"Thanks."

"Any time," he says, looking down at our still-locked hands.

Unsure if they should still be touching, I pull away. Fast.

"Hey, everything okay?" he asks.

"Uh-huh, yeah sure."

"Well, then where to?"

Shoot. Our plans. Here I've been sweating for

hours about sneaking out Dad's boat, but haven't spent a minute thinking about what to do instead.

So again we stare at each other and listen to the frogs chirping in the bushes.

As I will my brain to think.

Finally I settle on my usual routine. It's nothing special, but right now it's better than creeping around the backyard with Liggy.

"Why don't we head down to the harbor," I say, "and grab some ice cream on the way? We can listen to the band from the Whaler and chill, and if you decide you'd rather see Benny and the crew, they'll only be a few feet away."

Logan laughs. "Well it's not night fishing but I guess I'll take it. Though I doubt my mind's going to change about seeing Sardi."

"All right then," I say, as I head in the direction of Islamorada's only convenience store. And try not to remember that this is what I used to do with Benny.

CHAPTER NINE

"So this is Rosalie's on a Friday night?" asks Logan, staring at the swirling lights and sounds above.

"The way you made it sound, I thought it was going to be much worse."

"Believe me, it is when you're sitting right next to the band."

"You saying this isn't the typical experience?"

I laugh. "Well not everyone gets to enjoy the music with ice cream on one of the best fishing boats around."

Logan digs his plastic spoon into our pint of Cherry Garcia, pulling out a scoop pure sprinkles as I recline in the bow of the Whaler.

"Looks like we poured too many in," I say, pointing at his spoon.

"Too many sprinkles? Nonsense. There's no such thing."

I laugh and reach for the pint, digging around until I get a full scoop of ice cream and cherries. Relief floods through my veins, washing away my fears of sneaking out the boat and crashing into unmarked coral reefs, or of running into Kip or another one of Dad's friends. Logan runs his hand through his hair and sings along to the Jimmy Buffet song blasting above. Cheeseburger in Paradise. For the first time ever, it doesn't annoy me.

"So I have something to ask you," I say, feeling bolder with the music. "I might need a favor. Something involving an engine."

Logan's eyes perk up at the mention. "Does this mean we can change your spark plugs after all?"

I laugh. "Even better. My dad said I'm banned from the Whaler all weekend because of the shark. But he said if I could get that old skiff in the garage working, I could take that out instead."

"And let me guess. You have no idea how to fix it."

My cheeks burn as Logan puffs out his chest, a little too excited at the notion of being needed.

"Not no idea," I say, "but I thought since you were into this stuff, you might be interested in helping."

He grins until his eyes become two slits. "Well, I'd

be honored to help."

"Thanks. You free tomorrow?"

"And every day this week."

"Good. This could take a while."

Logan nods, his eyes brighter than usual. "Hey, there's nothing I like more than getting dirty with an engine."

At this I laugh, barely noticing as one song rolls into the next.

"So are all these boats used for fishing?" Logan asks, scanning the bobbing skiffs and motor boats all around us.

I shrug. "Most of them. Fishing is a pretty big business around here."

"Yeah, that's what my dad says, though I'd love to know more."

I raise my brow, still surprised by Nick's sudden interest, especially given how lightly he took his lessons on the charter.

"My dad's always traveling for work," Logan says, "and finds it goes better when he learns about the local culture. Really knows what the people are all about."

Ah, finally. An explanation for Nick's curiosity. I laugh at myself for all my doubts, for my inability to relax and enjoy Logan's company. But then, with all the competition between charter captains, it's rare that I spend much time talking about fishing. Except with Benny and Dad, that is.

"Well, most of the charters here are broken into two camps. Half of them are like the one we took you on, where we go into the backcountry flats, you know the shallow waters, and we hunt for bonefish. Really, that is Islamorada's specialty."

Logan nods, urging me to continue. I smile, surprised by how good it feels to talk about fishing with someone other than Dad or Benny. Especially since Logan seems so interested, like he's actually listening. So I clear my throat and keep talking.

"But there's still a lot of other fish out there, good sport fish in deeper waters. Those big boats over there," I say pointing toward Dad's Blackfin, "that's what people use to go after fish in deeper water. The sailfish and wahoo and stuff. We run some of those charters too, but the bonefish are what we focus on."

"And that's where you come in," Logan says smiling.

Again, my cheeks flush. "Not exactly. I just like that sort of fishing better. Always have."

"Well that, and you're good at finding secret spots."

My throat tightens at his words. "Wait. I never said anything about secret spots. Who have you been talking to now?"

Logan shrugs. "No one but Benny," he says, pausing. "He mentioned something about you tracking fish spots at the bonfire, after you left."

I breathe in deep, my fury at Benny growing. Leave it to him to drop one of my secrets just to make friends. Unbelievable.

"Well I wouldn't believe everything Benny says. He tends to exaggerate."

Logan laughs, then points straight ahead, toward the lone sailboat tied up to the edge of the far dock. "Looks like he's quite the acrobat as well."

"Huh?" I ask, following his gaze.

And that's when I see it. Benny and Marina, holding onto the boom of Rory Pinder's sailboat.

"That is so weird," I say. "What are they doing over there? That boat's Rory's pride and joy. He washes it down and checks it out religiously. If they mess anything up, he'll know."

Logan squints his eyes, then shrugs. "Looks like they're just talking. That shouldn't hurt anything, right?"

"No, I guess not. But hanging from the boom like that is dangerous." I throw down my spoon and jump up, ready to walk over, when Logan stops me.

"I know you're worried, but it's probably better not to interfere," he says. "Maybe they just want a little alone time."

I sigh, knowing Logan's right. The worst thing I could do is annoy Benny. "Well I just hope they're careful," I say. "Because one little scuff mark and Rory will be throwing a fit tomorrow at the dock office. He uses that baby every afternoon for those sunset cruise rides arranged by the hotels and likes everything to be perfect for his guests."

"Oh, so that's why they picked that boat then," Logan says, relaxing.

"Huh?" I ask, raising an eyebrow.

"You said he runs cruises for the hotels. So he probably works for Marina's mom. Meaning Rory could have given them permission to chill there," says Logan.

But I just shake my head. "Impossible. The Becco Lodge faces the Atlantic. Rory only goes to the hotels on the Bay."

"All right then, so then they're just looking for somewhere to hang out. A sailboat could be pretty romantic."

"I guess," I say, still craning my neck to see what's going on with Benny.

But Logan's moving closer now, blocking my view. And that's when he turns to me and leans in, inching closer to me on the bow.

My heart pounds so hard I can feel it against my ribs as he approaches. I'm not sure if I want to follow his lead or punch him for getting so close. And in that moment I am frozen, speechless, unaware of what I should do or say.

So when his hands reach for mine, I pull away. Stand up on the bow.

And look back at Benny.

"Uh, sorry," I say, folding my arms around my chest. "But it really looks like there's something going on out there."

Logan's now sitting back in his seat, his face set in a frown. "I thought we already determined everything was fine?"

"Yeah, I know, but look. Benny is definitely messing with the boat."

Logan sighs. "Hey, are you sure I didn't do something wrong?"

I turn back from Benny and look at Logan, at the way his hair's now covering the corners of his eyes.

"No, nothing," I say. "I just really want to make sure everything's okay with Benny."

Logan nods and as he drifts back to silence I decide not to think about what just almost happened. Or whether or not I wanted it to happen at all. Instead I stare out at Benny, watching as he shakes Rory Pinder's boom as if he were trying to tear it from the mast, then creeps over to the front of the mast and shakes that too, before scaling it like a tree.

I turn to Logan, ready to make my case that whatever Benny's up to is not normal, but when I look at the way he's staring out into the water, I decide not to break his gaze.

So I watch alone, in silence as Benny inches up a few feet then whispers to Marina. I stick out my neck and try to catch the conversation in the wind, but we're too far away to hear. Or to make out exactly what Marina is bringing over to Benny. All I can tell is that it's small. And shiny.

Logan turns to me before I can identify the object. "If this is really bugging you so much, just walk over," he says. "I know Benny's your best friend. Guess I'd be concerned too."

I sigh, relieved to have Logan on my side. The feeling surprises me and all at once I wonder why I thought I needed Logan's approval in the first place. Logan's right. Benny's my best friend. Why wouldn't I go over? It's then that I think of Marina, and how she's never too eager to see me. Again, I slump down in my chair.

"Well, as long as he's on time tomorrow, I guess I can let this go," I say.

"On time for what?"

"Boat repairs. I told him to come over and help us clean up the skiff."

"Ah yes, of course, the motor," he says, his mood lightening. "What time do you want me?"

"How about 9:00?"

"Sounds perfect," Logan says.

Just as a scream breaks out below.

We turn back to the sailboat to see Marina shrieking, her arms waving in the air. My eyes dart up, looking for signs of Benny, but all I can see is the tall metal mast of the sailboat, swaying back and forth as Marina runs from side to side, her hands now pointing to a shadow in the watery abyss.

"What's going on?" Logan asks, standing.

"We better go find out," I say.

Together we slip off the Whaler and onto the dock, prepared to confront Marina and Benny. I scold myself for not going sooner, for not stopping Benny from doing whatever stupid thing he's done.

As we round the corner leading from the Whaler to the main dock, Logan starts to slow. We're only a few boats down from the sailboat now, but Logan seems in no rush to get to Marina. Instead he freezes. Then he grabs my hand, crushing my fingers as his arm tenses.

I try to break away, but he clamps down harder.

"Logan, what's wrong?" I ask.

He mutters something under his breath, then takes a step back.

I follow his gaze downward, from the dock to the water. Just moments ago the water was quiet. Asleep.

But now it's rippling. Fast.

Before I can open my mouth to tell this to Logan, a loud pop pierces the air.

Once. Twice. Three times.

It's like firecrackers. A whole string of them.

Loud.

Fast.

Staccato.

Logan grabs my waist and throws me down onto the dock. He rolls over on top of me, sliding me toward the rubber bumper protecting the edge. We miss falling into the harbor by inches. Not that I care. The explosions are still coming rapid fire. They drown out the steel drums and noisy tourists and celebrating locals at Rosalie's. That is, if anyone is still celebrating.

I bring my hands to my ears and close my eyes tight. Logan and I lay there, shivering. Then everything grows quiet. Still.

I sit up. The explosions have subsided, leaving nothing but a thin haze of smoke and the smell of burned popcorn. And that's when I remember. How could I forget? The Fourth of July is only days away. Of course it was fireworks. Could it really be anything else?

Logan seems to think it is. He pushes me back onto the dock before I can stand. "Stay down a little longer," he whispers.

I hit the green glow button on my Timex watch and highlight the date. "It's just fireworks," I mouth.

He frowns. "Maybe. Let's just get out of here."

"But, but, what if it was something serious? We need to go look for Benny and Marina."

Logan shakes his head. "I'm sure they're fine. But we need to leave. Now."

He helps me to my feet and I can't help but feel

sick to my stomach as we crawl up the ramp one rung at a time, hiding in the shadows as the tourists above carry on again like nothing's wrong. Singing with the band and ordering drinks and throwing scraps of bread into the water for the birds. Maybe they actually saw the fireworks. Maybe that's why they're not scared.

When we reach the top of the ramp, I look back one last time, still hoping to catch a glimpse of Benny or Marina. But the sailboat is quiet now, meaning Logan is probably right. After the noise, they probably hid as well. So I send Benny a quick text asking if he's okay, saying I heard shots or fireworks or something at the harbor. At least that way he knows I care. And that someone is willing to help if he needs it.

Then I turn back to Logan, and together we walk to the edge of the parking lot in silence. As soon as we reach the street, Logan breaks out into a run. I breathe in deep then take off after him, my legs burning as I try to keep up. As we reach the road, two cop cars and a fire truck speed into the Rosalie's parking lot. We take a few steps back to avoid being hit.

"Still think it was just fireworks?" asks Logan.

"Probably," I say. "Shooting fireworks down here is illegal. Kip probably called the cops."

"Would they really send two cars and a fire truck if it was just a couple kids messing around?"

"I...I don't know." I shake my head, unable to

imagine them as anything else. "They had to be fireworks. It's almost July Fourth. People just freaked out because they're not used to hearing them down there."

"Come on, Piper. Have you ever heard fireworks like that? There were no lights and there were too many fast pops for cherry bombs. And firecrackers, well they never get that loud. If you ask me, someone on that dock was shooting a gun."

"You sound like an expert."

"I moved from outside of Detroit. I saw a lot of this stuff."

"Saw what? Fireworks? Or gunshots?"

Logan grimaces, then looks away. "Let's not worry about that right now. It's more important we get home in one piece."

The way he says it freaks me out, unleashing a rash of goose bumps over my skin. Because it's clear that Logan knows what he's talking about. That there's a chance the popping at the dock wasn't just fireworks.

But since when does Islamorada have gunshots? The island has always been safe. Idyllic. Old fashioned. I cling to this as we head toward my house and pray that Benny texts me back. Only five minutes later my phone still hasn't received any messages.

"Do you think everyone at Rosalie's is okay?" I ask, my voice wavering.

Logan doesn't answer. He's staring straight ahead, his lips pursed. I start to ask him again when a pair of high beams comes bounding around the corner. I catch a glimpse of red paint and oversized wheels. It's Dad, driving like a madman, taking the narrow turn about twenty miles an hour too fast. When his headlights reach our faces, the truck skids to a stop.

Logan wraps his hand around my arm and starts pulling. His legs look ready to break into another run. "Do you know who that is?"

"Yeah, my dad." I whisper the words just as the driver's door swings open.

"Piper, honey, are you okay?" Dad's running now, around the bed of the truck and over the pile of shells littering the side of the road.

"Yeah, I'm fine. We're just coming from Rosalie's."

"When did you leave? Did you hear the gunshots? I just got word from Kip."

"Oh my God...gunshots?" Even though Logan has spent the last fifteen minutes trying to convince me of the danger, hearing the truth out loud feels like a punch in the face. But instead of falling or fainting like I imagine Marina or Sardi would do, I stand tall. Try to act strong.

Logan just shakes his head. "We got out of there as soon as we heard them, sir," he says. "Most of the people thought they were fireworks, but it sounded a little loud for that."

"Smart decision," says Dad, loosening his shoulders. "And your other friends? They got back okay?"

I nod, thankful that Benny lives in the opposite direction. "Yeah, Benny's walking home the other girls, they all live over near Becco," I say, hoping he won't ask any more questions.

Luckily, Dad only nods, pleased with my explanation. "Good," he says, nodding his head. "According to Kip, it's absolute chaos down there now. Guess after the first round, there was another. A few witnesses said it was some lunatic shooting at the water, probably thinking they spotted that bull shark."

"Let's hope they got the shark," I say.

"I wouldn't count on it. Kip says they haven't found any floating carcasses yet. Meaning your Whaler is still beached, got it?"

"Understood. Logan and Benny are going to help rebuild that old skiff in the morning. We're hoping to get it out for tomorrow night's low tide."

A smile creeps up Dad's crinkled face. "Sounds like a good plan, but don't get too frustrated if it takes a little longer than a morning to get it running. That engine's got a lot of problems."

Logan's eyes perk up as Dad walks around back to the truck, signaling us to get in.

"All right, Logan, which way is home?" Dad asks, fumbling with his massive nest of keys.

"We're on Heron Circle, number 34."

Dad turns the truck toward the southern tip of the island, speeding by the graveyard of abandoned vacation rentals on his way to Heron Circle.

As the conversation turns to the skiff's dying motor, I rest my head on the glass window and let my eyelids fall. But no sooner have I started thinking about sleep, than we're pulling into Logan's driveway. Not really a surprise since the island's barely two miles long, but still. After today, all I can think about is sleep.

Logan says goodbye, thanking Dad for the ride and promising to be over by 9:00 tomorrow morning. I barely hear his voice as Dad replies, then drives away. Three more minutes pass. Then, Dad throws the car into park and gives me a shake.

"We're home, baby," he says.

"Thanks for picking us up," I say, opening the car door, then trudging inside.

"No, thank you for getting the hell out of there as soon as things got fishy. You've got a good head on your shoulders. Seems this Logan does too."

I nod and find myself agreeing. Logan may not be the most easy-to-read guy in the world, but there is something about him that's intriguing. The way he asks so many questions, is so interested in what I do. And now the whole getting-us-off-the-docks business. Somehow I just can't see Benny doing the same thing.

I head back to my room, letting my mind dream

about what I will say to Logan when I see him in the morning. But as I play out the different scenarios in my head, I realize that right now I'm too tired to figure out anything. All I want to do is crawl into my soft cotton comforter, and collection of down-filled pillows.

But as soon as I open the door, I know it's going to be a bean bag night. Liggy has used her snout to open up my unlocked window and is now perched on top of my bed. And she's got my favorite bathing suit in her mouth.

"Liggy, come on, not tonight," I say, reaching for a free bikini strap. I start to pull, but she refuses to loosen her grip. "Ugh, you couldn't just stay outside tonight, could you?"

Liggy gives me a look reminding me of my promise to let her sleep inside.

"All right, you can stay," I say, "but really, it's no better in here tonight than it is outside. Dad's got us conserving energy again. No air conditioning when the temperature falls below 80."

Liggy opens her mouth to yawn, dropping the colorful nylon onto my bed.

"Ah, finally!" I grab the saliva-covered bathing suit and drop it into my hamper. "Now, how about we move to the beanbag?"

Liggy grunts then jumps to the floor, having added beanbag to her vocabulary years ago. As soon as she's settled, I grab my favorite pillow and throw my arm around Liggy's neck. It may not be how I expected to spend my evening, but there's something comforting about snuggling up close to a best friend.

So I forgive Liggy's bad manners and make a note to lock my window before I leave tomorrow morning. Then my eyes close, ready finally for sleep. Only a nagging thought in the back of my brain won't stop bothering me. Every time I get close to passing out, it's there, hard and long like how my heart's been beating all night ever since Logan grabbed my hand.

Yet this thought isn't about Logan. It's Benny. I still have no idea what he was doing on Rory Pinder's sailboat with Marina. Or if he escaped after all that gunfire. I reach my hand to my nightstand and feel around until I come across my cell phone. He still hasn't texted me back. So I hit my first speed dial and wait for his phone to ring. But it clicks over to voicemail immediately. I debate leaving a message, but decide against it. If the phone's going straight to message, then chances are he's turned it off. Meaning he's probably asleep. And I need to wait until morning for any answers.

I hunker down once again next to a passed out Liggy and tighten my grip on her chest. And this time when my eyes close, I am greeted by visions of Logan and the Whaler and Rosalie's, along with the sneaking suspicion that maybe Benny isn't as perfect as he once seemed.

CHAPTER TEN

My eyes peel open at exactly 7:00 a.m. All I want to do is roll over and go back to sleep. But something's stopping me. Something big and heavy and furry. That's drooling all over my leg.

"Liggy, come on, it's Saturday." I push her over to the edge of the beanbag and crawl up onto my bed.

My eyes shut immediately. Sleep starts to return. Just about at the same second that Liggy jumps on top of me.

"Fine, girl, I get it. You need to go out." I pull myself out of bed and like a zombie, pull open my window just enough for Liggy to leap out. Then I collapse back onto the bed. Only this time, my eyes stay open. So much for sleeping in late.

After throwing on a t-shirt and shorts, I walk into the kitchen where there's a note from Mom and Dad. They've gone to Key West for the morning to shop for boat parts. I'm to be careful working on the motor, and to offer Logan some of Mom's Key Lime pie.

At the end of the note is a P.S. reminding me to stay out of the Whaler. Below it is a P.P.S. demanding me not to go swimming.

Scribbled below that in Dad's chicken-scratch handwriting — a stark contrast to Mom's loops and swirls that flow above — is a P.P.P.S. telling me that Kip's Coast Guard unit thinks they found the guy who fired shots last night at the dock. And no, he didn't shoot any people or kill the shark. Though he did pierce a few holes in a fiberglass cooler that fell off Rick Johnson's boat. Message being, tie down the equipment on the boats this morning, and make sure there's no damage. If there is, report it to the marina, then call Kip. He's turned the suspected sharpshooter over to the police and can get us in touch with the right person if anything's happened.

Leave it to Dad to run away to Key West without checking on the boats. Good thing I got up early. With two hours to go until Logan or Benny are expected at the house, there's just enough time for a quick check down at the harbor. So I down a glass of orange juice, then start off for harbor, ready to inspect the boats, and maybe conduct a little detective work of my own.

But the harbor looks the same this morning, just as it did the day before. The docks are stained with nothing but salt. No blood drops or stray bullets or even clumps of hair, like the cops always seem to find on CSI. Not there really should be any, if all that got shot was Rick Johnson's cooler.

I try not to think too much about last night's gunfire and instead focus on checking out Dad's two boats and my Whaler. With everything looking under control, I head back home just in time to make a quick breakfast of crab and eggs.

I crack two eggs into a pan and let them cook. In the fridge, I search the shelves until I find a plastic carton of crabmeat. As I close the refrigerator door, I hear a rustling behind me. Spinning around, I scream.

"Smells good in here, what's cooking," says Logan. He's grinning from ear to ear, acting like he didn't just barge in on me for the second time in two days.

"Whoa! You're early," I say, my stomach still up in my esophagus from the shock.

"The door was open. Liggy told me I should come in."

My face starts overheating as he walks toward the kitchen table. "Right. I'm sure," I say, rolling my shoulders in an attempt to force my nerves into relaxation.

"Okay, actually Liggy was sleeping," Logan says.

"But the door was open, and I rang the bell twice. When no one answered, I figured your parents were out. I remember your dad saying something yesterday about Key West."

I nod, relieved to hear that Logan's just observant. Not a stalker. And that he's acting just like he did yesterday, before I pulled away from him on the boat. For a moment I wonder if his stomach's jumping as much as mine is, but then I figure it doesn't matter. Today's mission is all about fixing the boat motor. Worrying about Logan will do nothing but consume energy I can't waste. Not if I want to get back out practicing, that is.

"So, do you have enough food for two?" Logan asks, eying the frying pan.

"Sure, grab a couple plates." I crack two more eggs into the pan and add the crab meat, letting it all cook up into a pretty scramble. Then I pile it onto two plates and hand one to Logan.

He raises his eyebrow, then stares down at the plate. "This isn't just eggs, is it?"

"Egg and crab, my favorite. Try it, you'll like it."

Logan stabs a small piece of egg and turns it around, inspecting the end of his fork. When he's sure it's devoid of all crab, he takes a bite. "Not bad," he says.

I laugh. "That doesn't count. You didn't even try the crab."

"Yeah, well."

"Come on, don't tell me you're afraid."

"Never. Here, how's this?" He scoops up a big lump of egg and crab and brings it to his lips. "Does this count?"

"If you eat it."

"Then here goes." He waves his fork around like an airplane, then opens his mouth wide.

For a moment he just sits there silent, chewing, and licking his lips.

"Well?" I ask.

"It's delicious," he says. "Tastes better than it smells. Who would've thought you could eat seafood for breakfast."

"I told you," I say, shoveling the eggs into my mouth in three bites. "After you finish, should we start on the motor?"

"Sure, I've got my tools outside."

"Then, let's head to the garage," I say, leading the way to the back yard.

With the garage door open and the sunlight streaming in, the skiff looks even older than usual. But, seeing as it's four feet longer and six inches taller than the Whaler, it's hard to debate that it's safer. The boat looks like a tank with a sturdy double hull that lets it rip through the water without swaying at all, making it almost impossible to capsize. Or get tossed around by a shark.

"So what do we do first?" I ask, as my eyes drift from the boat to the tools laid out beside it.

"First we try to start her up. See what happens." Logan climbs inside the boat and reaches for the key.

"No! Stop!"

"What?" he says, dropping the key.

"You can't start a motor out of the water. You'll ruin it. We need to fill a garbage can with water so we submerge the bottom half of the outboard."

Logan's face turns red as he jumps off the boat. "Good thing you're here. I forgot a boat's pretty different than a car."

"Let's hope not too different."

Logan follows me around the side of the house. Together, we fill a large metal can with water from the hose. After submerging the prop in the can, we're ready to try again. So I take a few steps back and tie Liggy to the orange tree – she's never been a fan of loud noises and the last thing I want is for her to start charging the can like it's some predator – as Logan turns the key. The motor clicks. Then dies.

"Huh. Is this thing hooked up to the battery?" Logan asks.

"Of course. Dad and I checked all the obvious things last spring," I say.

Logan folds his top lip over his bottom, then jumps off the boat and walks around to the back of the boat. I decide to go inside and grab some more orange juice just as he pulls the protective plastic top off the outboard. But inside, my cell phone beckons more than the juice. A quick tap on the keys confirms what I already know. No new calls. No text messages. No word from Benny. With the oven clock flashing 8:30, it's still too early to call his cell. And Mr. and Mrs. Benitez have probably left for the restaurant hours ago. Meaning there's nothing to do but wait and talk to Benny when he shows up in another half hour.

As Logan works on the outboard, the clock hand on my watch turns more slowly than the tide. Every minute that passes, all I can think of is that we are 60 seconds closer to Benny's arrival and learning about what really happened last night on the docks.

Out in the yard, I pick clovers and buttercups between glances at my phone. Then I count the blossoms on the orange tree that seem to never turn into oranges and inspect Liggy for bugs or thorns that might've gotten stuck in her fur.

Every few minutes my head jerks up in response to a curse or scream from Logan. I debate going over to help a few times, but in the end, decide to keep my distance. I've seen enough of these projects to know that getting involved usually leads only to disaster. That whole two heads are better than one thing definitely doesn't apply to situations when only one head can peer over the motor.

So when Logan calms down and starts clanging his

tools against the inside of the motor, I let out my breath and give Liggy a massage. That is, after checking my cell phone another ten times.

And that's when I hear Logan calling. "We're ready to roll," he says.

"Wow, already?" I reach for my watch. 10:30. Could Logan have fixed the engine in only two hours? Thinking back to the six-hour day I clocked with Dad last March, I doubt it but decide to keep quiet. Logan did say he was good with cars. Maybe he knows what he's doing after all.

As Logan wipes his hands on a rag and starts to climb back into the boat for the inaugural key turning, I stand up out of the grasses and take a long look down our street in the direction of Benny's house.

A strip of black pavement and weary palm trees, stagnant in the thick, motionless heat, meet my gaze. No cars or walkers or runners or anyone else is on the road. Meaning there's still no sign of Benny.

Logan shoves the key into the ignition, oblivious to my distraction. "Here it goes," he says.

The motor sputters to life, the prop shooting a tail of water into the sky.

"Oh my God it works!" I yell.

"Come on, don't tell me you doubted me."

"No, of course not. But two hours, geez. That was quick."

Logan hops down from the boat and grins. "You

had a corroded kill switch that was shorting out the motor. All I had to do was disconnect it. Would've had this working a lot sooner, but I tried a lot of other things first."

"And you knew all that from working on cars?" I ask, pretty sure that cars don't exactly have a kill switch for shutting off the motor.

Logan winks. "Actually I looked up common outboard problems on Google. Though it was my mad mechanic skills that helped me disconnect that wire."

"Seriously?" I punch his arm with a laugh.

Logan pretends to be hurt, then lifts me over his head. I let out a scream and he drops me to the ground, leaving me dizzy and flushed.

"So should we launch it?" he asks, his eyes sparkling.

"Yes, we should! It's perfect timing too. The tide will be low in an hour so we can get in some reconnaissance."

"Wait, some what?"

I bring my hand to my mouth, shocked that I've let the words escape. That in such a short time I've told Logan not only about the Whaler and the turtle nest and how to catch a bonefish, but that I've mentioned my secret fish research as well. I debate backpedaling and changing my story, or telling him that reconnaissance is some special kind of practice.

But then I think back to last night and how easy it

is to just talk to Logan. No complaining or putting down what I want to do or say. He just listens. And is eager to help, as evidenced by his presence here at the skiff. Like Dad said, he's got a good head on his shoulders. And that's not even mentioning his eyes, which have been growing on me ever since he looked into mine last night.

But do sparkling eyes and a few offers of help really make Logan worthy of my secrets? Right now, I have no idea. So I decide to dismiss the comment, hoping he'll forget about the mention.

"I'll fill you in later," I say with a wave of my hand. "Right now we just need to get this trailer hooked up to the truck so we can take her to the boat ramp at Rosalie's..."

My voice drifts as I remember that first, the truck isn't here, and second, I can't drive, even if it was. "On second thought, we may have to wait for my parents."

As if reading my mind, Logan pulls out his cell phone and starting dialing. "Hey Dad, can you meet me over at Piper's with the Explorer? We've got a boat we need to, uh, get in the water and her dad isn't home."

I stare at Logan as he rattles on with his dad, trying to use the words I've taught him so he sounds like a local, instead of a Michigan transplant. Using phrases like "get it in the water" and "before the tide goes down."

Hiding my grin in my cell screen, I check the time, then my messages. It's 11:00 and Benny hasn't even had the decency to type out 140 characters to let me know where he is.

"My dad's going to swing by with our SUV. He should be here in ten minutes, max."

"Great," I say. "Let me just call Benny in case he's on his way over."

"Oh yeah, I forgot he was supposed to stop by. What time is it?"

"11:00."

"Sounds like someone had a late night."

"Yeah, me. Liggy kept me up until after 1:00 a.m."

"That deer. She's so demanding."

"Tell me about it." I dial Benny's number as Logan fills Liggy's dish with water. After three rings, his line clicks to voicemail. Again, it's the Benny rap. Instead of leaving a message, I slide open my phone's keyboard and pound out a text. *U cming ovr?* I write. I'm still waiting for the response when good old Nick, sporting an orange polka-dotted t-shirt, pulls into our drive.

"Why hello Miss Piper, I hear you need some towing services," he says, laughing like he did on Dad's boat.

Only this time it feels good to play along. "We sure do. We've gotta get this boat in the water ASAP. We do have a fishing tournament to practice for!"

"You can say that again," says Nick with a wink.

"Your dad's taking me out to practice some more tomorrow. He says I'm getting pretty good, not that I should be telling you, seeing as you're the competition."

By the time we reach the dock and the boat is in the water, I'm so tired I can't even think about fishing. And I'm pretty sure that if Logan hadn't just fixed the motor and called his dad and dragged that skiff all the way down the boat ramp, he would be too. But of course, being as he's high on the type of adrenaline that comes from charging into new experiences instead of the kind that comes from praying you don't screw up, he's rearing to go. Ready to see what my fishing practice is all about.

Except that I'm still not sure I want to tell him all my secrets yet. Because the only people that really know about my reconnaissance missions are Dad and Benny. Telling Logan would mean widening my net of confidants. But with Benny not around, I'm running out of options. Because the tide is low. And I can't miss another day of practice.

"Let me just try Benny one more time before we go," I say, still hopeful.

Logan's lips twitch like he's about to talk but he stays silent. So I dial Benny's phone and again hang up as soon as I get his rap.

"Can we go now?" Logan asks.

"I guess. Just let me go stash my phone up at the

marina desk so it doesn't get soaked."

"Here, take mine too."

The marina desk is hopping today with a whole army of college guys running around in even tackier outfits than my Wesley's Fishing Charter shirt. I turn away as one of Benny's cousins passes by, a distant relative I've only met once at a few barbecues and pig roasts outside of the restaurant. Even though part of me wants to jump in front of him and ask about Benny, I know it doesn't make sense. A cousin he sees twice a year isn't going to have any intel on where Benny is today. And last night when the shots were fired, the marina was closed. So I hand over the phones to Nadine, the woman who's been working the front desk since I could walk, then head back down to the skiff where Logan's got the motor revving and the old canvas bimini top stretched out over the steering console like a beach umbrella.

"Ready?" Logan's slathering on sunscreen from an old tube that's probably been sitting on the bow of that skiff for the past three years. But, instead of saying anything I just watch as he rubs it into his chest then moves onto his face, and am surprised to find myself admiring his freckled skin. Sun certainly hasn't been pounding down on him any. Not like it does on me and Benny at least.

I sigh. It's hard not to draw comparisons now that Logan's shirtless and sitting in the driver's seat. And acting a lot like my sidekick. Which up until today has always been Benny.

For a moment, I think I hear Benny's voice, but when I turn, no one's there but Logan, untying our bowline from the dock. I motion for him to take a seat, then move over to the center console and grab the steering wheel. As soon as I turn the key, the motor roars to life, no problem.

"So where are we off to now?" Logan asks as we cruise by the docks.

I push down on the throttle, then give the boat some speed. "I guess to Coral Cove, on the west side of the island. It's not really a popular fishing spot, but I've been meaning to check it out."

Logan frowns. "Why are we wasting our time on a spot that's not used much?"

I take a deep breath and try not to laugh. Here I am, the girl that doesn't tell anybody anything. Who wouldn't even tell Sardi that I was working on my dad's boat for the summer. Or that my family owned a boat at all. And I'm about to tell this stranger, this guy from Michigan, everything. But then, Logan's really not just some guy. He helped me fix the skiff, and patch the Whaler. He even hooked a bonefish, even if he couldn't reel him in. And without Benny to help me practice, I don't have much of a choice.

So I open my mouth and start talking as the boat speeds by the edge of Rosalie's. Logan's face grows wrinkled as I delve into the intricacies of reconnaissance. His eyes widen as I tell him about the different kinds of shrimp. And stinging hydroids.

When I pull back on the accelerator and throw the motor into neutral, Logan is shaking his head and begging me to tell him more. But there's no time to focus on the technicalities of what I do and why I do it. Because there's a thick coat of brine shrimp covering the surface of the water. More than I've seen put together this month. Maybe all year. All in a place that no one ever visits except maybe to snorkel.

So I run to my GPS, punch in our coordinates, and then start writing furiously. The weather. The water conditions. The number of shrimp. Every detail gets recorded.

And with every word I write, I feel myself getting closer to being the Bonefish Scramble champion.

CHAPTER ELEVEN

"That was incredible," says Logan as we pull back into the dock. "My hands are still shaking." He straightens his arms and looks down at his hands, wobbling in the breeze.

I smile but try to act like it's not a big deal, like I see shrimp pockets like that all the time. Okay, so maybe he's caught on that finding that many shrimp is not normal. But still. After just divulging the biggest secret I have to a guy that's still pretty new to this fishing thing, I don't want to give up too much. Although, I'm pretty sure he knows we saw something big, given my running and jumping and shouting when we found the shrimp. And I'm almost certain that all he's going to do with the information is bottle it up until the tournament, seeing as I'm one of the only people he even knows on the island.

As we tie up the old skiff next to my Whaler – which looks even more like a bath toy now that it's next to an actual boat – Sardi waves at us from the dock. I look at my watch. Of course. 1:00. Meaning Dad's got to be back from Key West and out with his afternoon charter. And Sardi's probably finishing another fish sandwich with her fellow camp counselors. Not exactly my favorite crowd. But this time, I fight the instinct to run.

"I should probably go talk to her. See if she knows what was going on last night with Benny." I try to sound annoyed, but my hands are shaking so much that I'm hiding them under a life jacket and pretending to clean the bow.

"Want me to go with you?" Logan asks.

I shake my head. "Might be better if it's just the two of us."

"All right, I'll be in the parking lot if you need me. Who knows, maybe I can find that stingray again."

My cheeks grow hot. "Tide's coming in, so if he was trapped again, he might've darted out by now."

Logan nods and heads toward the saltwater ditch separating the parking lot from Rosalie's. I wait until he's settled on the footbridge, peering into the water, before walking back to Sardi.

"We missed you last night," she says as soon as I get near. "It was epic. Just epic! Everything started out pretty normal except for me and Travis were getting so close which was absolutely amazing, and Benny and Marina were kind of in a funky mood, but then they left early to go back to Marina's and like ten minutes later there was chaos! Pure chaos! Did you know that someone was down here with a *gun*? And that they might've even shot a *person*?"

Sardi's even more animated than usual today, her hands flapping like a pelican's wings as she retells the tale of the gunshots – not one round, but two! Isn't it crazy, two rounds of gunshots! But this part of the story I already know. I'm more interested in what happened with Benny. So as she finishes going through the list of rumors, from the bull shark to a drunken tourist and all the other swirling stories that old fishermen come up with when they have nothing else to do, I work on directing her back to Benny.

"It sounds like Benny and Marina really missed out on the action," I say.

Sardi nods her head so fast I worry she'll get whiplash. "They totally did. I mean, the Coast Guard's claiming that it was some tourist just shooting at a cooler, but I don't buy it. There were too many shots. And you should've seen everyone's reactions. First we all got quiet. Then we decided it was firecrackers or something and the band started playing. But then a few minutes later there were cop cars and more shots and things got really crazy!"

"Yeah, it sounds like it. I'm sorry I missed it. What did Marina say when you filled her in?"

"Oh, I never got to tell her really, with them packing up this morning and everything. And now they're gone for a week, or at least that's what I think she said, but our conversation this morning was so short. I barely got to talk to her for two minutes and now that they're on a trip together I don't want to interrupt..."

"A trip?" My throat tightens, as I think back to Benny's insistence that he'd be over this morning at 9:00, but as angry as I am, I decide to play along. "Oh yeah, that's right. I forgot that was this week."

"Yeah, isn't it so romantic? I wish Travis would take me away somewhere..."

"Yeah. Definitely. Well I should get going. See you later." I wipe a bead of sweat off my chin, cutting Sardi off before she can start talking about the wonderful trip with Travis she will never take. Now that the topic has moved off Benny, I know there's no going back. So I wave goodbye and run back to Logan.

"Find anything out about Benny?" he asks from the footbridge. One look down and I can see there's no stingray, but a couple parrot fish are putting on quite a show, their green and purple scales shimmering in the afternoon sunlight.

"She claims Benny and Marina are away for the week. Did Benny mention anything about that to you?" I ask.

Logan shakes his head.

"Me either. In fact, he promised me he'd be here. We were supposed to spend all week practicing for the tournament," I say, my voice wavering.

"Aw, don't worry, I'm sure he'll turn up. He's probably just at Marina's trying to lay low from Sardi."

My body stiffens. "But what if he's not?"

"Then I'll suck it up and help you with that tournament practice. I did all right today, didn't I?"

I nod my head and try not to let him see that I'm losing it, but before I know it, the tears are flowing. As are all my fears about the tournament. And having to do it alone. Without Benny.

"Hey, Piper, calm down. What's wrong?" Logan says.

"It's just that I need Benny," I say between sobs. "He's the only one that knows how to maneuver the boat and net the fish and really manage everything when I'm fishing. I've spent years preparing for this tournament and now Dad's finally letting me enter it on my own. How could Benny ditch me? He's supposed to be my best friend!"

"He didn't ditch you. I guarantee you he's somewhere on the island." Logan throws his arms around me before I can complain. The thick scent of salt fills my nose as my cheeks squish up against his faded gray t-shirt. "We'll stop by the Becco Lodge and see if he's there, okay?"

After a few sniffles, I pull away from Logan and nod. "Okay. But what if he's still missing?"

"Oh I don't know. We try his house?"

My feet drag along the hot asphalt all the way to the Becco Lodge. Logan tries to make conversation, saying that he's sure he can learn how to maneuver a boat and net a fish, but I'm not listening. All I can do is replay the scene last night of Benny and Marina down at the docks. According to Sardi, Benny was walking Marina home when that happened. Meaning they lied to her too.

But were they making up a story because they wanted some time to themselves, to hole up at the resort and work on Marina's purses and do whatever else it is they do now? Or is it because of something more dangerous. Something that involves Marina screaming on Rory Pinder's boat. After Benny was scaling the mast?

Besides a few guests lying around the pool, the Becco Lodge is empty. Peering into Marina's guesthouse reveals nothing but an empty room and sterile kitchenette. No purses strewn on the table, no bags of Dorito's lying near the sofa. Just blue tile floor and black granite countertops and a spray bottle of Fantastic on the coffee table. Someone's been cleaning up. Meaning someone else has probably moved out.

"Looks like they're gone," I say, fighting back another wave of tears.

"Not necessarily," says Logan, moving around to the back. He peers in another set of windows and laughs. "She moved her stuff to the back room. It's a mess."

I jump up on my toes and look for myself. Sure enough, mounds of clothing and purses cover both double beds. Loose fabrics and strings of beads hide the dresser. "Guess the maid was only cleaning the main room."

"Yeah, though it does look like they might be away. Someone was sifting through this stuff in a hurry."

"Maybe we should check with her mom," I say and before I can even think about what I'm doing, I'm running toward the reception desk in the main lobby. But the only person manning the desk is a college girl who doesn't look much older than me.

"Ugh, Marina, I could kill that girl right now," the receptionist says in between snaps of gum. "She promised me she'd stay here and help run the front desk while her mom was away at that conference, and then first thing this morning, she announces that she's going with her. Says she just has to get away."

"So the trip wasn't planned?" I ask.

"Nope, and now all morning I've been running

around like crazy, trying to keep our guests happy and accommodate all these people that want to go on our sunset cruise. Of course Rory's boat just has to malfunction the one day we're understaffed."

I take a step back as she mentions Rory. "Wait, what happened to his boat?"

The girl shrugs. "No clue. All I know is that the Tarpon Bay Resort called early this morning asking if we could book six people on our boat since theirs was out of commission. I of course said yes, but then all these other people started calling in from resorts down the island looking for space too, and I've been turning them down all day. It's amazing how many people are obsessed with these sunset cruises. All these calls have like quadrupled our call volume. And left me exhausted."

I nod, trying to look sympathetic. "Sounds like Marina picked a bad time to take off."

"Tell me about it. Though, I guess there was no way to know. Especially since the summer has been pretty quiet."

"Right. So, uh, did anyone else go with them on the trip?" I ask, hoping the question doesn't sound too out of place.

"I'm not sure," she says, just as the phone starts ringing.

We take this as our cue to leave. Neither one of us speaks until we're halfway down the drive leading back to the main road.

"So something happened to Rory Pinder's boat. Why do I feel like that is not a coincidence," I say.

Logan sighs. "Because it probably isn't. Though in all honesty, I didn't see them do anything but talk. If something happened to the boat, it was probably an accident."

"Maybe," I say. "Though Benny climbing up the mast was weird. Not that I can think of any reason why he'd want to hurt Rory's boat."

"Yeah, who knows. Maybe he saw something funny before the gunshots started and wanted a better look. I'm sure there's a logical explanation."

I frown. "I wish we could just find Benny and ask him. I mean, I can't imagine him going with Marina and her mom on a business trip. I just can't see his parents letting him do that."

"Hmm, guess there's only one way to find out." Logan grabs my arm and starts pulling. He doesn't let go until we're outside of Oswardo's.

"And why are we here?" I ask as he releases his grip. My clothes are stained with salt and my hair hangs limp down my back, like a tangle of fishing line that's been knotted up by a bad cast. Not exactly the best way to walk in on Benny's parents. But apparently Logan's encounter yesterday was not enough to teach him of the wrath of Mrs. Benitez.

Before I can object again, he's got the edge of the

wooden door in his hands and he's swinging it back, disappearing inside the restaurant. As a cool rush of air-conditioned air prickles my skin, I decide to follow. But first, I say a prayer that we'll get out alive.

As soon as I enter the main door, the interrogation begins. "Oh Piper! Back so soon and again, no one calls to tell me a thing! And you brought Benny's friend too. Why please, sit down, let us get you something to eat. We were just getting ready to close until dinnertime but I have a wonderful avocado and tomato salad with green chilies. You will eat some salad, won't you? It's very fresh. Got the avocados off the truck today and the tomatoes are straight from our yard," says Mrs. Benitez.

I breathe in and smile. "Of course we'd like some salad. That would be great. But we can't stay long, we are just out looking for Benny. We thought maybe he'd be working," I say, and for a second I wonder if I'm going to hell for all the lies I'm telling these days, first to Dad about the Whaler and the shark and almost sneaking out the Blackfin and now to Sardi and Mrs. Benitez. I mean, Mrs. Benitez is practically a saint. Lying to her about looking for Benny when I know he's been up to no good with Marina has got to be bad. Worse than even those lies to Dad. Or the Coast Guard.

But the way Mrs. Benitez's face falls when I mention Benny's name tells me she's under no illusions about this being an ordinary visit. "He didn't tell you?" she asks, her eyebrow raised.

I start to shake my head as Logan cuts in. "He said something about helping out Marina and her mom, but we didn't know when that was."

Mrs. Benitez nods slow enough for us to see the sun spots freckled across the bottom of her chin. "He went to Miami. Not for a day. But for five."

"Oh," I say, almost choking on my breath. So he is gone. For five days. Meaning five days without tournament practice. And five days of wondering about what happened last night on the dock.

Sensing my hesitation, Logan jumps in. "Did he tell you what they're doing there? Is he helping Marina's mom with some hotel stuff?"

"Yes, there is some conference or something. Marina wanted a friend to hang out with during the day. I told my Benny, boys that go on trips like this end up doing bad things. But, he goes anyway. What am I to do? He doesn't listen. Just packs up his bag last night and kisses me goodbye."

"And you haven't heard from him since?" I ask as one of Benny's cousins arrives with two platters of tomato and avocado salad. Logan takes a bite of avocado, then plays with the tomatoes covering his dish. Which is more than I can do seeing as Benny's disappearing act has got my stomach tangled up in knots.

"Oh no, I heard from Benny today, around noon," says Mrs. Benitez. "He was shopping in some fancy stores and he found me my favorite soaps. Ivory Garden they're called. You can't get them anywhere on the island, but my Benny said he was getting me a mountain of them to keep at home and at the restaurant too. They make these lotions that are so good for your hands, especially after a hard day's work."

"Well that was nice of him," Logan says.

"Yes, I guess it makes the trip okay. But I still don't like him spending so much time with this girl. She's not like you, Piper. With you I never worry. Good parents, a nice home. But I know nothing about this Marina. Oh, I don't know what to do with him! At least he got me the soaps."

"I'm sure Benny's not doing anything wrong, Mrs. Benitez," I say, hoping I sound at least a little convincing.

Mrs. Benitez frowns. "That Benny. When he gets back, he's grounded for the rest of year. No more anything. Here you are such a good girl, helping your dad all summer and coming to visit me. My Benny, he never helps. Even when I ask him to, he just leaves and he doesn't even call. I swear, if he's not back soon, I'm sending his father up to get him. Pull him right out of that mess he's made himself..."

"Marina's a nice girl, Mrs. Benitez. Her mom is

too. I am sure she's a good chaperone," I say.

"Yes, right. My Benny will not even let me speak to her mother to make sure. Ah, that boy he drives me crazy! He wouldn't even go visit his Uncle Carlos when I asked him. I said if you are going all the way to Miami, you should visit your family. And he refused!"

The conversation breaks up as a young family carting a double stroller walks into the restaurant. In just seconds, the waiters abandon their closing routine and start setting a table. Mrs. Benitez runs over and welcomes them to the island. They're tourists. Down from Ft. Lauderdale for the day. Stopping off on their way to Key West. Is it too late for lunch? Of course not. Sit down. We'll bring you some tomato and avocado salad straight away. On the house.

Logan and I use the distraction to slip out the back. I wave to the cooks in the kitchen before the door slams behind us.

"So they are really in Miami," I say. "For a week."

"Not a week. Just until Friday."

"Whatever. Isn't it weird they left on a Saturday? Don't most conventions start on Mondays? And why wouldn't Benny let his mom talk to Marina's mom? It just sounds so sketchy."

Logan sighs. "If we hadn't seen them on the dock last night, we wouldn't think anything was weird."

"Except we did. And Benny didn't tell me he was going away. He had plans to come over today, Logan, and he blew me off. He's ignored like ten of my texts. And the tournament's only five weeks away!" I bring my hands up to my mouth as the words slip out.

"It's going to be okay, I promise. I'll help you practice. I'm good with cars, remember? How hard can driving a boat be?"

"That's not it," I say, my entire body shaking. "Or not everything. It's the entry fee. We still haven't paid. And the money's due by Friday. No exceptions."

"So?" he says, still acting unconcerned. "I'll cover Benny's half. We don't need him..."

I slap Logan's arm before he can continue. "No, Logan, we do. The entry fee is $700 and I've only got $350. Benny has the rest."

He sits down on the curb outside of the restaurant, deflated. "It really costs that much?"

I nod.

"And your dad can't just lend you the rest?"

"He doesn't have the money to lend."

"Well I've got about $50 at home. I can ask my parents for some more. My dad's so into the tournament now, I'm sure he'll understand if I need some money to participate."

"But that's not fair," I say. "This is my mess, not yours."

"No. What's not fair is Benny disappearing without paying for the tournament."

"Even so, I refuse to take your money, even if your

dad is willing to pay." My eyes blink away a stream of tears before they can start falling.

"Fine, but the offer still stands," he says. "Is there anything I can do to help in the meantime?"

I nod. "Help me practice," I say, surprising even myself with the ease at which the words slip out. "If we practice all week, I won't lose any time. We'll just have to pray that Benny gets back early enough Friday to fork over the cash."

"I'm sure he will," Logan says, sounding a little too optimistic.

Instead of encouraging me, his words just deepen my worry.

"I hope so. But I can't help thinking something else is going on. That he's mad at me or something, or wants to bail on the tournament."

At this, Logan smiles and I almost laugh at the contrast, at seeing the boy with sad eyes playing the optimist.

"Don't worry," he says. "If Benny bails, then we'll do it without him. And we don't share any of the winnings."

"Thank you," I say and my eyes well with tears as Logan rattles on, talking about how he plans to become an even better fisherman than Benny. Relief washes over my face at his proclamation. Even if I know he'll probably fall short of his goal, it's good to have someone on my side. Who understands that the tournament is important. And is willing to help, without a lot of whining or hidden expectations.

Though as Logan stands up and dusts off his jean shorts, again my mind drifts to Benny. Benny who would never wear jeans on a boat. Who knows so naturally how to read the water and bait a hook and sniff out bonefish. And when Logan asks if I want to practice, I feel deflated, exhausted, as if Benny has taken part of me with him to Miami. But still I nod, knowing that by offering to help, Logan has given me a gift. One I can't afford to refuse.

"So should we head back to the skiff?" he asks, shooting me a smile. "The tide should be pretty high, you know. That means good fishing, right?"

"I guess so," I say. "But today let's just work on boat handling. I'm not in the mood to fish."

CHAPTER TWELVE

"You know moping around all night isn't going to make Benny get here any faster," Logan says as we sit there on the dock, our feet dangling on the water. "Friday is still a good ten hours away."

It's Thursday afternoon about an hour before sunset and the Rosalie's dinner crowd is starting to trickle in as the last of the charter boats offloads its tired, suntanned guests.

"I haven't moped all day," I say as I crane my neck, trying to see what the tourists have hauled in. I catch a glimpse of a grouper and smile, hoping they know enough to have Rosalie's cook it for them. "We fished all day and visited two coves. I call that progress. Especially after yesterday's boat handling session."

"Except that all you talked about both days was how mad you are at Benny."

"Well do you blame me? Him taking off with all that money."

"No, I don't, but I think you need to get your mind off it."

"And how do you suggest I do that?" I ask, smiling, enjoying the easy banter we've perfected over four days of practice on the boat.

Logan sighs, kicking his feet up in the water until he's whipped the surface into a bubbly foam. "Go out with me," he says.

I turn to him and stare as my mind jumps back to the night down the docks, back when he leaned in and I pulled away, too occupied with Benny to realize that the new kid, the unknown quantity with long hair and sad eyes that darted from side to side, who excited Sardi and Marina while creeping me out, was trying to look at me. And maybe do something more.

But one week and countless fishing lessons later, and the mystery of Logan has faded into friendship. His eyes, no longer sad, look crystal clear as he stares ahead and asks me again.

"We don't have to do anything fancy," he says. "But it could be fun, you know, to do something other than fishing." His words come out short and quick, as if he's already thought them out.

I smile and nod as my cheeks burn. Is Logan asking me on a date? Or is he just bored with cutting bait and driving the Whaler? In need of a friend, especially now that Benny's gone? I try to replay the past week's interactions in my head for clues, but with Logan waiting for a response I don't have time to think. So I just smile and nod as I try to piece together his meaning. Which judging from the way he's looking into my eyes is a whole lot different than what Benny means when he asks me to pick up a pint of ice cream for the Whaler.

"So is that a yes then?" Logan asks, still staring as I fumble over my words.

"Yeah, uh, of course. What do you want to do?" I say, and as soon as the words pour out, I realize I mean them. That I am excited to spend a night out with Logan.

He smiles. "You're the expert. You tell me."

"Well, you've pretty much seen my routine. Fishing, reconnaissance and ice cream on the Whaler. There's not much else to do."

Logan brings his hand to his chin and strokes it. Thinking. "How about a picnic then?" he asks. "By the turtles. You still haven't shown me the nest."

My throat tightens as Logan mentions the only other place I love as much as the Whaler. "Whoa, good call. That sounds perfect."

"Really?"

I nod, still impressed he remembers the nest at all.

"Great. Then what do you want to eat? I'll go place an order for some food now."

I laugh as Logan hops up, feet dripping, and starts walking toward Rosalie's.

"Get me a fish sandwich," I say, drying off my legs. Part of me wants to run after him and make sure he doesn't pay for everything himself, to make sure that if this isn't a date he doesn't think I'm being a freeloader. But the way he walks off makes me think that handing him a twenty might insult him. He's trying to do something nice. A treat. I'll pay next time, I tell myself as I once again return to his exact phrase. "Go out with me." Definitely sounds more like a date than a regular night out. But if it is, then shouldn't I be running home to wash my hair and put on something nice? I wish Sardi was here to help me interpret, but then telling Sardi would mean broadcasting my situation to the entire world. Or at least half the island. And since when would I put on something nice anyway? Even if it was a date?

Logan returns a few minutes later balancing a cardboard tray on his arm. He's grinning from ear to ear and from the way he reaches for my hand with no hesitation, no sideways glance or punch to my side, I can tell that this means something. Big.

So I grab his fingers and hold them tight as we

begin our walk to the nest.

It doesn't take long before Marina's abandoned guest cottage comes into view, along with the garden of ferns and grasses hugging its side. I guide Logan toward the small trail I carved out early in the week and smile, happy to have the lead.

"Is this it?" Logan asks, stepping over a cluster of cacti.

"Uh-huh. Can't see much right now, but in a couple months, it'll look completely different," I say, pointing to the mound of sand I covered with the dragnet. "They'll be hundreds of tiny turtles digging themselves out of the sand and crawling toward the ocean."

"Sounds pretty amazing."

"It is."

"I can't wait to see it." Logan looks into my eyes as he shifts the cardboard box of food from arm to arm.

We find a spot of moist, hard sand and place the box between us before digging into the spread. The fish tastes great as always, crisp and fresh and flaky, but even as I savor each bite I find myself looking back at Logan. He's fumbling with a ketchup packet. Then dunking in his fries. Concentrating on his food and looking cuter with every bite.

A shudder runs down my spine as I realize that being with Logan is making me feel freer, more alive. So when Logan looks up and asks if I want to go swimming after we eat, I clap in excitement then shed down to my bathing suit and dive right in, letting him follow a second later.

The water is barely cooler than the air, but still it feels good against my burning skin as together we splash and dive and laugh until the sun sinks below the horizon. As the last orange clouds dissolve into the purple sky, we leave the surf exhausted, yet somehow closer. Not just friends. But more.

And as we reach the beach, with the waves lapping on the shore and the half moon rising overhead, with the whole world looking peaceful and quiet and nothing around but a few terns and flames from the Becco Lodge torches, Logan kisses me. Immediately I'm mesmerized. Dazzled. Left with a cloak of goose bumps as Logan grabs my neck and draws me closer. I debate pulling away and taking a breath, telling him that I don't know what I'm doing or if I should be doing it, but with no time to untangle my thoughts, I instead cling to his arms and focus on his stare, turning off my mind for a few precious seconds.

When my thoughts return, there's no longer any doubt. All I want is to kiss Logan back. So I let him hold me tight and stroke my hair and laugh under his breath as a bird grabs a piece of loose netting and carries it back to its nest.

My gaze again turns to his eyes, now sparkling in the moonlight. Not looking sad or angry or even nervous. Just alive. Like I feel now.

Soon all I can hear is our two hearts, pumping wildly like a set of steel drums. He kisses me deeply now, even deeper than before. A moment later, he pulls away. Smiles. I smile back and stare. First at his face, then at the world around us. In this moment, nothing exists but Logan and the terns and the dancing waves rolling in from the ocean, one after another in perfect cadence like they have since the beginning of time. And I say a quick prayer, begging them never to stop.

"Should we head back home?" Logan asks, whispering the words, his hands still entangled in my hair.

I look back out to the ocean, then nod. "Guess we should. Don't want to disturb the turtles."

Logan places my hand in his and leads us out of the grasses and weeds, using the path I paved before. On the edge of the beach, he turns and kisses me again. Shorter this time, but just as urgent.

"You are the most interesting girl I've ever met," he says, resuming his pace.

"You're not too bad yourself. For a guy from Michigan," I say.

He smiles, then swings his arm until our hands are rising and dropping like the waves at our backs. "Hey, Islamorada is home now," he says and my hands burn as he grips my hand tighter.

"Does this mean you're gonna start talking like a local?"

Logan laughs. "I'm trying," he says as we round the corner onto my street.

Liggy's hanging out by the fence gate tonight, so I reach over the fence to give her a pet, unsure of how Logan and I are supposed to say goodbye.

Luckily, Logan is a little less shy. He picks me up and twirls me around, bringing me back to the ground only when I point out that it's barely 9:00 and my parents are probably very much awake inside.

Then I kiss his cheek and open the gate, first petting Liggy and then running into the house, where I say hi to Mom and Dad then skip on into my room, willing sleep to find me as thoughts of Logan and the turtles and the sparkling moonlight take turns rolling through my head.

Before I know it, the morning light is creeping through my window, bringing with it lingering memories of last night's picnic. And kiss.

For once I wish Liggy was with me on the beanbag, licking my face and listening to me talk, but today I am alone. Not even Mom and Dad are home this morning –they're already off running errands – though I'm not ready to tell them the news yet anyway. Because practicing for the Scramble requires spending a lot of unsupervised time on the water. Hours they might start trying to account for if they were to know

Logan and me were more than friends.

So instead I pull myself out of bed and boot up my computer, ready to review the week's reconnaissance results. But as the computer loads, it hits me. Today isn't just Friday. It's the due date for entering the Scramble.

And the day Benny gets home.

Just then, my phone rings. Could it be Benny? Home already?

I peer down at the caller ID. It's a text from Logan. Asking if I'm awake.

"Of course, come over," I text back, heading to my dresser in search of an outfit. I pull out a clean shirt and shorts, then pause, staring at myself in the mirror. I look like my usual self, skin tanned and hair wild, no different than I looked before I met Logan. Only inside I can tell something's changed.

So instead of running out like usual I spend a few extra minutes on my hair, running through a brush until it shines. Then I throw on some lip gloss before writing a note to my parents and heading out to fill Liggy's water dish.

Logan greets me just as Liggy starts slurping from her dish. "You ready for this?" he asks.

I turn to find him in a pair of sunglasses and his signature black t-shirt and jean shorts. "Guess so," I say. "Though Benny better have a good explanation."

Logan nods, then reaches for my hand.

I grab on and look into his eyes. Smile.

He bends down just enough to reach my cheek with a kiss. The touch sends sparks down my spine and into my toes, making it hard to walk without losing my flip flops. And I wish we could be just going to spend another day on the boat instead of on our way to see Benny and secure the Scramble entry fee.

A strong breeze whips my hair in front of my eyes and into my mouth as we head toward the Lodge. I breathe a sigh of relief when the Becco lobby sign comes into view. A few minutes inside would do my hair some good. Or at least give me some time to get it into a ponytail.

"You want to try here or Marina's guesthouse?" asks Logan as we reach the door.

"Let's try this first," I say, my hair elastic already in my hand.

Logan opens the door and waits for me to enter.

The same girl from Saturday is working the desk. "Oh hey Charlene," I say. "We were looking for Marina. Do you know if she's back yet?"

Charlene smiles. "Not yet, but I just got off the phone with her mom. They're planning on getting here around noon, so you've got another couple hours. Want me to tell her you stopped by?"

"Nah, that's okay. We'll be in the area, so we'll just check in around then."

"Sure thing," she says, returning to her magazine.

Outside, I hold my arms and try to control their trembles. If Benny gets back around 12:00, I should have more than enough time to secure his half of the Bonefish Scramble entry fee and run it down to the tournament office next to Rosalie's. But lately, hardly anything's gone to plan. And seeing as he's ignored my fifteen texts and phone calls, it's hard to feel too optimistic.

Logan seems to read my mood. "Let's do something while we wait. Want to check the turtle nest?"

I take a deep breath and nod. Checking the turtles always lifts my mood. And right now, I can use a distraction. So together we head toward the back of the resort. But at the edge of the sand, we find that the grasses and ferns that just last night hid the turtle's sandy clearing now lying limp in the sand. It's hard to tell if they've been trampled or just starved of water.

Even though Becco Lodge has got a serious sprinkler system, I pray that it's the latter as I grab Logan's hand and creep between the wilted plants, edging closer to the fence I constructed last week with the dragnet.

Yet before I can even see the net, Logan stops without warning.

I smash into his chest, my head bouncing off his ribcage. "Hey, what's that about?"

Logan looks away, then steps to the side. "Hey, do you want to do something else? Maybe checking the turtles wasn't a good idea after all."

"Uh, Logan? What's going on?" I push him to the side, then stare.

"I'm so sorry, Piper. I don't know what happened."

"Oh my God. The nest." I cry. "But just last night it was fine!"

"I know. It looks like something got into it after we left." He whispers the words and tries to guide me backwards on the path, toward the Becco Lodge and the missing Benny and our $300 short Bonefish Scramble entry fee.

But I refuse to go. Refuse to believe that the turtles are lost. So instead I look down right into the sand. At the gaping hole that used to be a mound of hope. And the devastation Logan's trying to hide.

CHAPTER THIRTEEN

The tears start fast. Hard. Hot. Singeing my skin as they evaporate into the salty air. And I find myself wishing that my hopes and prayers and cries could fix the cracked eggshells lying by my feet.

"I can't believe this. They're gone. All gone." I whisper between sobs. "The first turtle nest in months and it's ruined. They're all gone! Murdered!"

Logan brings my face into his chest for the second time this week. "Looks like an animal, judging by the prints."

"Yeah, probably a raccoon. I should've known we needed a stronger fence."

"No, covering the eggs at all was amazing. You did

nothing wrong."

"But I could have done more! I should have called one of the turtle groups, but Turtle Save lost their funding last year when the number of turtles dropped. And I didn't know who else to call!" I'm yelling now, loud enough for the guests back at Becco Lodge to hear me, but I don't care. And Logan doesn't try to stop me.

He just stares at the ground, then crouches down next to the caved-in nest. "Hey, look over here," he says. "I don't think that raccoon got all the eggs. There's only a few cracked shells. Didn't you say that turtles lay hundreds of these things?"

I nod, unconvinced. Loggerhead eggs need a constant temperature, much cooler than the hundred degree air roasting the outer layer of sand. An animal's digging could disrupt that. Let in a shot of killer air. And even if it didn't, even if the eaten eggs were from the side of the pile, or were loners dropped away from the main nest, chances are whatever animal did this will be back for another meal.

My knees buckle and I drop to the sand in front of the shards of shell. I turn them over in my palm, admire the soft, leathery surface. Cringe at the yolk-stained interior, grown hard and dry in the summer sun. "They never had a chance. I should've done more. Called in the Coast Guard, or that animal protection group on Key West."

I wait for Logan's response, but he remains quiet.

Looking up, I see him at the perimeter of the fence, pulling on the netting and examining imprints in the sand.

"Oh Logan, forget it. It's useless. I failed. They're all dead," I say.

"No," he says sounding so certain that I almost believe him. But I don't so I continue to cry into the cracked shells littering the sand.

"Piper, there are some animal tracks and it does look like something's gotten to one side of the nest. But I've covered up the hole and there's still got to be hundreds of eggs left. So maybe we can't save them all. But we can save the rest."

"It's too late. It's so hot today. The air probably boiled them. If the eggs get hotter than 90 degrees, it's over," I say.

"Give me your hand."

"Huh?"

"Just do it. Palm side out."

I open my hand and thrust it toward him. Logan opens his and lets a pile of moist dirt hit my fingers.

"What are you doing?" I ask, wiping them off.

"Showing you that the turtles have a chance. The dirt from the hole is still cool. If we mend this fence, they might make it after all."

My throat tightens, then relaxes. "Maybe," I say. "But we're going to need a lot more than a flimsy dragnet to ward off these intruders."

"Good thing I have an idea." Logan grabs a log and moves it next to the nest. "Go ask the front desk if we can borrow a shovel. There is no way we are letting another raccoon get into this nest."

In the lobby, Charlene confirms that Benny and Marina still have not returned. They're running late, stuck in traffic an hour away. Making their arrival time closer to 2:00. I let out a sigh, angry at the traffic but relieved to hear there should still be enough time to get the bonefish entry fee from Benny.

"Hey can we borrow a shovel for a minute? We're helping Marina with some planting out back," I say on my way out.

The girl nods. "Of course, help yourself to whatever you need from the utility shed."

I smile, then head to the back of the Lodge. The air in the shed is hot and thick and smells like a family of mice has moved into the neighborhood. With my nose plugged, I move forward, grab two shovels, and run to fresh air.

Back at the turtle nest, Logan has assembled a huge collection of driftwood and separated it into three piles of different sizes. There are thick logs, medium-sized branches, and smaller twigs and shoots.

"We're going to make a barrier out of wood," he says, "but this time not just on the surface. We're going to bury it in the sand."

"Huh," I say, impressed. "That might just work."

"Not might. Will," he says, grabbing a shovel.

He places the spade next to our netting and smashes his foot down on the metal. Picking up the other shovel, I do the same. We work in silence for what feels like hours, moving sand, positioning logs, packing a mixture of twigs and sand back around the logs. Our shirts are drenched in mud and sweat when we finish. My legs hurt so much that they are shaking, my hands burning from a constellation of new blisters.

"Do you think this will hold?" I ask.

"Depends. If you were a raccoon, would you mess with this?"

My eyes pass over the three foot high barrier encircling the nest. "No, I think this is safe. Especially since the logs go two feet down."

"Thank God," says Logan. "I'm dying out here."

I laugh. "It's 2:15 now, we should probably go check on Benny."

We retreat out of the shrubs, and are placing our shovels on the side of the ferns and grasses when I notice the front door of Marina's guesthouse swaying in the breeze.

"Hey, look! I think they're back," I say.

We run to the villa and storm inside without knocking. Marina's on the couch watching TV. Benny's standing in the small kitchen, chugging a glass of water.

"Benny, finally," I say. "I was starting to think you

wouldn't make it!"

"Oh hey guys," Benny says. "What happened to you? You're both a mess!"

I look down at my shirt and shrug. "We had to reinforce the fence around the turtle nest. Some predators got in last night, but thanks to Logan we got it patched up in no time."

"God, you and your turtles. Glad you found someone willing to listen to your rants. Sorry Logan, I feel for you, man." Benny laughs, as if he's expecting Logan to join in.

Logan just stares back.

"Anyway, what do you need, Pipes? Marina and I were just going to take a quick nap. It's been an exhausting trip. We've been in traffic on the bridge for hours. A truck full of tomatoes apparently jackknifed at mile marker 97. Not a good way to end the trip."

"That sucks," I say, "I didn't mean to interrupt, but today's the last day to enter the Bonefish Scramble. I've got all the paperwork complete, so all I need is your bit of the entry fee. If you give it to me, I can run down the forms so you can relax."

"Oh. I'm sorry," says Benny, rubbing a thick bandage covering the top of his arm. "I forgot that was today..."

"No worries. You made it back just in time."

"Well actually," Benny looks to Marina, then stares at the ground. "I meant to tell you earlier, only I didn't want to do it by text. And my phone service was a little shaky in Miami. But Marina and I have been talking. And we were thinking that maybe I should pull out of the tournament."

My mouth drops as Marina walks over.

"Yeah sorry," she says, "but that weekend's always so busy at the hotel and my mom could really use some extra help around here."

I lean back into the wall and stare at Benny's lips. "Wait. So did you just say you're backing out?"

"Look, Pipes, I'm sorry. I know how much it means to you."

At this point, I don't know what I want to do more. Run out crying, or kick him in the shins. I settle somewhere in the middle and start screaming.

"How much it means to me? Don't you mean us? Jesus Benny! We've been practicing for this for years! We've been preparing for this tournament for our whole lives!"

"You have," says Benny, "I'm just the sidekick."

"That's not true. You fish just as well as I do!"

"Right, that's why your dad won't even let me bait a line. We both know I've never been great at this stuff."

"What are you talking about? You're amazing Benny, the best boat handler I know." I gasp for air as my head spins.

"Look, Piper, I know I said I'd help you with the tournament. And yeah, the idea of winning all that money is pretty great. I know it would help your parents with the charter business and help you get known in the big-time fishing circles. But there's nothing in it for me. I don't want to be a fisherman. And there's a lot of other ways to make money."

"But what about your mom? And the restaurant? I thought you said they were struggling too!"

"Hey, they're no worse off than anyone else. It's not like $12,000 is going to turn around their whole business. They need tourists, not pocket change."

"Since when is $12,000 pocket change?"

Benny shakes his head. "Pipes, I'm sorry, but I've changed my mind. I don't need the money and I see no reason to spend the next few weeks on a little boat trying to catch my millionth bonefish. Just face it, Marina needs me more than you do."

"But Benny, without you I don't stand a chance! You're the only one who can drive the boat. Who actually understands me!"

"Well I guess you better start looking for someone else then, because I'm sick of it. Sick of the weeds, and all the boat trips, and your crazy reconnaissance missions. Like you can actually predict where the fish are. It's ridiculous. Completely insane! You might not be ready to grow up, but I am."

Benny's words hurt more than ten hydroid stings rolled into one. "You can't mean that, Benny." I whisper, looking first at his face, and then away.

"I'm sorry, I really am, but I'm done with this fishing thing. I've got football to worry about, and Marina needs my help now. I just don't have the time."

I steady myself on the wall to keep from crumbling to the ground. "Well I'm sorry you feel that way, but just so you know, if you don't pay your half of the entry fee, you know the money we saved together, then I can't enter either. It's $700 a boat, remember?"

Benny sighs. "Fine. You're right. A deal's a deal." He reaches into his pocket and pulls out the wad of cash he's been adding to for over a year now. Only this time it looks thinner than I remember.

"I'm not sure I can spare $350, but how does $100 sound?" he asks.

"What? $100! Benny, what happened to all the money we saved? That my dad basically gave us specifically for this tournament?"

"Hey, I earned that money," he says. "And I need it now for other things. Why are you so mad? I said I'd still contribute."

"But $100 isn't enough. Meaning I've spent the last year working for nothing." The tears well in the corner of my eyes, but I blink them away, not wanting Benny to see me cry.

Yet he knows me well enough to see them anyway, to look away and sigh. Then bite his lip. Turn to Marina, then back to me. "Fine, take whatever's left," he says. "I think there's a little more than $200. I'm sure your dad can cover the rest."

"I doubt it, but thanks anyway," I say.

For a moment his eyes weaken, revealing a glimmer of the old Benny underneath.

"Pipes, I'm sorry, but you're going to have to win this one without me." He whispers, then blinks, and in that instant, he's walking back to Marina on the couch. And the Benny I've always loved is gone.

"Guess we should be going then," says Logan, tightening his hand around my arm. "We'll see you guys later. Have a good nap."

The door slams behind us, but I barely hear the noise. Just like I don't feel my feet as they shuffle across the sandy walkway leading to the road. All I can see is Benny's face. All I can hear are his final words.

"Are you okay?" asks Logan.

I shake my head. "Take me home."

"I'll take you home," he says, "but first, we're going to enter that tournament."

My eyes fill with tears and my nose starts running, blurring my words as I try to respond. "How? I don't think there's even $100 here, Logan, and I only have my $350. Entering the tournament is impossible now. Completely impossible!"

Logan eases the money wad from my hand and flips through the bills. "He's got $225, and I've got $50, remember. I'll just ask my dad for a little more. I told you before, he's happy to contribute."

I bite my lip until I can taste blood. "You don't have to do this," I say.

"Yes, I do," he says, "because we are not giving up. You are going to win this thing, Piper, whether Benny is there or not."

"I wish I could believe you," I say, before losing myself in a deep fog.

CHAPTER FOURTEEN

"Hang on, Logan, let me go check on her. I think she's still in bed, but she told me last night she was feeling a little better. And if you ask me, she got over this flu days ago. This here looks like nothing but a case of pre-tournament jitters." Dad's voice echoes through the house as I throw a pillow over my head and roll back toward the window.

"Yeah, I talked to her last night," says Logan. "She said she wanted to practice today."

"Thank God. It's about time she got out of this house. I don't think she's spent this much time indoors since she was a baby and even then…"

I lose Dad's voice as Liggy ramps up her

scratching on my window. She's been pawing at it for the past hour, but today, I'm not letting her in. Yesterday I let her spend the day right next to me and all I did was spend ten hours listening to her high pitched snore. Usually a pleasure, but not really an effective distraction. Which is probably why I agreed to see Logan today in the first place. Well that and the fact that he's stopped by every day this week. If I ignore him much longer, Mom might actually kill me. Or make me start helping her around the house, which might be worse than confronting Logan. And thinking about the stupid Bonefish Scramble that's getting closer and closer with every day.

Dad barges into my room with a smile, barking at me to get dressed and finally leave the house. "Logan's here and this time, you're not telling him to leave. He said you agreed to go fishing with him last night and right now I'm thinking that is just the medicine you need."

I moan. "Fine, tell him I'll be out in a minute."

"Hallelujah, she lives!" he says, slamming the door. "Logan, she'll be right out. Can I get you anything while you wait?"

With a sigh, I scoot out of bed and throw on another bikini, tank, and shorts combination. Then I grab a hair elastic and gather my frizzy strands into a thick knot, without bothering to run a brush through the ends. When I reach the kitchen, Dad is frying some eggs and lobster, while Logan looks on.

"Hey, there she is. See, I told you she's looking healthier. Now you guys better get going," Dad says, flipping the eggs. "The tide will be high in an hour, meaning it is perfect fishing conditions."

"Okay, we're going," I say.

"Have fun, and be careful. They still haven't caught that shark, you know," Dad says.

"Yeah, yeah, we know." I grab Logan's hand and pull him out of the house.

In the yard, Logan stops me, shaking his head. "So are you done feeling sorry? Ready to practice? We only have three weeks, you know."

I frown, as the guilt from pushing Logan away all week comes flooding back. "Yeah, I'm sorry. I...I just needed some time to think."

"Yeah, I know. I talked about it with your dad. He took me fishing a couple times, you know."

I raise an eyebrow. "Really?"

"Yep. We went out with my dad. Don't you remember him coming into your room and asking you to come with us? We went out on Wednesday and Thursday."

My shoulders fall. "I'm sorry. Everything from the past few days is kind of blurry."

Logan puts his hands around me and brings me in close. "I know it's been a terrible week, Pipes, but please. I only want to help. Next time something happens, don't push me away. I'm not like Benny. I'm not the one who abandoned you."

I nod as we start the walk down to Rosalie's. "I know, I'm sorry, I just freaked. Losing Benny in the tournament was such a shock. I mean I still don't know if I'm ready... Maybe we should just go lie on the beach or something. I think I need another day off."

Logan frowns. "But I want to show you my new fishing skills. And you've already lost a week of practice. What about your reconnaissance?"

"The tide's too high for reconnaissance. And those waves look pretty bad," I say, pointing to the water as we reach the docks.

"No worse than that day we went out two weeks ago," says Logan.

"But we weren't really working on boat handling then," I say, "or how to actually land a fish."

Logan sighs. "Well I need to learn sometime, Piper. The weather may not be perfect during the tournament."

"True, but I really don't feel like shouting instructions over three-foot surf."

"Okay, then what do you want to do? Is there anything we can practice from land?"

"Not really." The words come out sharper than I expected, but I do nothing to take them back. Instead I cross my arms over my chest and stare out into the distance, trying not to cry.

"Piper, there's only three weeks until the tournament. We're never going to be ready in time unless we start practicing."

"Even if we practice every minute until the first gun, we don't stand a chance without Benny," I say.

Logan's eyebrows tighten. "Not only have I sunk $75 into this thing but I've shown up at your house every day for a week just to get told you're too sick to see me. And now you finally agree to leave the house and you're telling me we're going to lose? Before we've even practiced? Come on, Piper, snap out of it. Benny's a jerk. You don't need him. I'm here to help. I care about you, remember?"

I lift my eyes to his, wanting to grab his hand and tell him that he's right, that I know I'm being annoying and difficult. But something inside me won't let the words come out. "I really don't think going out today is a good idea," I say. "Maybe we should just go home."

"Fine, if that's what you want, then fine. I'll leave. But remember, Piper, I offered. And just because you're pissed at Benny, doesn't mean you're the only one here with problems. I just moved a thousand miles away to the middle of nowhere. And you don't see me complaining all the time. You say you want to be some famous fisherman, but look at you! You can't even get over a stupid fight with an annoying little dweeb. You'll never make it unless you learn to quit complaining and toughen up."

My mouth hangs open as Logan backs away. "Where did that come from?"

"What? You think you're the only one that can have an attitude?"

I bite my lip. "At the moment I think my problems are a little more serious than just moving to a different town." Beads of sweat start dripping from my forehead.

"Right because you know so much about it. I left behind a girlfriend, my football team, a job. Everything I knew. And why? To come here. The middle of nowhere!"

I open my mouth, ready to scream. To tell him that Islamorada is the fishing capital of the world. Hardly the same as Michigan. But something stops me. Makes me look up. Into Logan's very sad eyes. "You had a girlfriend?" I whisper.

Logan frowns. "Yeah, I did. But we knew that the long distance thing would never work so we ended it. And I worked part-time at a local mechanic's shop when I wasn't in school or playing football. Oh, and a month before we moved down here my best friend died. There? You happy? Now you know all about my pathetic life. Makes yours not look so bad now, right?"

Heavy teardrops fall onto my sandals as I catch the side of Logan's face. He's walking away now, his arms swaying violently from side to side as he disappears across the Rosalie's footbridge. His pace quickens as he crosses the parking lot. Not once does he look back. My heart yearns to chase after him, to apologize for being so rude, for caring so much about stupid Benny. But my legs won't move. Just like my mouth, they've stopped working, leaving me standing there on the pavement with a salty puddle forming by my feet.

"Hey Piper, you okay?" calls Kip from the docks. He's tying up the Coast Guard boat, probably taking a break from all that patrolling for the bull shark.

I find my voice before he can get close enough to see I'm crying. "Yeah, I'm fine."

"All right, just making sure that guy wasn't bothering you," Kip says.

I nod. "No, it's fine. He's a friend."

As Kip walks toward the ramp leading off the docks, I yell goodbye and bolt to the bathroom. I splash a gallon of cold water on my face. And then another. But nothing can wash away the stain hiding under the skin. The realization that I've just lost Logan. My last friend. Gone. All because of my big mouth.

So I wander out and slip down to the docks when no one is looking. It's after 10:00 now and Rosalie's is beginning to fill with tourists and locals who've slept in just to have an excuse to visit Rosalie's for brunch. Sardi will probably be stopping by soon, if she isn't there already. But then ever since the shooting two weeks back, her parents haven't let her spend as much time near the docks. At first it seemed like a blessing, but right now even seeing Sardi doesn't seem like a bad thing. At least it would be someone to talk to. Even if she would probably say something about my hair.

Hidden among the docked boats, I duck into my Whaler and sprawl out over the tiny bench seat in the bow.

Shedding my tank top, I strip to my bathing suit, deciding to get some sun even though I'm short on sunscreen. Sometimes it feels good to get burned. Same way two negatives make a positive, I guess. So I take some time to really think. About Benny. And Marina. And Logan. But my thoughts are so jumbled and my head is throbbing so much that every time I think of any one of them, all I can do is cry.

So instead I close my eyes tight and focus on the rocking of the boat. Up. Down. Up. Down. It sways along with the rolling waves that have snuck into the harbor. Ready to carry out the tide. And as the tide moves out, I drift away with it, until even the salty breeze tickling my face becomes nothing more than a memory.

But after what feels like a minute, I jolt awake. Someone's yelling. A guy. Who's close by. And he's saying my name.

"Please don't tell me you've been lying down here

all day now," he says.

My hands flail over the side of the bench seat as I open my eyes. It's Logan, already jumping onto the Whaler, a fishing pole in hand.

"Logan? Huh? What are you doing here?" I ask, thinking back to our fight. After this morning I was pretty sure we'd never speak again.

But Logan just smiles and makes himself at home on the seat next to the steering wheel. "It's 4:00. The tide's coming in again. Your dad said this was the perfect time for practice."

Hearing his even tone, I sit up straight. "But, uh, what about the wind?" I ask, hoping he'll admit that it's still too rough to go out. And let me retreat back to my safe cocoon on the bow.

But Logan just keeps grinning. "Wind died down about an hour ago."

"And you really want to go fishing?" I ask.

He shrugs.

"I thought we aren't talking," I say.

"We aren't."

"Then why are you here?"

Another shrug. "I ran into Sardi. Seems that on an island the size of a pancake, your social options are pretty limited."

The vision of Logan running from Sardi makes me smile. "So does that mean I get a second chance?"

"Only if I do."

"I don't know, I was enjoying my nap," I say, not that I mean it. Because the more he talks, the more my anger melts right into the waves splashing over the bow. I mean, if it's not worth stewing over Benny, then there's nothing to gain by stewing over Logan either. Except maybe a sure-fire last place finish in the Scramble. And no matter how angry I get at both of them, I can't let that happen. Not without a fight.

Luckily, Logan seems to read my mind. "I really am sorry, Piper," he says. "I had no right to throw all that crap on you earlier. What happened is in the past. And you had no way of knowing."

I sigh. "Well I'm sorry too. I was being ridiculous, getting so worked up about Benny. You're right, we can do this without him. And the tournament is supposed to be fun, not some horrible death march."

Logan shakes his head. "No, it's okay. You want to win, I get it. I want you to win too. And not just for the money. But because you're amazing out there. And everyone should know it."

I bite down on my lip and stare into his eyes. "I'm so sorry, Logan. I can't believe how awful I've been. Especially after what you said about your friend..."

Logan cuts me off. "Don't worry about it. There was no way you could've known."

"How, how'd it happen?" I ask, not sure I'm prepared for the answer.

He reaches for my hand, and for a brief moment

his eyes look even sadder than when I first saw him staring at that stranded stingray.

"I haven't told anybody before, he says. "Not since we left. Part of the reason we moved was to give me a fresh start. Usually when Nick gets sent on these assignments, my mom and me, we just stay back home and he visits on weekends. This time we decided to go with him, even if the assignment is technically only for a year. We'd thought we'd see if we liked it, if maybe we could make the island a permanent home. After Sammy died, it just seemed like the right thing. To move away. You know, forget about the past."

My spine stiffens as Logan pauses for air. A fresh start? Moving away? For a second I wonder if he's about to confess to some horrible crime. Maybe there's more to Logan than just some football star who likes to work on cars.

But of course, I'm way too interested in the other part, the part about Islamorada being his home, to worry about the other.

"Does this mean you're planning to stay here long-term?" I ask.

He looks away, then nods. "My mom and dad have been looking at houses for weeks. They're thinking of buying something."

My blood pumps hard against my veins as Logan's eyes grow sadder. "You know, you uh, don't have to tell me what happened with your friend if you don't want to."

Logan breathes in deep. "No, I do. I mean I don't, but I think it might help. It happened about four months ago now. God I can't believe it's been so long. Every time I close my eyes, I still see the whole scene. Every time I try to sleep. He's there, screaming. And I'm just standing there like an idiot, not doing a damn thing."

I jump over to Logan's seat as he keeps talking. Even though he's looking away, he grabs my thigh and squeezes.

"It was a Thursday. Spring football practice had just ended and Sammy and me decided to get in a few extra hours down at the shop. We weren't supposed to be working again until Monday but the carnival was in town and I really wanted a few extra bucks to take out Carly, my girlfriend. In the town I'm from, there's not a lot going on, so the carnival is a big deal. And my dad had been between work assignments for a while, so I knew I wasn't going to get any meal tickets from him. So I convinced Sam to come down with me and help out for a few hours."

His voice cracks as he tries to smile. In my mind, I picture Logan, his skin still white and pale, probably wearing one of his black t-shirts and those baggy jeans with the frayed hems he likes to wear at night when it's cooler. I can see his long hair all slicked back, his gold chain peeking out from the rim of his shirt. And then I picture Sammy, looking very much the same. A football guy. Tough. The stars of the school.

"So anyway, this guy comes in with a big SUV. A Suburban. One of those huge cars that can sit like a million people. He asks for an oil change. It was simple. Routine. So our boss tells Sammy to work on that and I'm supposed to take care of this tire rotation on a sedan we've already got up on the lift. But you see, it's a really small shop. We've only got one lift. So Sammy has to lift the car manually using a jack. Not a big deal usually, but it meant he had to position the jack under the car on the frame, pump it up, and then start the oil change. So there was this extra step."

Logan turns back to me and I rub his arm, telling him he doesn't need to go on. But he just shakes his head and keeps talking.

"I was in the middle of taking off one of the tires with another kid in the shop. Sammy had the car up on the jack and was getting ready to go under and change the oil. When we used the jack, we were supposed to have a spotter nearby in case anything went wrong, so I asked if he needed any help. But Sammy did this stuff alone all the time so he just said he was all good. So I just made some stupid joke about the girl he was seeing – she uh, had this really funny way of laughing so I was always teasing him – and I went back to my job.

"I'd just gotten the front driver's side wheel off

when I heard the crash coming from the right. Me and Eddie, the other kid in the shop, we dropped the tires and went running. But it was too late. The car was already on top of Sammy."

My mouth falls open as Logan shivers. I curl my toes around the bait well handle on the bottom of the boat. Logan grabs my hands and buries his head into my lap.

"The car was too heavy, Piper. We tried to lift it, but we couldn't. And the worst part was, I could hear him screaming, begging us to get him out. So Eddie dialed 911 and I threw under another jack and I pumped it up as fast as I could. By now our boss had come out from the back room hollering, and he grabbed another jack too and together we pulled him out. Sammy was alive then, still talking, and I was so relieved. I thought he was going to be okay. But then when the ambulance got there, he started to drift away. By the time they got him to the hospital, he was in a coma. He hung on for another week. But he never woke up."

"I, I, don't know what to say."

I fumble over the words as my arms wrap around Logan. He's hugging me back, sobbing, saying how it was all his fault. How he was supposed to be the spotter, how he let his friend die.

I try to tell him that it's not true, that there was no way of knowing the car was going to fall. And what was wrong with that boss, leaving a bunch of high school kids alone in the shop?

Logan hugs tighter, then releases his grip.

"After Sammy died, I never thought I'd do anything again. All I could do was sleep and blare my music and hide in my room. And I stayed in there so long that when I did come out even the sunlight coming in our kitchen window hurt. By that time, Carly didn't want anything to do with me, Eddie had moved on to a different job, and school was over. No one on the football team knew what to say. And neither did my parents. At that point, the last thing I thought I'd ever do again was work on cars.

"But you know, after a month passed, I found myself missing it. So one day I went out and I washed down my dad's car. And then the next day, I checked the oil. The next weekend, I was cleaning his sparkplugs. And six weeks after Sammy died, I was underneath a car, changing the oil.

"Because the thing was, as much as I wanted to, I couldn't stay away. Fixing cars is what I'm good at. It's part of what makes me tick. And it's always going to be a part of me, even if I do hope that one day I'm the guy designing them, instead of rotating the tires. But it's just like you and fishing. There's some things you just can't give up on. Even if you want to."

I breathe in deep and run my hands through my knotted hair.

"Logan, you are stronger than I could ever be. I don't think I'd ever come out of my room if I lost someone. I mean, here Benny just acts like an idiot and I freak out. And I wish I could just get back up and act like everything is okay, like you did. But this tournament isn't like fixing a car. I can't do it on my own. There are too many moving parts with the boat, and netting, and measuring and everything else. And I can't just ease back into it either. There's no time."

"That's why you've got me, Piper. Like I said, I may not be as experienced as Benny, but I know a thing or two about fighting for what's important. And right now, I can think of nothing more important than winning the Bonefish Scramble."

"You mean that?"

"Completely."

Silently, I stand up and jump to the dock. I untie the stern first, then the bow. I breathe deep as the lines splash into the harbor, freeing the Whaler from its harbor detention. The bull shark may be loose, but I don't care. I need to be free, on the boat I love best.

Logan catches my glance, then turns to the steering console.

I nod.

He flicks the key.

And then we fly out of the harbor, the wind whipping our hair and causing our eyes to tear.

CHAPTER FIFTEEN

"So it really has to be pink huh?" asks Logan as I hand him a skimmer, the bonefish equivalent of a fishing lure, and instruct him to tie it onto the line.

"The fish like pink. Believe me, I've tried all colors. This works the best."

"Did we use pink with your dad?"

I shake my head. "Think we're going to give away all our secrets to the tourists?"

Logan laughs as he ties the hook to the line, reminding me of why I decided to give him a chance to learn the ropes. Despite the time crunch, we're doing better than expected. In two weeks, Logan has come a long way. From reconnaissance to boat handling to fish netting, we've covered everything, even if it has been a crash course. The only thing we haven't done is catch any prize-worthy bonefish. A bit of a concern seeing as the tournament is now just eight days away, but I'm trying not to worry. Yet. There's still the shrimp pocket we saw a few weeks back at Coral Cove. Not to mention Lignumvitae, the next place on my list to check.

"So where do you get these things anyway?" asks Logan, pointing to his line. "My dad bought hooks the other day, but none of them look quite like this."

"They don't sell them everywhere," I say. "These ones I get specially made from a small stand that sells citrus fruit. They make them by hand on the side. Only a few people know where to get them, and that's a good thing. Because these babies work. If there's fish around, this is the rig you want to have."

Again, Logan's laugh fills my ears. "So why is it we only caught two yesterday then?"

"Because you spooked the fish!" I punch his arm and shake my head. Yesterday was the day he brought a radio on board. Good for ambience, he said. Yeah, right. Music on the water is good for a lot of things. Like swimming. Laying in the sun. And getting closer to Logan. But catching bonefish? Not really. It's a miracle we caught two. A testament to my reconnaissance. But this I don't tell Logan. Better he think it was his mad fishing skills. Right now he needs the confidence. Something I'm still a little short on, even if I am enjoying all the time teaching Logan. But who wouldn't enjoy teaching the most caring guy I've ever met how to fish? Memorizing the tan lines on his feet from the flip flops I begged him not to wear, counting the freckles that just started popping up on his nose this week.

Okay, okay, so maybe not everyone would find freckles and tan lines attractive. But right now I do. Because with Logan, we're a team. I tell him a fact about the tides or the waters or the grasses, and he remembers. I start guiding the boat to a specific channel or cove and he wants to know why.

It's like how me and Benny used to be. Though right now I'm beyond feeling nostalgic. Benny made his choices, and I've made mine. And while the future of the Bonefish Scramble is yet to be determined, the more time I spend with Logan, the more I realize it's better to work with someone who's really on my side. Oh, and who doesn't mind swimming in the weeds.

We spend the rest of the morning in the cove around the bend in the island, right where we found the masses of shrimp congregating a couple weeks back. The shrimp are still here, and the bonefish are too.

We catch six in about four hours, a good haul by anyone's standards, but none of the fish is any larger than before. So after recording their measurements and comparing them to the fish we caught yesterday on the other side of the island – one of yesterday's was bigger, but there were far less fish – we start up the engine and head back for the harbor.

Logan guides us in, letting the boat glide right into our slip like a pro. The landing is so beautiful I almost cry, but then I remember that with Logan's obsession with cars, it's no surprise he's turning out to be so good with boats. Boats handle differently than cars, but not that differently. And even though he's only 16, Logan's known how to drive for years.

"Man, I'm starving," he says, killing the motor.

"Me too," I say, wondering if he's heard my growling stomach. "Want to come to my house? We could grab some sandwiches there if you want."

"I really don't know if I can wait that long," he says, as if the half-mile walk takes longer than ten minutes.

"Well where should we go then? Your house is farther," I say, leaving out the part about how I'd rather not see Nick. Lately every time we stop by all he does is quiz me on bonefish. It's exhausting, having to play dumb all the time and make sure none of my secrets slip out.

"Wanna eat here?" He motions to the bustling deck above us.

"Uh, you sure?" I ask, knowing deep down that there really is no reason not to eat at Rosalie's. Except that I could use the ten bucks a fish sandwich costs on a few more bonefish rigs. And that at this time of day we're bound to see Sardi. And oh yeah, lately Benny and Marina have been hanging out here too. It's no easy feat to ignore Benny and Marina on the Rosalie's deck. Especially at lunchtime. During the week. When there's only a handful of occupied tables.

"Come on, Piper, I'm starving. And besides, we haven't seen Benny around in days."

"What about Sardi?"

He shrugs. "Right now I'd rather deal with her than walk a mile for a peanut butter sandwich."

"Point taken," I say as I follow him toward Rosalie's back deck. Getting lunch here might not be how I'd like to spend my afternoon, but after all the time Logan's put into fishing practice, I know I owe him at least an hour for lunch.

The deck is more crowded than usual, reminding us that the tournament is less than two weeks away. Tourists have already started descending on the area. Large RVs fill the parking lot, as do a couple of banners advertising the tournament's start next Thursday. The smell of fried fish, usually a favorite, makes my stomach sick as I catch a glimpse of Wyatt Jacoby. Last year's tournament winner, here in the flesh.

"Hey look, it's Wyatt Jacoby in the flesh," Logan says, shaking me as our waitress leads us to a table.

Apparently I've been staring, and not too subtly either. Good thing for me is that most people down here stare at people like Wyatt Jacoby. In the sport fishing capital of the world, people like him are God. And the fact that he's got TV cameras swarming him just makes the effect worse.

"Yep, that's him," I say, my voice a whisper.

"You know, in person, he looks so much smaller. I never thought he'd be so scrawny," Logan says.

"He doesn't look like much, but he's really strong. And he always pays big money to a local guide so he knows all the best spots," I say, wondering who he's bribed this year.

"Well if that's the case, then he doesn't stand a chance."

"What do you mean? He won last year and came in second the year before."

"But last year you weren't in the tournament."

I sigh. "Not on my own, but I was on Dad's boat. We caught a lot of fish too, just none of them was big enough to take first prize."

"Well this year's going to be different. You said it yourself, you've been practicing every day for a year."

"Yeah, pretty much since we lost last year. You know after that tournament Dad threatened to close down the charter business? Only thing that convinced him to keep with it was the fact that I was into it. He didn't want to kill my one interest, you know? Even if it meant money would be tighter than if he went out and got a regular job."

Logan smiles. "I've met your dad, Piper. You may have been the excuse, but I guarantee you he had no intention of closing the business. Fishing is his life too."

"Perhaps," I say, turning to the menu. Daily special is fried grouper sandwiches and hush puppies, same as it's been for the last ten years.

The waitress walks over with two Cokes we didn't have to order – even with my recent hiatus from lunch here, they still know my order by heart – then she pulls out a small pad and asks for our food order, more for Logan's benefit than mine.

He decides to be adventurous, ordering a whole platter of fried seafood. Clams, shrimp, scallops, grouper. Enough food for three people, really, but I don't comment. I just stick to my grouper and hush puppies, then take a long sip of syrupy Coke.

The food arrives just as Wyatt Jacoby gets up from the bar and heads down to the docks. I crane my neck, trying to see which fishing boat he's walking toward, but just as he reaches the row of fishing charters, a voice calls out from behind me.

"OhmiGod Piper! Finally! I haven't seen you in so long! Ever since the shooting I've pretty much been banned from Rosalie's but then when they opened the beaches back up my parents finally caved! I heard they never caught that shark, can you believe it? It's insane!"

I take in a deep breath and turn to face Sardi. "Hey, it's good to see you too. Yeah, the shark probably went out to sea, or more likely moved on to another island."

Sardi pulls up a chair and plops down between me and Logan. "So how have you both been? I heard that you and Benny had a falling out. I hope it's nothing serious though because he and Marina have been acting so cute together. You really have to see it!"

"Uh, I'd rather not," says Logan.

"Yeah, okay, but anyway you really should make up. We've been hanging out a lot. I think Marina's having a big pool party tonight. You guys should stop by!"

I shake my head. "Thanks for the invite, but Logan and I are busy. We've got a lot of work to do to get ready for the tournament."

Sardi squeals. "Oh yes! That's right! Did you see Wyatt Jacoby was here? I totally didn't think he'd be back after he conquered the tournament last year, but rumor is that he had such a good time that he convinced the Expedition Channel to do a special episode on the tournament. If it does well, they might make it into a show. All about Wyatt Jacoby taking on Islamorada!"

"Sounds cool," I mutter, not thinking it's cool at

all. Islamorada is about local fishing spots. Untouched flats. Overgrown coves. Not the glitzy Wyatt Jacoby.

I pop a hush puppy into my mouth as Sardi steals a handful of fries from Logan's heaping platter. "Hope you don't mind," she says.

Logan just nods and picks up a fried shrimp.

"By the way, have you guys heard that there is a total infestation of iguanas overtaking the island now," says Sardi, her eyes growing even wider.

"Uh, not really," I say, trying to remember the last time I even saw an iguana anywhere but on the rocks lining the bay.

"Oh God, Piper, you are always so out of the loop. And here it's been all anyone's talked about all day down here. Apparently some tourists came back to their room last night to find two five foot iguanas sprawled out on the bed. Isn't that insane? The people freaked out so much that the hotel had to close down an entire block of rooms to make sure there wasn't a whole nest or something."

"Huh, that's weird," says Logan. "I didn't know iguanas traveled in packs."

"They don't, not usually anyway," I say.

Sardi drums her fingers against the table, already losing interest. "Yeah, I'm definitely not an iguana expert. All I know is that a bunch of people were moving to the Becco now and there's some pretty ridiculous reviews of the whole thing posted online.

There's even pictures of it and everything, and let me tell you, out of the water those iguanas look gross."

"Yeah, I'm sure," says Logan, cutting her off. "Hey Piper, I'm actually thinking I've gotten a little too much sun today. I'm feeling pretty sick. Wanna wrap up this food and head to my place?"

I nod, then jump from my seat and head to the bar where they stash the Styrofoam containers. I walk back quickly and start dumping in our plates as Logan hails our waitress.

"It was good to see you, Sardi," I say, as Logan finishes with the bill.

"Oh yeah, definitely. I hope you feel better, Logan, and you really should think about coming tonight to the party. It should be a good time."

"Yeah maybe," Logan says. "See ya, Sardi."

"Bye guys! Take good care of Logan, Piper!"

I try not to roll my eyes as Logan grabs my hand.

"OhmiGod you two are even cuter than Benny and Marina. Just adorable! I always ask Travis to hold my hand but he never does. Something about his hands getting sweaty…"

We leave Sardi talking to herself and walk out into the parking lot.

"Want to finish eating on the boat?" Logan asks.

"How about my house? It's closer to the Lodge."

"Good idea."

We walk for ten minutes until my house comes

into sight. Mom is out for the afternoon doing her weekly volunteering at Theater of the Sea, and Dad's out fishing with Nick, trying to get him ready for the tournament.

So I get another bowl of water for Liggy – I swear that deer drinks more than any other animal I've ever seen – give her a quick kiss on her head, then join Logan in the kitchen. He's already placed our lunches on a tray and thrown the fries in the toaster oven to warm up. I pour two glasses of fresh squeezed orange juice – Mom doesn't allow soda – then join Logan at the table.

"So how often do iguanas find their way into hotel bedrooms?" Logan asks.

"About as often as Rory Pinder's sailboat malfunctions," I say.

"Funny that both situations seem to help out Becco."

"Yeah, some sort of coincidence."

"So what do you want to do? Should we just ignore it?"

"I don't know," I say. "There's a chance that these really are just unrelated incidents. But if Benny and Marina are going around vandalizing property, they could be in trouble. These things usually don't end well."

"Though throwing iguanas in someone's room is hardly vandalism."

"It is if the hotel loses money."

"True. But then maybe Benny hasn't been so open to conversation lately. Maybe we should just let it go. Might be more worth our time to sneak in some afternoon fishing."

I cringe. "Yeah, maybe," I say, turning the facts over in my head. Part of me wants to forget the whole thing and jet out in the Whaler with Logan, but the other part can't stop thinking that by not confronting Benny, I'm giving up on my best friend.

"God leave it to Benny to go muck everything up," I say. "I'm sorry Logan, but as angry as Benny is at me, I don't think I can let this go."

Logan nods. "Why don't we go check on the turtle nest then? It will give us an excuse for being in the area."

"Good idea," I say, wiping my sweaty palms on my shorts.

"So to the turtles then?" asks Logan.

"Yeah, the turtles. And then onto the sharks."

CHAPTER SIXTEEN

Fort Loggerhead is still intact, overlooking the gentle waves of the Atlantic. I unclench my fists as Logan finishes his full inspection, relieved there are no deep holes leading under the branches. No breaks in the netting from ambitious birds. No tracks in the sand from curious humans.

"I hope they're still alive." I whisper the words as I lean against a nearby scrub pine, pull off a cluster of needles and spin them in my hand. As their sap covers my palms, I break them into pieces and scatter them into the air.

"They definitely are. The soil was still cool, remember?"

"Yeah, I know. Fingers crossed, right?"

Logan nods. "How much longer until they hatch?"

"They take 80 days usually. I saw the turtle laying them the same day we first took you and your dad out on the charter."

"Well we moved down here at the end of May. I'm pretty sure I met you during the second week of June. And what is it now, mid-August?"

"Uh-huh. Those eggs probably don't have much time left. We should start checking them more frequently. Like every day around sunset. They usually hatch at night. We'll need to remove the barriers so the hatchlings can swim to the water."

"Should we take them off now?" Logan asks.

I run over the math in my head. If we met the second week of June, then it's been about two months now that the eggs have been incubating. Most of June and all of July. Plus the first week in August, leaving us with a couple weeks left. Ten to twenty days depending on the actual date we met.

"Let's leave them on until next week. Right now I think we're still at least ten days away," I say.

"Fair enough. Anything else we need to do here?"

I stare back at the nest and run over the checklist in my head. But with the eggs secure and still weeks away from hatching, there isn't much else to do. Meaning it's almost time to see Benny. For the first time since he bailed on the tournament.

My feet refuse to move as Logan starts walking toward the tiny path we've cut into the brush, leading back to the Lodge. I want to scream out and tell Logan that I've made a mistake, that confronting Benny is stupid and we've got no right to get involved. But as much as I want to say this, I don't.

Because deep down, I know we have to confront him. Benny may be swimming with sharks, but didn't he save me from the jaws of one a month earlier? What kind of friend would I be if I didn't do the same? Even if we aren't speaking.

So I dig my feet into the sandy soil and trudge ahead first to the path, and then across the beach where the old bonfire pit is stacked high with a pile of old branches. Getting ready for tonight's party. Definitely not something I want to be a part of.

From the outside, Marina's summer home base, the guesthouse, looks deserted. The shades are pulled and the front door closed, not propped open like it usually is. But as we draw closer, the sounds of satellite TV become clearer. Sounds like a baseball game. Or maybe a sports movie. Either way, it means someone's here. Definitely Marina. And probably Benny.

Logan knocks on the door before I can prepare for the encounter. Words and thoughts and ideas swim through my head as Marina opens it. She looks beautiful today, like always. Only this time she looks different somehow. Tired. Exhausted, actually. Like she's been up half the night.

My gaze keeps drifting back to the dark circles staining the skin beneath her eyes, the mound of tangled blonde hair piled high on her head.

For a moment I look away, annoyed that even with her hair and makeup a mess, her face still glistens in the light, her eyes as bright and fragile as a piece of sea glass held up to the sun. But the thought passes with a blink.

Even though Marina's smiling, the crease between her eyes gives her away. Something is bothering her. And I've got a pretty good idea what it is.

"Hey guys, what's up?" Marina hesitates for a second before stepping aside and motioning for us to come in. Her arms look awkward as she waves us toward the sitting room, then folds them back up across her chest like a pair of wings.

I look to her face for hints of from where the discomfort is coming. Is she worried because she knows Benny won't be happy to see us? Or is it because she's fighting with him herself? Knowing that dark circles don't appear overnight, and that Benny and I are most definitely still not talking, I decide it is probably a little of both.

Not knowing the right thing to say, I breathe a sigh of relief when Logan opens his mouth, ready to slice the silence chilling the air conditioned room.

"So I'm sorry to barge over here, but I had a couple things I wanted to ask Benny," he says, as we shuffle into the entryway.

Marina smiles again and her lack of concern about us seeing Benny helps me relax. Maybe there really is a better explanation for those two unrelated incidents at the Tarpon Bay. Maybe Marina's dark circles are the result of stressing about the hotel. Or fighting with Benny. And if Benny's pissed at Marina, maybe he's not mad at me at all. Maybe he'll be happy we're here. Ask to be friends again. Maybe.

"Want something to drink?" Marina pulls out a six-pack of Dr. Pepper from her small refrigerator. It's not my favorite soda, but I take one anyway. It feels better to have something cool in my hands.

"Oh is that the Marlins game?" Logan asks, eying the television from the small kitchen table where Marina's led us. The room is empty except for a pile of purses strewn across the couch and a laptop on the coffee table. There's no sign of Benny in sight.

"I think so," Marina says with a wave of her hand. "Benny was watching it earlier. He's cleaning up now though in the other room. Let me grab him."

As Marina heads to check on Benny, Logan scoots onto the couch and grabs her computer. His eyes widen as he waves me over. "Look at this," he says.

I slide across the tile floor to join him just as the bedroom door swings open. Logan scoots back into the couch and averts his gaze, as if he was never looking at the computer at all.

"Hey guys," says Benny. He looks straight at me then turns his head, settling his stare on Logan.

"Hey man, what's up? We were just checking out the turtles, and thought we'd stop by," Logan says. "Terrible game going on with the Braves. Another three runs just came in the last inning. Looks like they're going to waste their whole bullpen today."

Benny shrugs. He's never been that into baseball. "Guess we're more of a football state."

"That's what I'm hoping. Hey man, it's almost time for football tryouts and we still haven't thrown the ball at all. We really should go out this week and practice. When's football camp start anyway, the last week in August?"

"Yeah, the day after the tournament. Think you'll be ready?" Benny asks.

"Sure, I've been running all summer. In the mornings, before it gets too hot. But we should get Travis over here one night this week. With three of us, we can run some real drills."

Benny hesitates before speaking. "That would be awesome. I really could use some help, but this week is pretty bad for me. I promised Marina's mom I'd help out with the hotel. They got some unexpected reservations this week and they're a little short staffed."

Logan slaps his hand on his knee. "Oh yeah, that's right. Sardi was telling us earlier that there was this big iguana infestation at one of the resorts. Maybe I'll just call Travis then, there's a lot the two of us can do. Do you have his number?"

"Uh, yeah, I guess," Benny says. He reaches into his pocket and grabs a cell phone. "Here, it's 305-555-4521. You should definitely give him a call, and then we can all practice when things slow down a bit."

"Yeah, maybe," says Logan. "Though starting next week I'll probably be swamped with the tournament up until camp starts. You sure you can't take some time off? Football camp can be pretty brutal if you're not ready for it. I know a week wouldn't do much, but it would help a little, even if we just focused on some basic drills."

Benny shifts in his chair, then turns back to Marina. "I really wish I could but unfortunately I've already promised Ms. Beccoli that I'd help out."

"Okay, okay, message received. So what are you going to be helping out with anyway? Helping Charlene with the front desk?"

Benny frowns. "Uh..."

"He's helping me finish the purses," Marina says, then bites her lip. Because we all know that Benny helping Marina with her purses is as likely as him swimming in the weeds.

"Funny, I heard he was helping out with

reservations," Logan says.

Marina raises an eyebrow. "What do you mean?"

"Oh nothing, just that the iguana attack on Tarpon Bay didn't sound like much of an accident," I say, breaking my silence. "I mean, when's the last time an iguana ventured far enough from the ocean to even get near a hotel room anyway? Especially seeing that the Tarpon's rooms aren't on the water."

Benny sighs. "I'm sure it's happened before."

"But right after Rory Pinder's boat ends up with a snapped line?" I ask.

"Wait. Who told you about that?" Marina asks. "Did Sardi know about that too?"

I shake my head. "No, but would it matter if she did?"

Marina walks over to the couch and sits down on the opposite side from Logan.

"Of course it wouldn't matter," Benny says. "Though it does sound like someone is starting rumors."

"Or putting two and two together." This time I catch Benny's stare and refuse to let go. For a moment, our eyes remain locked.

Then he breaks away, marching toward Marina and the couch. "If you have something to say, Piper, say it. Otherwise I suggest you leave. We really need to work."

"Oh yeah, on the purses. That's right," I say.

Benny lets out a growl. "Okay, I'm done. Goodbye, Piper."

Logan rises from the couch and joins me. "We'll catch up later, okay man? Let me know when you're free to practice."

"Sure, sounds good," he says.

"And stay off private property," I say under my breath.

Catching my words, Benny stands. "You just can't leave it alone, can you, Piper?"

"I would, except we saw you that night at the docks. On Rory Pinder's boat."

"OhmiGod, I told you someone was there, Benny!" says Marina, sitting up straight.

"So you admit being there," I say.

"What?" says Benny, "Marina shut up! You don't know what you're talking about!"

"Hey, don't talk to her that way," I say, walking up to Benny's face. Logan tries to take my arm and make me step away, but I refuse. Benny and I have had fights like this before. And as scary as he can look with his tanned muscles and furrowed brow, I know he isn't going to hurt me. With anything more than his words, anyway.

"I'll say whatever I want to whoever I want to, Piper." Benny shouts each word slowly, letting them bounce off the walls of the room. "And I'm telling you, Marina doesn't know what she's talking about."

228 Jackie Nastri Bardenwerper

"Look man, we all know that she does," says Logan, stepping forward. "That night we were hanging out on the Whaler and saw you chilling on Rory's boat for quite a while."

"So what the hell does it matter if we were down there. We were trying to get away from the crowds."

"Right. Then why is it that just hours after I see you climbing the mast, Rory is canceling his sunset cruises for the day?" I ask.

"I don't know, but cool it, okay. What I do on my time is none of your business."

I plant my feet into the ground and will myself not to punch Benny in the face. "Apparently not."

"Glad we agree. Now if you'll excuse me, I have to get back to work."

"Sure, no problem," says Logan. "Just one more thing. Next time you're planning on breaking an air conditioning system, I suggest you don't leave the search page up on your computer. Evidence like that can be pretty incriminating."

"Shit Marina, I told you to turn that thing off."

Marina's shoulders slump as she retreats to a corner. Part of me wants to run over and tell her everything is okay, that Benny overreacts all the time. But the other part's just too angry at Benny to break away and comfort someone else.

"So are you ready to come clean now?" I ask, looking Benny straight in the eye.

"What do you want me to say? Sounds like you've got it all figured out without me."

"Well then how about you tell me why," I say, "and then promise me you'll stop whatever it is you've got planned."

Marina buries her face in her hands and starts to cry. Benny narrows his eyes and huffs before running to her side.

"I'm sorry baby, I know I got a little worked up. But I didn't mean it at all, see? Everything's fine now. Just fine," he says, stroking her back.

"No Benny, it's not fine." The words sound dark and tired, just like Marina's eyes.

"I told him we needed to stop after Rory's boat," she says, "because that was dangerous enough, having to run and hide after all those shots rang out. I'm still not sure the shooter was a tourist looking for the shark. The way those shots were zipping by, I was convinced it was crazy Rory himself. Out to kill whoever was dumb enough to climb on his boat. Which is why me and Benny packed up and booked it to Miami with my mom. But then when we got back and Charlene told us that we were actually successful and that the sunset cruises had been booked all week, I started thinking maybe it wasn't the worst idea..."

"Wait, you're saying Rory was shooting at you?" I say, trying to make sense of Marina's words. Sure, we all know Rory loves his boat, and that he can act a little crazy, but crazy in a I'm-going-to-go-spear-fishing-in-my-pajamas-at-midnight kind of way. Not like a psychopath. Which makes the shooting theory unlikely. Unless he really does just care that much about his boat.

Benny seems to agree with my analysis. "No one shot at us. The shots were just nearby, so it seemed at the time that they could have been. Obviously, we thought it better to be safe than sorry. Though now that they say it was a tourist, I'm convinced that Rory had nothing to do with it."

"Which is why you moved ahead with the iguanas." I say.

Marina raises her mouth into a half smile, letting her guilt shine through. "That one he did on his own. I was too scared to touch them."

"Geez, how'd you get those things inside, anyway?" asks Logan, his shoulders loosening up. "Sardi said they were five feet long!"

Benny points to me. "Spend enough time with this girl and you pick up a few things. Rounding up iguanas is one of them."

"Hey, we haven't caught iguanas in years," I say, "and even then, it was only the babies."

"Yeah, too bad a small one wouldn't have made the same impression."

"I'll say," says Marina, "those stupid iguanas scared the guests so much we picked up six extra reservations. That's more than my purses will ever bring."

I shake my head and look up at Marina. "Even if they don't, wouldn't it be better to know that whatever they brought in, at least it was gotten the right way?"

"God Piper, quit the sermon," Benny says before Marina can respond.

I pull out my cell phone and snicker. "Well I can guarantee you that your mother would never go around vandalizing other restaurants just to fill hers. In fact, something tells me that if I called her right now she'd be very interested…"

"Stop it! Right now!" Benny swipes at my arm but I pull away before he can grab the phone.

"How about I promise not to say anything to Mrs. Benitez only if you promise to stop messing with other people's properties?"

"Fine," he says. "But just know the one you're really hurting is Marina. She needs the cash just as much as you do."

"And even she knew what you were doing was dumb. She was trying to do it the right way with her purses, remember? You're the only one I know who doesn't want to work." Out of the corner of my eye I see Marina, her eyes wider than I've ever seen them before. "Don't worry, Marina, Benny is good at being a jerk. But he's also good at apologizing when he's wrong. It's all about manners, right Benny?"

Benny growls for the second time of the day. "Seriously, Marina, I don't know why you ever let them in."

"And I don't know why we thought it was worth coming over. But I'll promise you this, Oswardo. If we hear Sardi or Rory or anyone else barking about more damage down at the resorts, I'm calling your mom on speed dial. And something tells me that even a barrel of Ivory Garden soaps wouldn't get you out of that one."

"You've made your point. Now goodbye. And please, don't come back."

"Does this mean we're not invited to the pool party?" I ask.

Benny makes a face that looks just about as scary as the bull shark.

"Don't listen to him, you're always welcome," Marina says, and for a minute I think that maybe I've underestimated her as well. Maybe she never saw me on the docks that June day in the first place. Maybe she's never really been that bad.

I thank Marina for the invitation and say goodbye before grabbing Logan's arm and heading back out into the oppressive August heat. Before I know it, we're enveloped in it, sweat beads forming on our foreheads.

"I always knew you were tough, but wow, you treated him rougher than a bonefish," Logan says as the cabin door slams behind us.

I laugh, releasing the jitters and tension bottled up inside. "Without your catch on the computer, we didn't have anything. Not to mention the way you set him up in the first place. The idea of Benny working on Marina's purses. It's priceless!"

Logan smiles, then leans in for a kiss. My cheeks blush as I close my eyes. Our lips brush lightly, like a rock skimming the surface of the ocean. Seconds later, we're running down the road, pebbles and broken seashells catching in our flip flops.

"You want to come over for a bit and hang out?" I ask, slowing my gait as we reach my house. The running has filled my veins with energy, made me eager to pick apart our conversation with Benny.

But Logan just frowns. "I actually gotta get home and help my dad with a few things," he says between breaths. "I promised I'd stay home tonight too. But I'll see you tomorrow first thing for practice, okay?"

I nod, hoping he can't tell I'm upset. "All right. Everything at home okay?"

"Sure, Nick's just bored. Wants some father-son time, you know?"

"Yeah don't worry about it," I say, opening the gate. "I should probably help Mom with some chores here anyway."

"Good. Then I'll see you tomorrow." Logan kisses my cheek then heads back to the road.

I wave goodbye before turning to Liggy, who's

waiting for me under the orange tree, her water dish empty. I bring it to the hose and fill it, then set it by her snout. Then I collapse onto the ground and hug her tightly, glad that even when the world's swirling around me, Liggy is always there under that orange tree. Ready for me to hold onto.

CHAPTER SEVENTEEN

The sun beats down on my shoulders as I check my watch. 10:00 a.m. and already it's so hot that the smell of burning skin envelops Logan and me as we sit there on the skiff, our feet dangling in the harbor. Not in the mood for a third-degree burn, I reach for the sunscreen. The bottle's almost empty – no surprise seeing as I go through three a week – so I squeeze the hot gel right onto my shoulders and start spreading.

"So do you think Benny stayed at the pool party all night and didn't sneak out to bust someone's air conditioner?" I ask as I wipe my greasy fingers on my board shorts.

"Well, it depends," says Logan. "Do you really

think he'd want to deal with the wrath of Mrs. Benitez?"

I laugh out loud as Logan sticks out his hands and pretends to choke a nonexistent Benny. "I'm sure you're right, last night was probably completely uneventful. Let's go fishing. Only seven days 'til the tournament, right?"

"Sure, just one problem."

"What?" I ask, not sure I can handle any more bad news.

"I'm not going out to sea until you give me a proper send-off."

"Which is?" I ask, raising my eyebrow.

Logan smiles, then leans in for a kiss. He doesn't pull away for a full minute. Even though we're down at the docks. In broad daylight. At 10:00 a.m. On a Wednesday.

"Ah, all better," Logan says, looking into my eyes.

"Better? Are you crazy? Half of the island is here! I give it ten minutes before my dad's running over here to ban us from unsupervised boat rides!"

"What? Since when is it wrong to kiss your girlfriend?" he says.

At that, I freeze. "Girlfriend?" I ask. Sure, Logan and I have been spending all our time together, and there's been quite a bit of kissing too. But hearing Logan call me his girlfriend out loud still gives me chills.

"Does this mean you're my boyfriend too then?" I ask, smiling back.

"If you want me to be," he says, his eyes shining.

"Well in that case...how can I say no?" I try to think of what to say next but in the burning sunlight, with boaters all around, all I can think of is escaping the harbor, of being alone with Logan. So I let my words linger and laugh at Logan's beaming smile as I flick on the motor and throw the throttle into reverse.

Minutes later, we're anchored at the ledge and fishing is the last thing on our minds. We've switched on the portable FM radio I usually only turn on for emergencies, to get weather reports when the VHF won't come in. But this time we've turned it onto a real station, one that actually plays music instead of just fishing reports.

With the music on, I feel safer, bolder. So I let Logan kiss me and run his hands down my back. And I don't even yell when he pulls away and jumps off the bow, folding his body into a cannonball before splashing into the water. Sure, the bull shark hasn't been caught and technically I'm still prohibited from swimming, but if Benny can vandalize boats and smuggle iguanas, somehow swimming at the ledge doesn't seem like a big deal.

"Want some company?" I ask as Logan surfaces in the water, his head and shoulders peeking above the surface.

"Obviously," he says.

I open the rear bait well and pull out two masks and snorkels. "Then it's time for some real fun," I say, then dive into the warm, salty water.

A school of grunts circles us, darting off into the shallows as the world below our toes comes into focus.

Logan's eyes open wide, then close as the corners of his mouth rise into a smile. I hear him try to talk, but the sounds are muffled, his voice no different than a dolphin calling her mate. A whale signaling to his pod. So I grab his hand and start swimming.

The water grows shallower as we head closer to the shore and the coral reefs protecting it like an orange peel. A pair of grouper hides next to a mustard yellow brain coral. Clownfish dart in and out of a nest of sea anemones, while a school of angelfish dance near my fingertips. The reef is as magical as ever today, and the water feels good on my cooked skin, as do the tips of Logan's fingers as they brush over my palm. We surface for a few breaths right as a fat parrotfish emerges from a hidden cave of coral.

Logan pushes his mask onto his forehead and gasps. "It's amazing," he says.

"It's my home," I say, then kick my feet downward like a dolphin, and dive deeper.

Once on the bottom, I inspect the reef and teems of tiny fish and plants intertwined in the threads of coral. As my air starts to dwindle, I find what I'm looking for.

A brown sand dollar lies half uncovered in a patch of sand. I lift it from its hiding place and take off to the surface. Logan's waiting right where I left him, only he's got his mask back on and his face is in the water, inspecting the spectacle below him.

I tickle his arm and he lifts his eyes to the surface.

"Finally, you're back! You just missed it but a humongous fish just went by. I don't know what it was but it was massive," he says. "It was almost as long as me."

"Did it have a funny mouth? Kind of like a beak?"

"Yeah, exactly."

"It was probably a tarpon then. They get pretty massive."

"Those are the fish we feed at that diner, right? The ones on the docks?"

"Yeah, exactly," I say, thinking of the lazy mornings we've been spending down at the southern tip of the island.

"So what do you have?" Logan asks, staring at my hand.

I smile. "It's a sand dollar. Really, it's a type of sea urchin, but if you take it home and leave it outside, it will turn white from the sun. I used to collect them as a kid. I'd find them on the beach and use them to create wind chimes and Christmas ornaments. After a big storm, you can find hundreds."

"Is this one for me then?" asks Logan.

"I'd like it to be, only this guy's still alive. But I wanted to show him to you anyway. Maybe we can find a dried one on the beach. It'd be more special anyway if we found it together."

"I couldn't agree more," says Logan. He grabs the delicate disc from my hand and runs his fingers over the bristly hairs covering its body. "It feels like a toothbrush!"

"Those are its spines," I say.

"Spines, huh. They look harmless to me," he says.

"Yeah, he wasn't made to defend against humans. More like fish."

"Well then, guess we better let him get back to it." Logan raises his hand into a salute and drops the sand dollar back down into the water. Then he wraps his arms around me and holds me close.

We reach the docks around mid-afternoon. Logan and I tie up the boat and give it a good rinse using the fresh water hose from Rosalie's. Then we run up the dock ramp and head towards the footbridge, ready to pick up some sandwiches at my house.

But before we reach the bridge, Sardi is calling out, asking if we've heard the latest story. Something about another island disaster.

I whip my head around so fast I can feel the muscles in my neck seize like they do when I jump into the ocean from the wrong angle. But before I can speak, Logan's got my arm and is directing me away.

"Let's deal with this later," he whispers into my ear. "Right now we need to go say hi."

"To who?" I ask.

He points to the parking lot, where Dad's truck has just pulled in. The bed is filled with fishing rods. The heavy duty types used for sailfish and mahi mahi and wahoo.

"Hey Sardi, sorry but we have to go," I say, trying to remember the day's charter schedule. With all the tournament training, Dad's been pretty easy on me the past month. I've only helped out a few times. But even so, I usually know when there's something important going on.

I bite my lip, hoping I haven't forgotten one of those times.

"Let's catch up later today, though, okay? I really want to hear what's going on."

Sardi nods then heads back toward the restaurant, giving me just enough time to place a few feet between me and Logan before walking over to Dad.

"Hi Piper, Logan, wasn't expecting to see you guys on the shore at this time," he says, reaching for the rods. "Shouldn't you be out in the flats searching for those bonefish?"

Logan walks over and helps him with the pile. "That's my fault, I told Piper I needed a break. I was getting a little sea sick out there."

Dad nods. "All that drifting in the grasses can do

that sometimes, especially in this heat. Tell you what, you guys have been working so hard lately, why don't you take a break? Come out with me today on the Blackfin. I've got a couple of tourists that just called me up, said they wanted to go after some wahoo. And you know how I hate to waste all that gas on just two people."

"Wahoo, that sounds awesome," I say. "But we were just going to grab some food. We're starving. And I don't think I have any charter t-shirts here. They're all at home."

Dad reaches into his back pocket and pulls out two twenties. "Go order us a few fish sandwiches. We'll eat them on the boat. We've got a half hour before our guests get here. And don't worry about the t-shirts. This time you're not working. You're coming as guests."

I take the money and look up into his eyes.

"But Dad? Are you sure? Taking us will definitely eat up more gas."

"But it will make the day worth it. Now, go place our order while Logan and I bring these rods down to the dock."

I roll the bills in my hand until they resembles a blade of grass. Then I walk to the counter at Rosalie's and order three fish sandwiches and French fries.

As I wait for the sandwiches, I scan the tables and chairs overlooking the dock. Sardi is still here, seated with Travis, and I debate going over and asking her to fill me in on the story. But without Logan here to catch me if I black out from anger, I decide that maybe it's not the best time to get involved.

So I fight the urge to run back to her table, or to sprint over to Oswardo's and tell Mrs. Benitez exactly what her son has been doing. Because the truth is that ever since the tourists have thinned, so have our recreational trips out into the ocean. Of course we've spent a lot of time out there with some experts, and even a few novices, who wanted to try their hand at the big game.

But a trip just for us? Where we get a turn in the fight chair? Now that doesn't happen every day. Or every month. So I decide once again that dealing with Benny will have to wait. The trip will make Dad happy. And showing Logan how to catch a wahoo will be exciting. Another new adventure. And after the way Benny's been treating me, the idea of letting him ruin another day just seems wrong.

Three cardboard plates of fish sandwiches arrive, steaming from the fryer, and I pop a huge wedge of fried potato into my mouth before balancing the three platters in my hands. My tongue burns and stomach growls as I walk down the ramp and think of ways to sneak another fry into my mouth. But with my hands overflowing with plates, I decide to wait. I've lost too many fish sandwiches in the harbor to risk it.

The wait pays off as I take the first bite into the crisp battered fish. The flaky grouper tastes so sweet that I don't even add any tartar sauce. Instead I eat the sandwich in two bites, then use the sauce for my fries.

Our guests, two skinny, older men, arrive just as we are finishing lunch and they look excited to get started. They've just run into Wyatt Jacoby on the docks and now have it in their minds that they're about to catch a monster. A real possibility in this part of the Keys, but still unlikely. Especially given that both their arms combined don't look strong enough to haul in a fat grunt, let alone a wahoo.

But the old men surprise us. They tell stories of past fishing trips for the entire hour ride out to the fishing grounds, about catching blue sharks, cod, and tuna up north. And when Dad yells out that we've got a wahoo on the line, they play rock paper scissors to determine who gets strapped in the chair first.

Even though the winner's arms are pulled so tight that his veins look like they're about to pop out of his skin, he lands the fish. In under an hour. Dad gaffs the prize and pulls him onto the boat. He's a big one. A prize. A fish to make Wyatt Jacoby proud.

"Now this one's a keeper," the man growls, pumping his fists.

"Aw, I doubt he's even fifty pounds. I can do better," says his friend, staring down at the fish that is most definitely more than fifty pounds.

But Dad just laughs and throws out the lines again, trolling the area until we get another hit.

"All right guys, it's on," he says, as I help strap contender number two into the hot seat.

The second fish doesn't take as long to reel in. But as soon as he reaches the boat, he starts jumping and thrashing and using his killer speed to make a final run.

The line tightens and I run over to the rod to adjust the clutch. By the time I reach the rod, the old fisherman's already letting out more line, and the fish is slipping farther into the ocean.

"Guess I got to reel him in all over again," he says, then gets to work, his arms wobbling like rubber as he takes two big pumps, rests, then repeats the process.

An hour of grunts and cursing follows before we see the fish again. But then he's there, banging against the side of the boat, exhausted, like the man in the chair. This time Logan gaffs the fish, just like I showed him with the bonefish. Dad whistles as Logan pulls him in like a pro, his arms not even flinching from the weight of the fish. The second wahoo is two inches shorter than the first, but twice as fat.

"See, told you I could do better," says the man, inspecting his catch.

His friend shakes his head. "Mine was longer. Yours is obese. Nothing special about that."

"That's what you say now. Wait until I have ten more pounds of meat than you do."

The men laugh, then reach into the cooler and pull out a couple beers.

"Okay, who's up next? Piper? Logan?" asks Dad.

"It's Logan's turn," I say, jumping around the boat.

Logan shakes his head, then walks over to the fighter chair. Dad lets out the lines and again starts trolling. It doesn't take long before we have another bite.

"The rod's going!" I yell to Dad.

He kills the motor and helps me give Logan the reel. "It's a big one," he says. "You can tell he's ready for a fight."

And fight he does. Every time Logan reels in two feet, he has to let out three so the fish doesn't break the line. He does this once, twice, ten times before I lose track of his progress. I throw three buckets of water on the line to keep it from smoking, and even then Logan yelps every time the metal rod hits his thigh. The reel is boiling. The line smoking. And the wahoo keeps darting farther away from the boat.

"And they say we're too old for the big ones," says one of the men. "We landed our fish in half the time!"

Logan grunts, then keeps reeling.

"His fish has got to be bigger," I say, then continue to cheer Logan on.

"Sure, bigger. In our day, young men never

complained. And they never took longer than an hour to reel in a little fish."

I look down at my watch. Sure enough, we're approaching the two hour mark. "Do you need any help? Want to take a break?" I whisper.

Logan shakes his head. "I'm a fisherman now, right? What kind of a fisherman would I be if I gave up?"

"That's the spirit," says one of the men.

Dad walks to the back of the boat and squints into the distance. "I still don't see that fish near the boat. When's the last time you let out more line?"

"I don't know, ten minutes maybe?" says Logan.

Dad smiles. "All right, well he has to get tired soon. Try not to let any more out for a while. Just keep reeling."

Logan does as he is told. By now his veins are popping just like the old men's were earlier. He's covered in so much sweat that his grey t-shirt looks almost black. But he doesn't give up. He just keeps reeling in that line until the fish emerges near the surface.

"Uh, Dad, I think we're going to need a bigger gaff," I say.

Everyone stares down at the water next to the boat. And gasps. Because attached to that line are the remnants of a wahoo. Hanging out of the razor-sharp jaws of a bull shark.

"Oh my God," I say, stepping back. The sight of its grey skin, it's black, blank eyes, sends chills down my spine. For a moment I can't move. Can't talk. Can't do anything but stand there and stare at the creature that wanted me dead.

"How'd you catch a shark on that thing?" asks one of the men, more interested in the strangeness of the whole thing than the danger of the bull shark.

"I, I don't know," says Dad. "We use metal leaders and line, but still. I wouldn't think our rigs would be strong enough for a shark. The hooks you use for sharks are much bigger."

Dad helps Logan get the rod into the holder. Logan unstraps himself from the seat, then stands behind me, letting me lean back into his wet t-shirt.

"I guess we should cut the line," Dad says. "Piper, can you get me a wire cutter?"

"Cut the line? Are you crazy?" says one of the men. "What you got there is a prize. You need to get him in the boat."

Dad shakes his head. "Boat's not big enough for that sucker. He's got to weigh over 400 pounds."

"Then let's tie him to the side. We can go in slow, maybe call the Coast Guard to help. You know I betcha this will make the news. Catching a wahoo that gets eaten by a bull shark. Boy, that sure doesn't happen every day."

"Good idea, let me give Kip a call now," Dad says,

walking toward the radio. "By the way, did you feel the second hit, Logan? When the shark bit the wahoo?"

"Uh, not really," Logan says. "The line just felt really heavy. I knew whatever it was, it was strong."

"Got that right." I walk to the bow for some air while the men struggle to tie the shark onto the side of the boat. Behind me I hear grunts and screams as the shark lets out a final thrash, then collapses in exhaustion. The old men cheer as they cover the shark's body with an old dragnet and tie its tail to the swim platform with the rope we usually use for the anchor.

I stay on the bow and try not to focus on the commotion as Dad starts guiding the boat back, happy to have a place where the shark's eyes can't reach me. Logan joins me on the bench seat and holds my hand low, so Dad can't see. By the time we reach the docks, the shivers are gone. But my heart is still racing. This I blame on Logan, instead of the shark.

A crowd surrounds us as we tie up the boat on the end of a large T-dock, instead of guiding it into the slip. Kip helps keep away the spectators then jumps onto the boat himself, running over to the side where we've tethered the shark.

"Holy Jesus," he says, bringing his hand to his mouth. "That thing is huge. And it's a bull shark all right. Wonder if it's the one that attacked all those boats."

"Could be," says Dad. "But then again, the waters are so full of 'em, it could just be a coincidence."

"Is he dead?" asks Kip.

"Think so. He stopped thrashing before we tied him up."

Kip and Logan help my Dad untie the shark from the boat. A dock worker meets them at the edge of the dock in a small Whaler like mine. Dad jumps in and together they haul the shark toward the hoist at the edge of the harbor. They hook the shark up to the bridle, then dock the Whaler and climb up the dock ramp.

We meet them on the edge of the concrete, where the hoist will bring up the shark. We've weighed the two wahoos by now, each coming in at just under 100 pounds, and said goodbye to the old men. Not that they've left the scene, just kind of melted into it, becoming lost in the early dinner crowd from Rosalie's.

The shark comes up slowly as a breeze tosses the bridle from side to side. When the shark reaches the pavement, I shriek, still not used to looking at his eyes. Even in death they're black. And wide open.

Dad guides Logan to the bridle and unhooks it from the hoist. A crew of men drags it to the scale, then steps back. Five hundred and thirty nine pounds. Practically a baby. For a bull shark, anyway.

But the crowd refuses to thin, especially when Logan walks up next to the dangling shark for pictures, and then starts pulling the half-eaten wahoo right out of its mouth. At this I look away. Take a deep breath. The news crews and marine biologists we called will be here soon. But my stomach's telling me it's a bad idea to wait. So I tell Dad I'm not feeling so well and think I need a break.

"Why don't you go grab a soda or something," he says, sensing the marine biologists from the corner of his eye. "The gruesome part will be done in a few minutes."

I nod, then duck into the crowd, leaving Logan with a local reporter and Dad to meet the scientists.

At the bar, I get a Coke and down it in two seconds. Then I'm given an ice cream sundae with orange slices – my favorite – on the house. I pick out the orange pieces and suck out the juices, letting the peel stick out of my lips like a mouth guard. I laugh, thinking of how Benny used to do the same thing. And that's when it all comes back. Benny. Marina. The vandalism.

Right as Logan comes running, yelling that they've gutted the shark. That they've seen the inside of his stomach. And found a jagged chunk of fiberglass inside.

CHAPTER EIGHTEEN

"So it was him, then. You caught our shark." I whisper the words as I drop my spoon into the melting ice cream.

"There's no way to tell completely, but they think it's him. Hard for sharks to get a bite of fiberglass unless they're pretty close to shore."

"No one knows it's from my boat, do they?"

Logan shakes his head. "Your secret's safe."

"Thank God. Though I'm afraid it's not the only secret that's safe right now."

Logan lifts his eyebrow.

"Benny." I say. "We need to talk to Sardi still. Find out if he broke his promise."

"Crap. You're right. I totally forgot."

"Me too. Until I sat down. What are we going to do?"

"How about we stop by the Lodge once we finish up? The scientists are taking the shark to their research facility. I decided to donate it to science."

"That was really cool of you," I say.

"Well I'm not about to stare at the shark that tried to kill you every day. Even if I do like knowing he's out of the water."

"Yeah, me too."

"So how about that ice cream?" Logan says, sitting down on a stool.

I push the bowl over in his direction. "Finish it. I don't have much of an appetite."

"Me either," he says. "But ice cream is just too good to pass up."

Logan dips in my spoon and fishes out the few remaining globs of vanilla. Then we thank the waitress and head back to the commotion on the docks. The crowd has dissipated, leaving only Dad, Kip, the scientists, and Rick, who really seems interested in whether or not the shark had any bullet holes. Or whether those crazies, which may or may not include Rory Pinder, were just shooting at his cooler.

"Did you find anything interesting?" I ask.

"Besides that piece of fiberglass, not much. Just a few Styrofoam containers that look a lot like the ones from Rosalie's," says Dad.

"Wow, so he's been in the harbor."

"That or he ate some boaters' trash."

"Any bullet holes?"

"Nope. Not a scratch on 'em," says Dad, trying to hide a smile. I look back at Rick who's just shaking his head. Still angry about the ruined cooler.

"Is there anything else we can do?" I ask.

Dad turns to Logan. "Get some ice on your arms. You're going to be hurting tomorrow, and Piper needs you in top form for next week's Scramble."

"Yes sir, I will be ready to go."

"Good, now get to it. Piper, I'll see you at home later, I've still got to clean up the boat."

"You sure you don't want our help?"

"Positive. And thanks for coming out, honey. We haven't drummed up that much excitement at the dock in years."

"Yeah, I can't remember the last time we had reporters meet us."

"I know. There should be a nice spread in tomorrow's papers. Maybe even a picture of Logan with the shark."

Dad winks, then turns back toward the ramp leading to the docks.

"Oh, and Dad?" I say as he walks away.

"Yeah?"

"Thanks for taking us out. It was a lot of fun."

"It was. We have to go out more often. It's worth the gas."

I wave goodbye and meet Logan, who's saying his goodbyes to the shark. He pats its sandpaper skin hard then thanks the scientists before joining me near the footbridge.

"They promised to give me some of its teeth. So I can make a necklace," he says.

"The teeth that almost killed me."

"Yikes, now that is too freaky to think about."

Without a word, we step onto the road and start heading toward the Lodge. The streets are quiet except for the rustling of the palm trees and chattering of the parakeets that have nested in their branches.

Logan grabs my hand and we slow our gait, taking time to watch one swoop down and grab a branch in its beak, then fly back up to its home, its feathers a flash of brilliant green against the dusky orange sky.

For the whole walk to Benny's, we pretend that everything is fine. That we are just going to check on the turtles. Or maybe on our way to dinner at the Lodge. Neither of us mentions Benny or Marina. And when we arrive at the guest house to find it all locked up, Logan just shrugs.

"We tried our best," he says. "And we still don't even know what happened. With Sardi, you never know. Could've been nothing at all."

"But something tells me it was."

"No way to know for sure."

I whip out my cell phone and punch in Benny's number. It clicks over to voicemail after seven rings.

"You don't think there's any way they got arrested last night or something, do you?" I ask after hanging up.

Logan shrugs. "There's always a chance. I mean, we've been pretty out of the loop all day. Though if it was something that major there's no way Sardi would've let you cut her off mid-story. Or that Kip wouldn't have mentioned it either."

I sigh. "I know you're right, though I still feel like maybe I should tell his parents," I say. "Maybe we should go to the restaurant."

"Why don't we give it another day? In case they really didn't do anything. We don't want to upset Mrs. Benitez for no reason."

"True. Mrs. Benitez can be scary. If she knew what was going on, she'd kill me. She'd probably tell my parents too. And that would be a mess we don't need. Especially before the Scramble."

Logan rests his arm on my shoulders as we walk back towards my house. "I'll see you in the morning," he says as we get close.

I lean in for a kiss, then hug him tightly. Logan hugs back even tighter. He lowers his head to mine and breathes in my hair. As he releases me, I smile, wishing I didn't have to go inside. But the light is fading and Liggy waiting for her water. So I turn to him and smile once more before joining my parents inside.

Sleep comes quickly after an exhausting day. I wake the next morning feeling refreshed, that is until my feet hit the ground and I'm reminded of all the pulling and heaving of yesterday when I helped Logan with the shark. And to think, I was just on the sidelines. Logan must be a mess. I pick up my cell phone and decide to find out. Judging by his voice, there's little denying that he's in pain.

"Did you ever get ice on your arms?" I ask.

He groans. "Apparently not enough."

"Should we take the day off then?"

Logan hesitates before responding. "Nah, let's go out. I need to get out of here anyway. Nick's driving me crazy."

I smile. "Let me guess. He still pumping you for fishing tips? You know, my dad is probably the best teacher out here. He can tell him a lot more than I can..."

"Yeah, whatever. Prying is just part of his job."

I smile at the thought of goofy Nick pumping locals for information. "About that. How's his documentary research coming? Who's he interviewed so far?"

Again, Logan hesitates. "Who knows, he's always out with someone," he says. "Should we meet at the boat in twenty?"

"Yeah sure," I say, happy to change the subject from Logan's crazy father.

"At which boat?"

"Let's take the old skiff today. It's bigger than the Whaler and easier to fish from. We'll probably want to use it in the tournament."

"Awesome, I'll see you there."

I get down to the harbor early, hoping to catch up with Sardi. But instead of finding her, I'm greeted by a slew of new faces and boats in the marina.

The docks are busier today, and not just because it's Friday. With the tournament starting on Thursday, things are really heating up. There are more fishermen around now, more skiffs in the water, hugging the docks that Rosalie's brings in only for the biggest tournaments of the year.

Logan and I meet at the boat in a hurry and push off the old skiff before anyone can see us. Then it's off to investigate the coves around the island before the tide gets too high. It's one of the last days we have for reconnaissance, and I need to be sure my notes are right. That I've got the best places for bonefish pinned down.

Yet even the coves are buzzing with activity, as are the backcountry flats a ways out, where the out-of-towners usually don't go. I bite my lip and stare at the competition, in their shiny skiffs, painted red and gray and blue.

"I can't go looking for shrimp with them staring," I say. "What if they figure out what I'm doing?"

Logan frowns. "What about the notes you've been taking for months now? Won't those be helpful enough without data for this week?"

I nod, trying to keep calm. "Yeah, they're good to have. And that cove we found a few weeks ago has been full of shrimp every time we go past. The problem is that there are other skiffs there. If they have good luck, they might plan on hitting the same spot during the tournament. And then there's nothing we can do. All of our advantage will be lost."

"What about your fish finder? Should we try using that?"

I shake my head. "No, it's useless for these types of fish. What we need are some new spots."

"Do we have enough time?"

I look at my watch. "The tide will be low for another two hours. How much gas do we have left?"

Logan walks to the stern and picks up the tiny red tank. "It feels half full."

"Good. Then it's time we go explore Lignumvitae Key."

"That's the island you can see from Rosalie's, right? Isn't that mainly covered in coral?"

"Yeah, a lot of it is, but there are also a few pockets of weeds. With any luck, they'll have some shrimp carcasses as well."

The motor roars to life as we zip across the glassy bay and head out toward Lignumvitae. I exhale as the island comes into focus. No one is there. Not a skiff or tourist ship or even any scientists. The island is ours alone.

Ever since I was little, I've been obsessed with the Lignumvitae Key. Only accessible by boat, it's an untouched haven for big leafy trees, white beaches, and more marine life than I could ever imagine.

As a kid, Dad used to take me and Mom there for picnics and lazy Saturdays. Sometimes we'd pull up to the small dock made for tourists and let the botanists guide us down the hidden interior trails. Other times we'd anchor the boat a few yards out and swim in to the island, me on my boogey board, and Mom in her inflatable raft, pointing out the different sea creatures mingling below.

"There's a blue striped grunt, oh, and a school of porkfish. Did you see that big boulder coral over there? It's just beautiful isn't it," she'd say, and I'd smile, knowing that even if Dad was the fisherman in the family, Mom was the one who could put a name to all those animals that to Dad, had always just been scenery, tangential to his game. Of catching the biggest bonefish, or sailfish, or wahoo, or whatever else he was trying to get on the line.

On the beach, I'd pretend that I was a lost girl,

that I'd survived a terrible shipwreck and was now destined to live out my days like the Swiss Family Robinson. And when I got older, even if the fantasies ended, my love for the island only grew stronger.

Lignumvitae became my special place. Where I could go to think, and no one could reach me. Not even by cell phone. It's Lignumvitae that gave me the name for Liggy.

So it seems almost fitting that with six days to go before my face-off with Wyatt Jacoby, Logan and me are circling the small outcroppings of coral, looking for sprigs of sea grasses and weeds.

And that when Logan starts yelling and pointing to a convex beach of green, my eyes begin to tear. Lignumvitae has always been filled with secrets. And right now, I'm relieved that it's decided to share them with me.

The water feels cooler here a mile offshore. Clearer too. I adjust my mask and snorkel and start checking the area. I steer clear of a clump of hydroids and focus on the weeds. A school of tiny angelfish surrounds me, their fins less than a centimeter long. Still babies, I think, and I swim further into the grasses. Baby fish means food that babies like to eat. Plankton. Algae. But shrimp? Not necessarily.

I surface and check in with Logan on the boat, tell him I need a little more time. Then I dunk my head into the water and drift down the shore, checking out the different species of grasses as I search for fish. Ten minutes pass before I am rewarded.

As I swim over a patch of sand hidden among the grasses, a huge school of pink Key shrimp surrounds me. I laugh into my snorkel, then shriek as a stream of water shoots right up my nose. Gasping for air, I reach the surface, crying for Logan.

"They're here, they're here! More shrimp than the last cove on Islamorada. This is the place, Logan. This is where we're going to catch the fish."

The afternoon passes in a flash as Logan and I bob like buoys over our new fishing spot. As the tide changes, we watch the fish change too. The baby angelfish retreat even closer to the shore. Right before the bonefish move back in. We sit there in silence as we spot first one, then ten bonefish, their silver scales glistening as they move through the afternoon sunlight. The shrimp are still there too, and the bonefish look hungry.

We see one of the smaller bonefish attack a shrimp at the bottom, a perfect example of the bonefish's tailing, as he rubs his mouth in the sand and lets his tail wave above him.

Seeing the textbook behavior makes me smile. Not only are the bonefish here, but they're feeding. Meaning they feel safe, even with the skiff bobbing above them.

We leave Lignumvitae with renewed hope about

the tournament. The next few days we will be busy preparing equipment, checking in with the tournament staff, making sure everything on the boat is legal. Tasks that usually make me nervous. That make me long for my reconnaissance, and my days spent drifting at sea. But now that we've got a new spot, one untouched by the competition, I am ready for the challenge. For once, everything is going to plan.

That is, until we reach the shore and my cell phone picks up signal. And I see that there's a voicemail. Not from my parents, or Sardi, or even Benny.

But from Marina.

And it sounds like she needs to talk.

CHAPTER NINETEEN

We're at a table at Rosalie's, having docked the skiff next to the Whaler, when I play the message again. I shudder at Marina's voice. She's trying to sound calm, but her voice sounds ten decibels louder than usual. I push the speaker button on the side of my phone and play the message for the third time. Logan bends over the phone and cups his hands over his ears, drowning out the moan of starting engines in the harbor.

"Hey Piper, this is Marina," starts the message. "Um, I know we don't usually hang out or anything, but I was thinking of going for a walk this afternoon and if you're free, or uh, not fishing, I'd like to talk.

Anyway, call me back when you get this."

"I still don't see what's so weird about it," says Logan. "So she wants to talk? It could be about anything. Maybe she's just lonely without her friends."

"Right, so she calls Piper Wesley, the girl most likely to know nothing about clothes, purses, and everything else she cares about. This girl is calling me for one thing, and that's advice on Benny."

Logan sighs. "Now I know you are probably one-hundred percent right, but remember, you do have more in common with Marina than just Benny."

I narrow my eyes. "Like what?"

"Parents with struggling businesses?"

I open my mouth to refute Logan, but then shut it. Because of course, he's right. Marina is just as much a part of the Islamorada ecosystem as I am. Meaning she's weathering the same storms, even if she is doing it in designer clothing.

"All right, so I guess I need to talk to her. But I'm so bad at this girl talk thing. I mean, I can barely handle ten minutes of Sardi!"

"Believe me, no one can take more than ten minutes of Sardi."

Logan smirks and I laugh, swatting his arm with my fist.

"So I guess I should call back Marina then," I say, my smile turning serious.

Logan stands up from the table, tousling my hair

as he walks by. "And I should spend some time with my mom and dad so they won't be mad when I disappear again tonight.'"

I turn back to Logan. "Tonight? I didn't know you had plans."

"That's because I haven't asked you yet."

"Asked me what?"

"To get dinner." Logan lets out a big grin and again goes for my hair. "I figured with all the practice we've been putting in, the least I could do was take you somewhere nice. You know, something fun. So we could relax."

"But you take me places all the time!" I say, thinking back to all the fish sandwiches at Rosalie's.

"Okay, well tonight I'm taking you somewhere far from Rosalie's, the Bass Pro Shop, turtle nest and the harbor. How does that sound?"

"Like I have no idea where we're going."

"Good, then it's a surprise. How about I swing by your place around 7:00 and we can head out from there. Does that give you enough time with Marina?"

I look down at my watch. It's only 3:35. "If I can't wrap up with Marina in three and a half hours, then you'll know I'm in trouble."

Logan chuckles as he kisses my cheek. "I'll see you at 7:00 then. Oh, and wear something nice. Tonight we're going to act like tourists."

Again I open my mouth to speak, but don't know

what to say. For the second time in ten minutes, I'm speechless. And I can't help thinking that this time, I like it.

As Logan fades into the distance, crossing the footbridge and then the parking lot, I turn back to my cell phone and push it around the table.

I know I should be calling Marina, but the idea of daydreaming about where Logan's taking me seems much more important. Could it be one the big fancy places on the beach, like Pierre's or Morada Bay? And if it is, how will he ever cover the tab? Or is he doing something sneaky, like having Nick serve us fried grouper in his backyard?

If it wasn't for the tourist comment, I'd put my money on Nick and fried fish. But something tells me tonight is more important. That whatever Logan has planned is big.

"Hey, I thought I'd find you here," Marina's voice catches me off guard, bringing me back to Rosalie's.

"Oh hi, I just got your message a few minutes ago. I was going to call you back."

Marina looks down at the table, and at my cell phone, dangling off the edge across from me. "It's okay if you weren't, you know. Going to call back."

My cheeks redden as I lean over and grab the phone. "So do you want to go somewhere quiet?"

Marina nods.

Knowing she's not super aquatic, I bypass the boat

and head for one of the main roads near Rosalie's. After passing an old strip motel filled with boisterous fishermen and cranked up radios, we slow our gait and relax our muscles. As if now we're home, where the street thins and noises revert back to the mundane.

I listen in awe of the sounds of everyday life, swirling all around us. Pots clanging against metal sinks. Orange trees rustling in the breeze. Kids screaming as outdoor faucets drip over their toes, washing away a day's worth of salt and sand and adventure.

"I'm sorry to bother you like this, Piper," Marina says, "but I know no one is closer to Benny than you. And I just really need your help to understand him."

I try to read Marina's face as she shuffles along, her eyes transfixed on the horizon. Is she really looking to me for relationship advice? About Benny? Because the kind of close I have with him is nothing like Marina. Benny hasn't talked to me in weeks. And even before that our conversations had become strained, centering mostly on his aversion to swimming in the weeds.

"Well, I'm happy to help," I say, "but honestly, me and Benny usually just talk fishing and swimming and stupid stuff. And I doubt that's what you're looking for..."

Marina stops me short as she buries her face in her hands. "I just don't know what to do. He's so freaking stubborn. I told him Becco didn't need the money that badly in the first place, but he just had to prove he could cut Rory Pinder's line without anyone knowing. And then, I admit, I thought the iguanas would be funny. But in the end, all those pranks got us was a couple nights of reservations. Not enough money to make a difference. So I told Benny it was time to cut it out. That's actually what I was telling him before you guys came in the other day..."

"So let me guess. Benny didn't stop."

"Well, no. He hasn't done anything else, yet. But he has all sorts of crazy ideas. Thing is, he thinks these things are funny."

"Ugh, that's Benny," I say, surprised to find myself on Marina's side.

Marina raises an eyebrow.

"He's always been easily amused."

She laughs as she pushes a strand of hair out of her face and flashes me a smile. It's the first honest exchange we've ever had. Our first conversation, if you don't count the ones with Benny in the middle, and I'm finding Marina's analysis of Benny to be pretty spot on. She may not look or act like me, but when it comes to Oswardo Benitez, she seems to find the same traits annoying.

"But really, I just don't know how to get him to stop thinking about these pranks," says Marina. "Maybe it was better when he was fishing all the time...I think now he's bored." She lowers her voice as she says the words, letting them scatter in the wind like the seeds of a dandelion.

"Hey, I begged him not to quit," I say.

She nods. "Any idea of how to make sure he doesn't do anything else stupid?"

"Yeah, threaten to cover him with sea grass."

Again she laughs. But this time she sounds nervous, so I decide to go give her some pointers on Benny. Earlier I'd feared that talking about Benny with his girlfriend would feel like betrayal, as if I would be revealing a piece of myself. But right now, it feels cathartic. Like I'm setting something free.

"Really, the best ammunition you've got is his mother. So lead with that," I say, "And if the wrath of Mrs. Benitez doesn't scare him, remind him that I'll go talk to her too, and I've got a lot more dirt on Benny than just a few iguanas. If that still doesn't work, just try to be his friend. Ask him what's wrong. He's usually only a jerk when something's really bothering him."

"Do you think this is one of those times?"

I sigh. "I honestly don't know. But the way we're not talking, I guess I probably wouldn't know, right?"

Marina frowns. "You know, I never did tell you I was sorry."

"For what?"

She breathes in deep, avoiding my eyes. "For

pressuring him to drop out of the tournament. But it's just that he used to come back all sunburned and angry, usually at you, actually. And I thought if he could just stop thinking about fishing and we could hang out more, he'd be happier. My friends were gone, Benny always seemed miserable. It seemed like the perfect solution. But all the extra time has done is tear us apart. I swear, it's like all those hours out there bickering with you, they kept him sane."

My eyes start to water as Marina picks up the pace. A couple weeks ago I would have decked her in the stomach for confessing something like that, for stealing Benny away.

But right now, all I am is sad. And confused.

If Benny's acting out because of me, then why is he still with Marina?

And not back on the skiff where he belongs?

But does Benny even belong there anymore? Now that his seat's been filled by Logan?

I let Marina vent for a few more minutes until the Becco Lodge comes into view. Right as she gets ready to say goodbye, I stop her.

"One more thing," I say, trying to keep my voice level. "I saw Sardi earlier and she said something about there being more island destruction. Any idea what she was talking about?"

"Oh, she probably heard about the damage on Key View Drive. A big palm tree came down last night during a thunderstorm and ruined a couple houses in the neighborhood. Scary stuff, those storms."

"Yeah, scary," I say, then wave goodbye. It's almost 5:00 now but there's one more thing to do before heading home. And it's just a small walk from Marina's cabin.

The turtle nest looks swollen today, brimming with promise and the hope of new life. There have been no more raccoons or birds or other visitors. Thank God. So I grab a piece of the dragnet and start pulling, ready to expose the mound of white to the world.

The net comes off easily, though the logs take a little more work. I remove the small sticks and debris shoved in between first, leaving the biggest pieces of driftwood for last. Sweat pours down my shirt as I dissemble the pile, but I don't stop to clean it.

Instead, with my eyes focused and mind drifting, I keep moving logs and smoothing sand until nothing stands between the turtles and ocean but a smooth strip of beach. And one heck of a journey.

As I walk home, I think about the challenges those babies have ahead and pray that at least some of the turtles will live to find these shores again.

Then I think about Benny. How he abandoned me, right when I needed him the most. And how it was Logan who forced me off my beanbag and back onto the skiff. Logan, who is probably getting ready right now to come over and pick me up. In less than an hour.

And I'm still covered in salt and seaweed.

I start to panic about the whole dressing-like-a-tourist thing as I walk into the house. Mom and Dad are there on the couch, watching the news, and seem oblivious to my nerves. So I take off my flip flops and join them, sitting down on a nearby chair. It's hard not to laugh at myself. Getting all worked up about another night with Logan. As if hasn't been my boyfriend now for a week.

"You have a good time with Logan today?" Dad asks as the news breaks for commercials.

"Yeah, we got in some good practice. We finalized our fishing spots for the tournament," I say.

"Good, I'm glad. Fishing for the next few days is going to be tedious, with all these out-of-towners around."

I smile.

"Oh, shh be quiet," Mom then says, pointing to the TV. "It's coming up now!"

I turn toward the screen. Dad hits the volume on the remote. Then, next thing I know I'm staring at Logan. And the bull shark.

The screen flows into a montage of video clips from the docks yesterday as the newscaster begins her voiceover. Dad, Logan, and me flash across the screen along with images of the docks, boats and of course, shark.

"Following a slew of shark sightings last month, it

looks like it is once again safe to head out into the water," she says. "Islamorada residents can rest easy tonight after the surprising catch by amateur fisherman Logan Cook. After signing up for a sport charter excursion for wahoo, he ended up with the heavy hook of the day, bringing in a 425 pound bull shark that experts believe is the same shark recently seen by boaters stalking the island coastline. The shark has been taken to the Key Marine center for further research. Scientists hope to use this opportunity to learn more about local migration and eating patterns of the bull shark around Islamorada."

The screen fades back to the newsroom as talk turns back to the week's heat wave that's been scorching the island.

"That was great," says Dad. "They got all of us in there. And they even mentioned Wesley's Charters!"

"Who knows, maybe it will help drum up some more business," says Mom.

"You should call up Logan, see if he saw it. Tell him we recorded it. In case he missed it."

I laugh. "How about you show it to him yourself? He's coming to pick me up in an hour."

"Great idea," says Dad. "Where are you guys off to tonight? Going down to Rosalie's again for the Friday night band?"

I bite down on my lip hard before responding. "Actually, I don't know where we're going. He said he was taking me out for dinner. And that he wanted it to be a surprise."

"Oh my gosh, Piper, is this a date?" asks Mom.

"Uh, I don't know," I say, slightly embarrassed that up until now I've been pretty elusive on the status of our relationship. "We just thought it would be cool to do something fun before the tournament. Logan's been working real hard to learn the ropes."

"Well I think that's great," says Mom. "You know, honey, Logan is really cute. You should think of wearing your hair down, and maybe even a little makeup. I can help you put it on if you'd like."

I bring my hands up to my tangled hair, for once thinking that Mom is probably right.

"And tell Logan to get here a little early so we can watch the newscast," says Dad. "I really want him to see it. He's only been here a few months and already he's a local celebrity!"

"Okay Dad, I'll tell him," I say, turning to Mom, "and uh, I don't know if I really want to wear too much makeup, but I guess a little couldn't hurt."

Mom claps her hands together and squeals. "Oh honey, I knew this day would come! Now you go get cleaned up and let me know when you're ready. This is so exciting!"

I smile, then retreat to my room. I stare at my tanned face in the mirror before stripping off my sandy board shorts and wrapping myself in a towel. Inside my stomach's churning, as my mind bats around thoughts of Benny. Marina. Logan. And of course, the tournament, which is coming all too fast. It's funny how the white caps always seem to crash ashore at the same time.

CHAPTER TWENTY

"Have a good time, honey, and we'll you see you later tonight. I can't wait to hear where you end up going," says Mom from the doorway. She lingers for a moment before Dad grabs her by the waist and eases her inside.

"Wow, I don't think I've ever seen your mom so excited," said Logan.

"Yeah, she was pretty psyched by the idea of a date," I say.

"Ah, so she thinks it's a date then?"

"Well I couldn't keep it a secret forever," I say.

Logan grins as we reach the road. He watches me stand there dumbfounded, not knowing which way to go.

"Ah, stumped aren't you? Face it, the suspense is killing you."

I laugh. "Actually, it is."

For the first time since I've left Marina, I feel my shoulders roll back into their normal position as I just enjoy being with Logan. All his jokes and funny looks. The way he sat with my Dad for twenty minutes watching the recording of his newscast close to ten times. And how he's zigzagging around the street, not committing to any direction long enough for me to know where we're going.

"I should've just blindfolded you," he says as I run over and jump on him piggy-back style.

"No, this is more fun," I say, sliding back down to the pavement. "Besides, even with my eyes closed I always know where I am. I know this island probably better than you know your own bedroom."

"Which is why planning a surprise for you is so fun. And challenging." Logan takes off down the street in the opposite direction of Rosalie's, sprinting between huffs of laughter.

I follow close behind, only catching him when he stops a few houses down from mine. Then I let him take my hand as we adjust to the feel of the road, still warm from the afternoon heat. When we reach the Overseas Highway, we head toward the southern tip of the island.

And when we reach the small bridge leading to Lower Matecumbe Key, we march right across, as if leaving the island is something we do every day. Sure, Lower Matecumbe technically is still Islamorada, and the bridge is only a few yards long, but somehow crossing the water with Logan is liberating. As if I'm leaving my swirling thoughts behind, back in the waters at Rosalie's.

Logan guides me toward Robbie's, the big marina where we sometimes feed the tarpon fish, as we climb off the bridge. "I figured we liked their diner so much, we should try the real restaurant. Maybe get away a little bit from Wyatt Jacoby and all the fishermen."

I smile, touched at Logan's own reconnaissance. "That sounds perfect. And I've actually never done more than pick up fish sandwiches here. So it's new for me too."

Logan grins. "Good. So your dad wasn't lying then."

"Oh my God, you asked my Dad?"

"Well... I had a few ideas that were, uh, in my budget. But I wanted to make sure it was someplace different."

"All right then, you're excused. But only because you did such a great job."

We walk through an entryway of palm fronds and tiki torches as we enter the restaurant. Logan inches ahead toward the hostess, ready to tell her we have a reservation. But before he can even spit out the word "Cook," he steps back, his cell phone vibrating.

"I'm so sorry, could you excuse me a sec?" he says, walking back toward the tiki lights.

"Is everything okay?" I ask.

He frowns. "I missed the call. But it looks like it came from Marina. Did she try calling you too?"

I reach for the bag slung across my body that Mom insisted I wear. Not quite a purse, but not quite a backpack. A perfect compromise, she'd said, but it still felt to me like trouble.

In my eyes, I'm either carting enough stuff to require a backpack, or I can take my phone and wallet and shove them in my pocket. A purse just adds a step. And tonight my theory is proved right as I sift through the bag and pull out my phone, which has six missed calls.

"Guess that's what I get for letting Mom put me in a skirt with no pockets," I say.

Logan turns to me, his eyes staring deep into mine. "The missed calls are worth it. You look beautiful."

He leans in for a kiss just as my phone buzzes. I meet his lips briefly, then pull back with just enough time to answer the call.

"Hello?" I say, with just enough attitude for Marina to know she's interrupting.

"Hey Piper, sorry to bother you for the millionth

time today, but I'm out with Benny... and we... could really....your help." Her voice fades in and out, as I catch every other word.

"Wait? What did you say? Can you speak up? There's bad signal."

"No, actually I can't talk louder, but we're in trouble. At the Tarpon Bay...we need a distraction."

"A distraction? How are we going to do that?"

"I don't know. Just get Rory...away...the pool..." The call cuts out completely and when I dial back, voicemail clicks in before a single ring.

I look at Logan and frown, knowing that our magical dinner, hidden among the palm fronds and tiki torches at Robbie's, is going to be cut short. Because once again, Benny's got me tangled up in the weeds.

"Let me guess. Benny's in trouble," Logan says, raising his brow.

I look down toward the ground, unable to face him. "I'm sorry."

"Is it really an emergency?" he asks. "Because I've kind of been looking forward to this for a while."

"I know, I know," I say, playing with my hands. "But Marina said they need us as the Tarpon Bay Resort now. That Rory Pinder's hunting them down and we need to distract him."

"What if we just let Rory find them?" Logan asks. "Maybe it would teach them a lesson. I mean, we've already warned him once now."

I sigh. "I'm sure you're right, but with Rory being so crazy I just don't think we can risk it. Who knows what he'd do to them."

Logan paces around the line of tiki torches, kicking the sand around them into a spray of dust. As the sand starts to settle, he walks back, arms folded and eyes narrowed.

"I'm sorry," I say again, trying to read his mood. "I don't want to go either."

"I know. But you're right," he says, already walking toward the bridge. "Benny's your friend. We have to go."

"Are you sure? I don't want you mad," I say, running after him.

"I'm not," he says. "Just annoyed. But I'm over it now. Who would've thought tonight would turn out so special, huh? Imagine, we've got a date with the one and only Rory Pinder and it wasn't even planned."

I laugh, thankful that Logan's acting like himself. Annoyed maybe, but okay. And right now, that's more than enough.

"Now Marina mentioned something about getting Rory away from the pool, so I guess we should head there," I say as we pick up the pace. "Though I wonder what Rory's doing at the Tarpon Bay pool in the first place."

"Maybe he was taking a swim."

"Or hanging out at the bar. But why he would be bothering Benny and Marina..."

"I bet he recognized them from the harbor. They did say they thought he was the one firing those gunshots."

"Yeah, maybe." I grind my feet into the ground and run harder, thankful I stuck to my flip flops instead of those wedge heels Mom and Sardi both love. But with no food in my stomach, my energy runs out with a half mile still to go. Of course the Tarpon Bay just has to be on the exact opposite side of Islamorada from Robbie's. Just our luck.

Logan slows along with me, then waits in silence for me to catch my breath. "So what are we going to do when we reach the pool?" He asks as my pulse stops pounding.

"I don't know. Maybe if we pretend we're guests going for a swim and make a big scene, Rory will stop whatever he's doing?"

"What if there are already guests swimming though? How will that help?"

"Good point," I said, my mind racing. "I guess I could go up and talk to him then. Ask if he's been fishing lately. He always has been friendly with my dad."

"Yeah, if he's pissed though, he might not want to talk."

"True. Though I bet if you went asking for a last-minute sunset cruise, he'd listen. Fridays are the only day when he doesn't do them, because of the band down at Rosalie's. But if you went and offered him the cash you were going to spend on dinner, I bet he'd take you up on it."

"You think that would work? The sun's already started to set."

I check my watch. 7:35. "It's that or we make a scene splashing around the pool. I don't know which is best."

"Guess we'll have to figure it out as we go," Logan says, as the green thatched roofs of the Tarpon Bay guest cottages come into view.

We sneak around the back to the beach adjacent to the pool. Then we take a few breaths and start walking slowly to the pool, as if we were coming from one of the guest cottages. Like the Becco Lodge, the Tarpon Bay is a luxury place known for its private accommodations and pristine views of the Atlantic.

But while the Becco promises peace and tranquility, the Tarpon has always been a little hotter, the type of place young couples gather for an after dinner drink by the pool, or to listen to the Top 40 DJ that comes in after 10pm on Saturdays. I've never spent much time at the Tarpon, and as we near the pool I'm surprised to see candlelit tables surrounding it.

"Maybe we should pretend we're coming for

dinner," I say to Logan, "and I will just pretend to run into Rory or something."

He nods without breaking a smile. "You know we could never afford a real meal here, Piper."

"Don't worry, we won't order anything but a soda."

He sighs, relieved.

And then the tables grow closer. Along with the pool. And right away we can see something is wrong. And stinking. Near the pool.

We cover our noses as we reach the tables, sliding in a pair of abandoned chairs toward a table still covered in untouched dinners. Then we shuffle toward the crowd congregating near the bar, and the crazy man yelling in the middle of it.

"They're in those bushes, I just know it! There's nowhere else they can be! Those stupid kids, I bet they're the same ones that cost me hundreds cutting the lines on my sailboat last week! Now who's coming with me?"

The crowd of young couples cheers, but no one volunteers to go with Rory, who's staggering about now, pointing to the dingy pool water, which on careful examination, appears to have pieces of grunt and lionfish floating on top.

"Oh God, they dumped the chum bucket," I say under my breath.

"The what?"

"It's a gross concoction of fish guts and blood. You

dump it in the water to attract the big fish. Dad used some the other day when we went wahoo fishing."

"Nasty stuff."

"Especially in a pool."

"So what do you want to do?"

"Let's offer to go with Rory. And lead him away from the pool."

Logan nods, then starts walking toward Rory. "Stay here." He whispers the words before turning back toward the bar.

Not sure what Logan is thinking, and not wanting to ruin his plan, I decide to listen and stay back, letting myself fade into the palm trees lining the candlelit pool. From there I watch as Logan mixes with the crowd, then moves front and center.

He walks up toward Rory and opens his mouth, then stops, closing his mouth tight. He takes two steps back in retreat before I hear the calling. And shouting. Of Nick's voice.

"Hey son, what are you doing here?" he says, motioning for Logan to join him at the far corner of the bar. "There's someone I'd like you to meet. This here is Wyatt Jacoby, the man behind the mask, so to speak."

At this I frown, as the face of Wyatt Jacoby comes into focus. How does Nick know Wyatt? The idea that Wyatt could be an interview subject seems unlikely, but then the way Logan tells it, Nick is always befriending everybody as part of his job. Meaning Nick probably went out for a drink, met Wyatt and got to talking about fishing. Especially given how interested in it he's become.

And it's then, with that realization, that Nick's interest in fishing has always seemed a little too intense, a little too probing, that I start to feel sick.

The feeling only gets worse when Wyatt talks. "Hey Logan, nice to meet you. I've heard a lot about you," he says, then turns, lowering his voice so low I can barely make out the words. But under his breath, with the light breeze swaying and stink of chum mixing with Rory Pinder's annoyed groans, I'm able to hear them.

"Thanks for all your help," he says. "Thanks for all your help."

A cold sweat breaks out over my forehead and arms and drips down the sides of my shirt as the words sink in.

Why is Wyatt thanking Logan for help?

Why is Nick talking to Wyatt in the first place?

And why are they here jammed into a crowded bar known more as a tourist destination than local hangout?

The questions haunt me, bringing me back again to Nick's obsession with fish. And the one fact that everyone who fishes on Islamorada knows about Wyatt. That he wins through bribes, usually to local guides and fishermen not involved in the tournament.

People with information and no reason not to accept a few bucks in exchange for revealing prime hot spots.

Of course, I am not a guide. And me and Dad, well we have invested pretty much everything into this tournament. But then, last year we came in second. And with the Expedition Channel shelling out big for another special on this year's tournament, Wyatt has a lot on the line.

Meaning hitting up a retired local could not be enough, especially since last year's snitch moved away after Rick told the whole charter crew at Rosalie's.

But could Nick really be a spy?

And then what does that make Logan?

And where does it leave me?

I back away toward the beach, unable to watch as Logan's nervous eyes dart from side to side, as he tries to excuse himself from the crowd by telling his dad he was just cutting through, on his way to the convenience store across the street.

Saliva catches in my throat and I gag as Nick convinces Logan to stay. They're talking to Rory now, trying to calm him down. But it's as if I've frozen, unable to hear or see or smell the world around me. All I can do is feel the fire burning inside me.

A minute passes before I realize that I'm crying. My stomach heaving with such intensity that it's a wonder I can stand up at all.

And it's then that I hear him. A familiar voice,

coaxing me into the brush.

"Hey Pipes, it's me," Benny says, emerging from behind a scrub pine. "Geez, are you okay?" he asks.

I try to motion with my finger to the scene before us, but just the thought of lifting my hand saps my energy.

Luckily, Benny already knows what's up. "I always knew that guy was trouble," he mutters, before grabbing me by my waist.

Then, as Logan and Nick talk to Rory, getting him to laugh at the stupidity of dumping a chum bucket into a pool, Benny drags me down the beach and through the cabins to the right of the Tarpon Bay pool, with Marina following behind. When we reach the road, he hugs me tight before speaking.

"Thanks for coming, Pipes," he says.

I try to nod as he and Marina continue talking, thanking me for my help and telling me everything is going to be all right. That even if Nick is an idiot, it doesn't mean Logan is. Or that he's done anything wrong.

But even as Benny talks, I can tell he doesn't believe it.

"Will you be all right here if we leave you?" Benny asks after a moment. "If not, we can bring you home, but we really should get away from here. You know, in case Rory does come looking."

This time when I try to shake my head, I feel it

move. "No, I'm fine. I think I need to walk," I say.

"Okay then, fine. Just call me when you get home so I know you're all right?"

I grind my teeth as Benny looks at me with concern, and I remember all the times lately I've asked him for help and gotten none. Without waiting for the feeling to pass, I wind up my arm, then let it go flying, punching Benny right in his ribs.

"Whoa, what the hell is that for?" Benny asks, stepping back.

"For being an idiot," I say. "For abandoning me before the tournament. For making me trust that loser back there."

I point back at the Tarpon as another torrent of tears overtakes my face.

"Hey, I didn't make you trust anyone. That was all you, Pipes. And I agree what I did tonight was dumb, but I thanked you for coming, didn't I?"

"Thank you doesn't solve anything," I say.

"Nor does blaming me for your mess."

Then Benny wraps his arm around Marina's shoulders and leads her down the road.

Leaving me there alone, stained with tears, in the middle of the deserted street.

CHAPTER TWENTY-ONE

The morning sunlight stings my eyes as I lay there awake on my beanbag. I kick Liggy's legs until she rolls over, giving me just enough room to bring my arm to my eyes. After rubbing them awake, I stare at my ceiling, wishing I could fly. That the stucco walls above me could open up wide and let me break free. Free to drift away to another beach, another tournament, another life.

For a moment, I think about what it would be like to live up north, where the waters are colder and fishing more dangerous. Where charter boats must combat snow and cold and swells much bigger than those that roll over the flats. But as Liggy drools on my leg, I cast these thoughts aside, trying instead to clear my mind.

As I lay there, trying to block out the world, my door opens.

I cringe, angry for not locking it.

"Hey Pipes, you up yet?" asks Dad, as he sticks a sliver of his face between the door and its frame.

"Yeah, getting up soon," I say.

He hesitates, then nods. "Logan's here and he seems pretty upset. Says he needs to talk to you right now. Everything go okay last night with your date?"

I breathe out deep, filling my stomach with warm, salty air. The movement disrupts Liggy who burps, then jumps to her feet with a yawn. After lifting my window to let her out into the yard, I rise from my knees to me feet, then turn to face Dad.

"Tell him to go home," I say. "I never want to see him again."

Dad sighs. "You sure about that honey? He seems pretty upset. You sure there wasn't just a misunderstanding?"

With that, I fall back to my beanbag and fill Dad in on an abridged version of the story of seeing Nick and Logan with Wyatt Jacoby. By the time I finish talking, Dad looks smaller, deflated.

"And to think I've been nothing but a friend to that man. Gave him all those lessons for no money. What scumbags. What, what..."

Dad pumps his fists in the air as he mutters obscenities under his breath. When he runs out of air, he stands there, panting, for a minute.

Then he wipes his brow and edges back to the door. "I better go tell Logan it's time for him to leave."

I nod, relieved when Dad spins around, closing my door on the way out. Even with a layer of stucco and plywood separating me from the hall, I hear Dad's voice rise as he tells Logan to leave followed by Logan's pleading, by his swearing that he's told Wyatt Jacoby absolutely nothing about my reconnaissance or my fishing spots or anything else.

"Then what about Nick?" Dad asks, his voice booming.

Logan stutters. "I'm sorry I can't control him," he says.

"And I'm sorry I can't trust you."

The front door slams and for a moment, all is quiet. But after a minute, the quiet feels worse than the yelling and I find myself running out of my room and into my father's arms.

"How can he do this? How can they both do this? To us? When we've done nothing but help them?" The words come out in a jumble, made worse by the tight grip Dad has on my head, which is drawn close to his chest.

"It's okay, baby, it's okay. Some people just aren't wired the same way. Don't have the same values or morals as the rest of us. Guess Nick is one of them."

I sigh, then keep crying as Dad holds me close. After a minute, he sets me free, retreating to the kitchen to get me a towel.

"I can't believe I trusted them," I say, shaking my head.

"You had no reason not to," Dad says. "Nick seemed strange, but like a normal enough guy. And I've always found Logan to be nothing but trustworthy."

I nod. "Me too," I say, fighting another wave of tears.

"You know, Pipes, it is possible Logan has nothing to do with this mess," Dad says. "Just because Nick's a jerk, doesn't mean Logan is too."

"But then why would Wyatt be thanking him too?" I ask, unable to forget Wyatt's last words.

At this, Dad shrugs, unable to provide an answer. "Want me to call up Nick? Get to the bottom of all this?"

I shake my head, not wanting to hear anymore.

"All right," Dad says, "I won't bring up Logan. But I am going to give him a call, just so he knows he's lost his spot on Wesley's Charters for the tournament."

I nod.

"You know, if you want to go out with me now, you can," he says, his tone soothing. "But if you want to reel Benny back in or bring another friend, that's fine too. I'm happy to go out solo, or maybe take your mom out for the day."

I let myself smile at the thought of Mom cutting bait. "Yeah, we'll figure it out," I say.

My legs feel like lead anchors as I excuse myself to my room, this time turning up the radio to drown out Dad's call with Nick. The thought of continuing on with the tournament without Logan or Benny has made every muscle ache, every breath hurt. My only comfort is that I have Dad in their place.

For the next two days, I leave my room only to go to the bathroom and eat, and even then most of my trips are combined, limiting the total time outside my four walls to less than an hour. Each day, Logan stops by and each day Dad tells me of his visits, growing less and less angry with Logan with each encounter.

"He claims he never told Nick anything meaningful, honey," he says. "And Nick says even what he told Wyatt is minimal. Now of course, we can't just believe them, but it could be the truth, at least about Logan," Dad says, each time beefing up his defense for Logan a little more.

By Wednesday, one day before the tournament, Dad is basically calling Logan innocent, saying he had a good talk with Nick down at Rosalie's, and that while he'll never consider the man a friend, he's forgiven him. Nick was doing his job, just as we were doing ours. It might never make sense to us, but truth is, not everything in this world does. Good news is that all the secrets or reconnaissance in the world can't guarantee Wyatt a fish. That comes down to luck, feel and love of the water, something I've got bushels of.

Only as I sit here alone in my room, it doesn't feel like I've got bushels of anything.

That afternoon, I decide to let Dad take me fishing. Together, we cruise by some of my old spots, and wave at the constellation of charter boats flooding our waters. After finding no shrimp – and landing no bonefish – Dad decides to cut the trip short, blaming our poor performance on the overcrowded waters, instead of the fact that I've lost my spark.

We reach the docks a few minutes later and head up toward the parking lot, bypassing Rosalie's on the way out.

"So you decide what to do about the tournament?" Dad asks as we reach the truck. "My offer still stands if you'd like to come out with me and your mom."

"You really got Mom to commit to going?"

Dad grins. "I think she was kind of excited at the idea of being there when you win."

"When I win? Dad, I'm not sure I want to even compete."

He sighs. "Pipes honey, I know this hasn't turned out how you'd like. But even still, you've done too much to just quit. The Scramble only comes once a year, and I'm not letting you miss it."

I frown, knowing Dad is right. And that if he

wants me there, he will bind me up and throw me on the boat before leaving me at home. So I bite down on my lip and nod.

"All right," I say, "in that case, I'm going out on my own skiff. Alone."

"You sure?" asks Dad.

"Completely," I say. "But only so I can throw Benny and Logan's entry money in their faces when I win the tournament."

Dad slaps himself on his leg and smiles. "Now that's the spirit," he says, jumping into the truck. "I knew you'd come around."

I leap into the passenger's seat beside him and laugh as a grin creeps over my face. Maybe fishing alone won't be so bad after all. Maybe it will be just the peace I need.

That night, I debate calling Benny and filling him in on what's happened, how our worst fears of Nick and Logan have indeed been confirmed. But seeing as Benny never responded to my call asking if he'd agreed to stop with the pranks, I decide it's better not to call. Because truth is, there's only so many times I can give him another chance. This time might just be that last straw.

As the moon rises higher into the sky, I decide to run down to Rosalie's to inspect the old skiff before the tournament. With the craziness of the last few days, I've skipped all my pre-tournament routines that usually get my mind ready for a day on the water. A necessary precaution, really, seeing as going down to Rosalie's would have meant an almost certain confrontation with Logan or Wyatt or a bunch of other charter captains I'd rather not see, only now it's left me nervous. And afraid that after all my practice and reconnaissance and saving every penny, I'm still not ready. Not ready at all.

Yet with the cover of darkness hiding my fears, I head into the hallway. If I'm to have any chance of catching anything tomorrow, I need to spend some time at the boat. So I say goodbye to Mom and Dad and slip out into the cool night air, thankful my mind has cleared with enough time for me to check my lures and practice casting my lines to make sure there aren't any unexpected snags or tangles.

When I reach the docks, I find the skiff bobbing lightly, same as Dad and I left it a few hours before. I climb aboard and head to the back bait well where I stashed my hooks and lures. The silvery pink threads glisten in the moonlight as I secure them in my hand then tie them onto my lines, being careful not to hook my fingers. The docks are quieting down now, as is Rosalie's above. Wyatt Jacoby and his camera crew left hours ago. Rick and a group of fishermen are just walking up the dock. I try to listen in on their banter, to see if they're discussing fishing tactics or secret spots, but all I can hear are some slurred words about some waitress at Wahoo's, a restaurant that's known just as much for its beer as food.

When I'm sure everything is in order, I grab onto the bow line and pull it tight until the side of the boat is flush against the dock. Then I let go of the line and jump onto the dock.

And almost knock Benny into the water.

Startled, I take a step back and cross my arms, sending a hook right into the flesh of my pinky.

I scream.

Benny smiles.

"What are you doing here?" I say. "You scared me half to death."

He shrugs. "Night before the tournament? I knew you'd be here."

"Well you're a little late. It's almost 10:00. I have to leave." I brush by his shoulders and start walking to the dock ramp.

"This the boat you're fishing in tomorrow?" he asks.

I nod.

"Logan did a great job fixing her up," he says.

"Guess so," I say.

"Hey I'm sorry I didn't call you back the other night," he says. "It's just that, well, I guess I've felt pretty awful about everything, but haven't known what to say."

"Oh, okay," I say, looking away so he can't read my eyes.

"I would've called the next day, but then I just figured I'd see you around Rosalie's or something."

"Well I've been home. You could've looked for me there."

He frowns. "Yeah, I kind of got roped into helping out at the restaurant for the afternoon."

"Whatever," I say, staring at his eyes. "I'm sick of your excuses."

This time, I brush by him, wanting nothing more than to run away back to Liggy and my beanbag and to the hum of Mom and Dad watching a movie in the living room. But Benny grabs onto my arm before I can pass by.

"Look, I'm sorry. I should have called," he says. "I should have thanked you. And checked in, to see if you were okay. I know that."

"To see if I was okay?" I ask, no longer trying to hide my tears. "How could I have been okay? After all that happened?"

Benny shakes his head, unable to meet my eyes, and it's that moment, that very second when he hesitates, that something inside me cracks. Once again Benny is letting me down, right when I need him the most. So I take a deep breath and try not to cry as the words continue to pour out of me like a river flowing over a levy.

"First you bail on the tournament, and then Logan turns out to be a spy out to *ruin* me and you think maybe you should have checked in to see if I was okay?"

I shout the words, spitting each out rapid fire, before continuing.

"Benny, I needed you, and you never even texted back to tell me if you were alive. Or if you'd finally realized that messing with Rory and the rest of the island is insane! You know all summer long, you've been running around trying to help Marina, and really you've done nothing but hurt the people we've always considered family."

Benny bows his head, then wipes his brow. "Yeah, I know. You're right. But then, Pipes, you always know what's right."

"Don't call me that," I say.

I'm gasping for air now, covered in sweat and salt. But all I can see and smell and taste is Benny. And the indifference that's dripping all over him, smelling worse than a bucket of old bait.

"Call you what?" he asks, tightening his brow.

"That nickname."

"But that's what I always call you."

"Yeah, back when we were friends."

"And what are we now?"

"I don't know Benny, acquaintances? Call it whatever you want to, but don't use the word friend."

"That's not fair," he says. "So we drifted apart a little this summer. What's the big deal?"

I look back at the skiff motor, then stare up at the stars.

"Fine, don't say anything," he says. "But the only reason I pulled back was because you were so jealous of Marina. All summer, every time I mentioned her name, you'd flinch or roll your eyes or try and change the subject. I'm sorry if I got sick of it and didn't want to deal with you anymore. Face it, for once you weren't most important and you hated it."

Every emotion floods through my veins as I stand there on the skiff. Frozen in place on the dock. Unable to reach the shore.

"Are you insane?" I say again. "I have never been anything but super nice to Marina. I went to her parties and I took her fishing and I never said a bad word about her at all, even when you bailed on the tournament. And when have I ever been most important? Try never."

"Right. And that's why you never stuck up for me when your dad wouldn't let me reel in any fish. Or why you never trusted me to keep track of your GPS coordinates when we were out doing reconnaissance. It's always been about you, Piper, the star fisherman."

"That's not true. Dad never let you reel in the fish because you always lost them. And I didn't let you write down coordinates because you usually got them wrong. You always want to be involved, but you never do the hard work. I wasn't trying to steal anything from you, Benny. I was the one covering!"

"You could have just talked to me."

"Same goes for you," I said.

"I'm not the one who's ending the friendship."

"Do you really think I'm the one to blame for this?" I say. "Because if that's what you think, then I think it's time to leave. I don't know why you even came here in the first place."

He sighs. "I don't know either. For some crazy reason I thought I missed you. And after all that happened, I thought you might have missed me. But I must have been mistaken. And to think I've spent all week worrying about you and that stupid tournament. I walked all the way out here as soon as I got off work just to see if you could use some help. If you wanted me as your partner in the tournament."

I gasp at the words, finding it hard to fight the relief that pulses through my veins at the thought of having Benny with me tomorrow. Of things being like they should. Like they always were. Only his offer rings hollow, feeling a lot like one of those Styrofoam coolers they're always filling up on the docks. At first glance, they look great, but as soon as you pick one up, you realize there's nothing to them.

"Benny, you never texted or called or did anything. After you saw what Logan did to me. And you just left, after all I did to help you."

"I know, Pipes, I know I've been awful and I'm

sorry. But I'm here now."

I open my mouth to speak, to tell Benny I forgive him and that everything's okay. Only my brain refuses to say them, and before I know it I'm shaking my head and looking away.

"But now's a little late, don't you think," I say, forcing myself to utter the words.

"I understand that you're pissed, but that doesn't mean I couldn't help out," says Benny. "I know how much you need to win this thing."

"But you can't help now. You're not even registered," I say.

"I saw the entry list posted at Rosalie's. I know you included my name."

I bite down on my lip hard. Until I can taste blood. "That's only because half the money was yours. But really, I'm fine. Without you."

"Pipes, I want to help. After all that you've done for me and Marina. Bailing us out at the Tarpon, not ratting me out to my mom...I owe you this."

"Benny, stop calling me that! I told you we're fine. Now if you'll excuse me I need to get home. I have an early morning tomorrow."

Benny stands at the foot of the dock, blocking the ramp to the parking lot. "Don't go," he says. "Piper, I need you."

"And I don't need you."

"But...but..."

I whip my head around and scowl. "But what?"

"I think I love you, Pipes."

The words hit me mid-step, as I'm hopping from boat to dock. Love? Me? Does he even know what that word means?

For a second, my feet wobble. The inky water of the harbor wells up, catching the side of my sneaker. I catch my balance just in time. Both feet on the dock, I cross my arms and prepare to run. Only my feet won't move.

Benny walks over and grabs my hand. He wipes a strand of hair out of my face. Whispers sorry in my ear. And then stares back into my eyes. I look away. Down at the water, and the small shiner fish shimmering below the surface.

"You don't mean it." I whisper and try to break free of his grasp.

He holds on tighter. "No, I do. I think I've always loved you. Since we were little. Why else would I spend half of my life in the weeds? Guess I just didn't know how to show it. Come to think of it, I still don't. But I want to try."

He leans in for a kiss.

I stand there. Motionless.

His face grows closer. His hair tickles my forehead. It's thicker, coarser, than I'm used to. A different sensation. Different than Logan.

Oh my God. Logan.

I pull away as the hole Logan's left rips open, burning my stomach once again as I'm flooded with thoughts of me and Logan on the skiff, with the turtles, on the Whaler, eating ice cream and then, then outside Tarpon Bay with Wyatt Jacoby.

Was that really the same Logan? Has my whole summer been nothing but one big lie?

"I'm sorry," I say to Benny, brushing him aside. "I can't do this. I, I don't know what I want, but I know I don't want this."

"What do you mean? We've been friends forever, Pipes. It's the only thing that makes sense," he says.

I raise my hand before he can talk. "Maybe once I thought I loved you," I say, staring into his eyes.

"But no. I know now that I don't. And you know, if Logan taught me one thing, it may be just that. I mean, all you ever did when we went fishing is complain. You wouldn't even swim in the weeds. And that's not even mentioning how you bailed on the tournament after promising to be my partner. Or how you wouldn't even help me try to save those poor turtles. Or how you've spent the last few weeks like a tyrant, hurting others who are struggling just as much as us! Benny, let's face it. We're different. Maybe it's time we acknowledge it."

His eyes grow wide. His shoulders slump. "Sounds like you've given this a lot of thought."

"Actually I haven't. That's just off the top of my

head. But if you want, I can keep going. Only I don't want to. I'm sick of fighting, Benny. I want you to stop acting like such a jerk and go back to the Benny I used to know. I want you to be my friend. Maybe we can work on that instead."

Benny clenches his fists. He reaches into his pocket and grabs a wad of paper. Crumbles it up into a tight ball. "God Piper, what is wrong with you?" he says, throwing the trash into the water.

"What are you talking about? And what are you doing?" I ask. "Pick that up right now."

"No," he says. "The ocean isn't going to die from a piece of paper."

"I don't get you," I say. "I said I wanted to be friends."

"Yeah, after you called me a jerk."

"Hey! All I said was that I care about you."

He sighs. "Yeah, I know. I'm sorry. I deserved that. It's just that I finally figured out things weren't working with Marina, and thought maybe it was because we were supposed to be together. But I guess I was wrong."

I bend down onto the dock and fish the floating paper out of the harbor. "Oh, so you broke up with Marina and thought you could come down here and just hook another girlfriend?"

He shakes his head, not saying a word.

"Well?"

Still nothing.

I stand up, brushing off my knees. "Oh. So she broke up with you, then. Let me guess, she dumped you the minute you got back from Tarpon Bay. You know, she was sick of your attitude too."

Again, silence.

"Look, I really have to get home. If you want to be friends, you can come by Rosalie's tomorrow afternoon. Tournament ends around 5 o'clock. Otherwise, I'll see you around."

"Wait Piper, don't go," he says.

"I have to," I say, turning to the ramp. "But like I said, come by tomorrow. Maybe then we can work something out."

I breathe in deep and walk up the ramp, forcing myself to look straight ahead. The air feels light and cool. As I reach the parking lot, I break into a run, not stopping until I'm home. When I walk in, Mom and Dad are asleep on the couch. I kiss the top of their foreheads goodnight and run back to my room. I throw on a pair of pink pajamas – probably the only pink clothing I own – then flop down on the bed.

As I lie there my skin all pins and needles, my mind refuses to shut off. All I can think about is Benny. Logan. The tournament. And the scratching at my window.

Liggy. Of course.

I slide up the glass and let her slip inside. She flies

through the space head first, landing on my beanbag in a heap.

"Oh Liggy," I say. "Where do I begin? The tournament's tomorrow and all I can think about is Benny and Logan. They're both just awful. Can you believe that Benny, trying to screw my head all up when he knows how important this is to me?"

Liggy opens her mouth and yawns. The smell of moldy berries fills the air.

I lean off the side of the bed and give her a pet. "You always are the best listener."

She opens her mouth again. This time, she sneezes.

I laugh. "So do you think I'm doing the right thing, saying no to Benny? Do you think I can really do this on my own?"

Liggy rolls over on the beanbag. Her breathing grows slow. Steady.

"Guess I've lost you too, huh girl?"

I turn off the light and try to get some sleep. But something's still nagging me.

It's the turtles. With all that's happened in the past few days, I've forgotten about the nest. The way the sand was cresting like a big balloon trying to rise up out of the sand. The hatching will be any day now. The eggs are ready. Only with the tournament tomorrow, I don't have the time to check up on them. Protect them from the dangers waiting in the grasses.

I reach for my laptop, hands trembling. Without

Turtle Save, I don't know who to call. But I need someone. After three months of caring for them, I can't let my babies down. So I Google "turtle save." Then "turtle rescue." My screen fills with places in California. One in Tampa. Then I see it. Turtle Watch. A national organization. With a field office in Miami. I grab my phone and punch in the number. The line rings, then clicks to the message machine. It's almost midnight. The machine is not a surprise. So I breathe deep and start talking.

"Hi, I am calling to report a loggerhead turtle nest in Islamorada, Florida. It is on the west side of the Becco Lodge property, right off the main path. There's a narrow footpath near a palm tree grove that leads to a small clearing where the nest is. We've been monitoring the spot for almost ninety days. We weren't sure the eggs were alive, but today the sand was cresting. If you can send a few volunteers down, that would be great. The eggs look ready to hatch any day."

I pause, then take a breath. Do I leave my name and number? Or just stay anonymous? Probably better to end the message. Last thing I need is Turtle Watch bothering me tomorrow. Because tomorrow's about the tournament. Nothing else. I've done all I can to help Benny. Forget about Logan. Save the turtles. Now all that's left is saving myself. And the future of Wesley Charters.

CHAPTER TWENTY-TWO

For most people, waking at 4:00 a.m. is a challenge. For me, it's as natural as casting a line. Which is why when my eyes pop open at 2:30 a.m., I'm not surprised. If anything I'm amazed I got as much sleep as I did, seeing as I'm about to embark on the most important tournament of the year alone.

So instead of turning over, giving Liggy a squeeze, and drifting back to sleep, I give into my tingling feet and let my eyes dart around the room. I've been asleep for only three hours, but my body has already decided that is all I'm getting.

I jump out of bed and walk over to Liggy. She snores, but doesn't move. One hard push does the job.

She grunts as she rises to her feet. The window open, I guide her outside. Liggy jumps.

I slam the window shut, making sure to lock it so she can't force it open with her snout. Then I dress quickly. Black board shorts, bright blue tank top. The rubber boat shoes that protect my feet. In the kitchen, I grab a banana, being careful not to make any noise. Mom and Dad won't be up for another two hours.

With the banana in hand, I creak open the back door and walk outside. It's warm and misty. Still dark. A crescent moon peeks out from the swirling fog. A few stars sparkle overhead. The streets are empty so I walk down the middle of the road, glancing at the rows of sleeping houses. Windows closed. Lights off. No morning papers littering the driveways. But the main lights to Rosalie's are on. It's probably the TV crews. Getting some night shots of the harbor before it gets busy.

Wyatt Jacoby's show always has a lot of scenery. Little montages they use to introduce a place. And break up the sometimes slow pace of the fishing. The thought of his camera crew filming makes my stomach turn as I wonder which of my secret spots they'll be filming today, figuring it's either the cove or Lignumvitae.

Determined to ignore the film crew, I jump over a nest of wires in the parking lot and head for the docks. It's Wyatt Jacoby's crew all right, though the star is nowhere to be seen. Probably still in his bed at the house down the street. The mansion they rented just for the occasion.

As the cameras pan in and out, catching the bobbing boats and sleeping pelicans, I decide to text home and let my parents know I'm safe.

But my pocket's empty. No cell phone. And I didn't even write Dad a note.

If only Rosalie's was a little closer, I think. But with a starlit mile standing between me and the house, I figure it makes more sense to stay.

When it gets a little later, I'll run down to the Coast Guard station and call home. Kip always lets me use his phone, and my parents will appreciate the extra hour of sleep.

With the decision made, I grab a rag and a bottle of Turtle Wax. Then I get to work on the skiff. Spreading the filmy paste. Buffing it dry.

The motion hurts my hands, but it's worth it to take off the last layer of grime and algae. To bring the boat to life. The old skiff looks magical as the camera crew's spotlights cast a purple haze over the early morning sky, bouncing off the slick fiberglass surface.

A voice from behind startles me. "I thought you did that yesterday, before dinner."

I turn back and see Dad in his Wesley's Charters shirt. Dressed and ready to go. "I did," I say. "But I thought another coat couldn't hurt."

He nods. "It never does. You know, sleep never hurts either though."

"Yeah, guess I was too hyped up for sleep."

"Or to remember your phone." He tosses my cell across the docks.

"Dad!" I yell and lean forward, catching the phone before it hits the water. "You could've ruined it!"

He laughs. "Just testing your reflexes. Though next time, try to remember it. Or at least write a note."

"Yeah, I know. How'd you know I'd be here anyway?"

"Biggest tournament set to start in a few hours? Where else would you be? I wouldn't have been surprised if you'd asked to sleep out here."

"Well, the thought did cross my mind," I say, noticing a shadow a few boats back. "What's that?" I ask pointing. "Someone else here already?"

Dad sighs. "Now don't get mad, but I found him on the docks. Sleeping on your Whaler to be exact. And I think you guys should talk."

My mouth drops as Logan walks out of the shadows. His hair blows in the wind, showing off his sleep-lined face and even whiter-than-usual complexion.

"Dad!" I say, throwing up my arms. "I don't have time. I can't lose my focus, not before the tournament."

"Now Piper, me and Logan had a good talk and I think you should really hear him out," Dad says.

Logan jumps in before I can speak. "Ten minutes, Pipes. Just give me ten minutes."

I fight the urge to run up and push him and Dad both into the water. But, not wanting to get disqualified before the tournament begins, I try to act civilized.

"Fine. But that's it," I say. "After that, I'm done."

Logan nods, then looks to Dad. "Thanks Mr. Wesley, for everything."

"Just don't make me regret this, son," he says.

Logan nods, then waves to Dad who promises to see me off before the tournament gets underway. I watch as Dad's shadow grows long and skinny under the spotlights lining the docks, disappearing only when he reaches the next row of boats.

"Sorry to barge in on you like this," Logan says, "but I've been looking for you all week. Calling, stopping by, camping on the Whaler. Did you get any of my messages?" he asks.

His voice squeaks on the last words and I look up into his eyes, surprised by the sound. His eyes look more gray than blue, more sad than alive.

"Yeah, I got them," I say. "But I just didn't see the point in talking. There's nothing you can do that can make telling my secrets to Wyatt Jacoby even half okay."

Logan grimaces. "No Pipes, no. It's not what you think. Really, I've been trying all week to explain..."

"To explain what? I heard what Wyatt said. And my dad already talked to Nick. We know you've been supplying them with information."

Logan blinks, then wipes his brow. "No, but that's the thing. I might have told them stuff, but never anything important. Nothing that would lead them to the bonefish at all. The only reason I said anything at all was to get Nick off my back."

"Oh, that's right. Because you were Daddy's spy right from the beginning, huh?"

Logan's shoulders slump as he bites down on his lip, then stares me in the eyes.

"I never told him anything, Pipes. Nothing important at all."

I try to look away but with his eyes burning into mine, I find myself staring back. At the boy I first met, the boy with the long hair, black t-shirts and sweltering jeans. The boy who helped save the turtles. Who gave me my first kiss. God, that kiss. As the memories flood back, I want nothing more than to run in for another. To tell Logan that everything is okay. That we can erase away the night at Tarpon Bay.

But of course, things don't work that way. It's not like we can clear Wyatt's brain. So I break the stare and look out into the water, breathing in the scents of the incoming tide.

"I'd love to believe you, Logan," I say, "but I can't. Everything you've told me has been a lie. How do I know this is any different?"

Logan breathes in, then sighs. "Pipes, I screwed up, I know I did," he says. "But you have to believe me, please. I might have lied about the little things, like what my dad does and why he was sent here, but the one thing I never lied about was us. Or how I feel about you. Do you really think if I was using you I woulda really stuck around so long?"

His eyes are pleading now, his forehead covered in perspiration. But dancing on the waves around us is the reflection of Wyatt Jacoby's film crew shooting above us. A truth too real to ignore.

"Logan, I'm sorry, but I really have to get ready."

"No!" he says, pounding his foot into the dock so hard that a school of shiner fish jumps through the surface of the water, mistaking the disturbance for a predator below.

"Piper, I have ruined a lot of things lately, and I admit I've been a jerk. I wanted to tell you so many times about my father, but I didn't want to lose you. And then that night at the Tarpon, I was so confused...but I never told Nick or Wyatt or anyone any of your secrets. Not one. I never want to hurt you."

"It's a little late for that," I say.

Logan bows his head to the spotlight-lit water. Then, he lifts it, craning his neck to the parking lot above.

"What if I could prove to you that I'm telling the

truth. That I never told my dad about your reconnaissance or secret spots or anything except for what your dad taught us on that first charter. Would you forgive me then? Let me help with the tournament?"

"Maybe," I say, "but proving that would be pretty impossible."

"No, I know a way," he says, extending his hand.

"Logan, it's too late. I don't have the time."

"Piper, please. I said ten minutes. It's only been three. Just come with me to the parking lot. If this doesn't convince you, then you never have to talk to me again."

The thought of never talking to Logan burns as I slowly grab his hand, letting him pull me onto the dock. I then let go of his arm, letting it fall to his side as I follow him up the ramp to the docks.

The sky is still dark and the docks empty. We should be home in bed, but instead we're here, on the docks, running towards the camera crew. And I can't help think that Logan's being here means something. Maybe something good.

But then we reach the summit and we're standing there, looking straight ahead at Wyatt's fancy cameras and a big spread of bagels and food. I take a step back, not wanting to enter a world I don't believe in. Logan turns back, begging me to follow, with his eyes as much as his lips.

"Okay," I say, pointing to my watch and he nods, knowing he's almost out of time.

He runs over to a truck in the distance, and when I join him I see that it's filled with LCD monitors and recording equipment, along with two Mac computers and a pair of guys wearing big hoodie sweatshirts and chugging Mountain Dew.

"Hey Dennis, Cal, how's it going," Logan says, slowing his pace.

"Oh Logan, hey. You're Nick's son, right?"

"Yup, that's me. How's the filming going?"

"Going well, just tying up a few loose ends. You know we're going live when the tournament begins so it's been a push, getting all the backstory edited in time."

"That's so awesome," Logan says, peering inside the van. "Do you think I can take a look? This is my friend Piper, she's gonna be in the tournament so she won't be able to watch the show. I told her you might be able to give her a sneak peek now."

"Oh, I'm not sure," says Dennis, looking back at the monitor. "I guess it wouldn't hurt. How much you want to see?"

"Nothing much," says Logan. "Just something small. Like a scene of Wyatt fishing."

Cal nods, pulling up the video. "You're in luck. I just finished putting together this footage from yesterday. Wyatt went on quite a streak. Here you guys, why don't you come in closer?"

Dennis hops down for the van making room around the monitor. Logan jumps in first, then stretches out his hand. Again, I hesitate before grabbing on.

"Now watch closely, in about two minutes he's gonna have a real fighter," Cal says, his bloodshot eyes beaming.

I nod, glancing at a pile of empty Mountain Dew cans before focusing on the screen. It's Wyatt all right, and he's inspecting his line, showing off his lure to the screen. I inch a little closer and narrow my eyes as I inspect the rigging. Sure enough, he's got an imitation shrimp on the end of his line. Just what we use on our charters.

Not what I use on my own. Quickly, I scan the other rods propped up on his boat, squinting my eyes to make out the lures dangling on the lines. Sure enough, they're all shrimp. Not a single pink lure in sight. And it's then that I let my eyes dance around to the water and grasses and beach. It's a familiar spot, but nowhere I've found fish in weeks. And the way Wyatt's talking, it sounds like this is his place. The spot he plans to use for the tournament.

Cal lets out a whoop as a bonefish grabs Wyatt's line and I find myself gasping, having forgotten to breathe.

"Pretty impressive, huh," Cal says, slapping his

leg. "Took me half the night to get the lighting right on that scene."

"Looks impressive, thanks for the peek," says Logan. "That's exactly what I wanted to see."

"Sure you don't want to see more?" asks Cal, his voice rising. "I've got another pretty cool scene I could pull up for you in a minute..."

"Nah, that's okay, man," says Logan. "Piper here's gotta get ready for the tournament."

Cal nods as we hop out of the van. "Well thanks for stopping by, and good luck. I'll be rooting for you to come in second."

"Second?" I say, turning back. "So you really don't think anyone could ever beat Wyatt."

Cal shrugs. "I don't know about that. Just know it's better to root for the boss."

Logan shakes hands with Cal and then Dennis before retreating toward the docks. "See anything interesting?" he asks once we are out of earshot.

"Maybe," I say, trying to contain the quaking in my stomach.

"I told you, I never gave anything to Nick. Nothing important at all. In fact, I pretty much led them the wrong way. All the way to the west of the island where we haven't found shrimp in weeks."

I nod as my mind races, trying to process the information. Of course the recording could mean nothing, the footage could be old. Or Wyatt could be saving all my secrets for the tournament. But given the size of Wyatt's smile, his detailed explanation of why he was using that shrimp for bait, somehow that feels wrong. Why would he focus on information he wasn't going to use?

I turn back to Logan and shake my head, realizing that for once, I actually have proof that Logan is telling the truth. But then if Logan's been telling the truth, then have I been unfair not to listen?

"Logan, I'm sorry," I say, my throat catching. "I should have called you back."

Logan comes in for a hug, then squeezes tight. "Hey, don't worry, everything's going to be fine. And there's nothing to be sorry for. I would've hated me too."

I nod, breathing in a breath of hot air through Logan's t-shirt. In the time since we've seen the footage, the sun has started to rise, illuminating the quickly-filling harbor. There's only an hour before first gun now, and I still have to check in with Dad and get my lines ready to go. But as I turn toward the dock ramp, ready to run down it, Logan stops me once more.

"You still looking for a partner?" he asks, looking me in the eyes.

This time, I smile. "I thought I already had one," I say, then pound down the ramp, onto the docks, and onto my future.

CHAPTER TWENTY-THREE

The gunshot is loud and smoky. It cuts through the air like a loon diving after its prey. It smells like burned eggs. Again I think of fireworks. Of that night down at the harbor. And then I think of Logan and his betrayal and the fact that I'm still not one-hundred percent sure he's innocent. But there's no time to think of that now. The gun has been shot. The tournament has started.

The harbor swells as almost a hundred fishing boats rev their engines and file out of the harbor. Logan and I get in line behind Dad's skiff as we enter the channel. Wyatt Jacoby is right behind, with a huge party boat full of cameras idling beside him. I keep our speed low, under the five mile an hour limit in the no wake zone, until we pass the rock pile a hundred yards out from Rosalie's. Then I push down the throttle, bringing the old skiff to a plane.

We cut through the fog and dart away from the first rays of sun. To the West. Mom and Dad head to the Northeastern cove where I first saw shrimp in May. Wyatt Jacoby takes off toward the South, very much in the direction of the spot in the video. I feel myself let out a breath I didn't know I was holding as a gaggle of boats follows him, cutting the water into a mild chop. A few boats head off on their own, settling in the weeds near Rosalie's. But the one thing they all do is stay near the main strip of islands. Logan and I are the only ones zipping across the deep water. In search of Lignumvitae.

As our engine whips the waves into a foamy froth, I wonder if I've made the right decision. Lignumvitae is a long way out. If the fish aren't here, we could lose hours driving to another spot. Especially if the wind kicks up the waves. I try to focus on our trip last week to the island. The teeming shrimp. And tailing bonefish. But it's hard to stay calm. My hands keep on shaking in beat with the motor until Lignumvitae unfolds itself on the horizon. A perfect picture of sparkling green and blue.

I pull back on the throttle and the motor wanes. The change in speed sends the bow deeper into the water. We're bobbing just inches from the waves now, the choppy water swirling around the hull. But today I don't spend much time looking at the higher-than-normal waves. Because right now my eyes are entranced by the small crest of coral and rock in front of us. The point of Lignumvitae.

The bushy leaves of the Lignum Vitae trees sway with the breeze as a group of iguanas sun themselves on the rocky beach, enjoying the only hours of sunlight when the rocks won't burn their tails. The weeds look tall and healthy, just as they did last week.

I kill the motor and let us drift into the grasses. Logan reaches for the anchor. He throws it into a shallow outcropping of coral, then pulls back on the line until it catches.

"Perfect," I say as he ties off the line on a cleat.

"Time to start fishing?" he asks.

I nod.

I open a bottle of water and take a swig. Logan moves to the bow and stares out into the weeds.

"See anything?"

"Not yet."

"Give it some time. They'll come," I say, inspecting the bubbles. The tide is dead high, and the water's not moving. Meaning the fish probably won't be hungry for another hour. So I grab my rod and prepare to check over the rig one last time.

That is, until I see it. A touch of silver in the

water. A small ripple in the surface.

"Oh my God, Logan. They're here!" I whisper, then let out my line and start jigging.

Logan reaches for the gaff and net, preparing for a possible catch.

I reel in the first cast slowly. Nothing takes the bait.

I cast again and let it sit in the water. A minute passes. Still nothing.

So I cast a third time, deep into the weeds.

And something hits.

Something big.

The rod bends forward and I flick back the barrel, letting out a whirl of more line. The fish takes it and swims closer to shore, dodging and darting between a maze of weeds and coral.

"He's really running," I scream. "We could lose him in the weeds!"

"What should I do?" asks Logan.

"Pull up the anchor!"

Logan runs to the bow and uncleats the line. I turn away and focus on my bending rod. I let the fish take a little more line, then close off the barrel. I've let him run enough. Now it's time to reel him in. I fight the fish with my hands off the rod handle as I push the rod up towards the sky. When the tip is high in the air, I start dropping the tip, reeling in the slack line furiously, before the fish can bolt away with it.

"Anchor's up," Logan screams as I fight to lift the tip of the rod.

"Thanks," I say. I try to laugh but all that comes out are a few low huffs. My arms are burning and I still haven't gotten a single glimpse of the fish.

I reel in again, but something feels wrong. The weight is gone. The line is slack.

"Crap!" I scream. "He cut the line! We lost him!"

Logan runs to my side. "How did that happen? Did I do something wrong?"

I sigh, hoping he can't see the sadness in my eyes. "No, it just happens sometimes. When the fish goes under a piece of coral or something. It's okay. We'll get the next one," I say.

Only the next one is small and skinny, barely a foot long. I debate throwing him back into the water, but Logan convinces me to keep him.

"If no one catches anything big, this could be the winner," he says, but I know he doesn't believe it. It's hard to think of this fish as much more than a piece of bait.

The sun beats down on our backs as it rises higher in the sky. I start the motor and move us farther down the beach, letting the skiff drift straight into a new bed of weeds. "Hopefully this will work better," I say. "Tides moving again, the fishing should pick up."

Only the fish don't seem ready to eat. I make out a school of shrimp near the surface, but they're just drifting calmly. No fear or worry from any large fish below. I tie on a new jig – one of the pink ones I bought last week – and cast it into the weeds.

The rod bends down fast, then pops up toward the sky.

A hit.

But no fish.

Whatever it was is gone. Before I can even set the hook.

Logan sees the frustration building on my face and walks over next to me. Asks if I want him to cast a line. Let me rest in the bow. We've already got one bonefish, even if he's small. Maybe that will be enough. Maybe the fish aren't biting anywhere today.

"Give me ten more minutes here," I say. "If we don't get anything on this next cast, we should head off to a new spot. Maybe try that cove near Rosalie's. We've had some luck there."

Logan nods, not saying what's on both of our minds. That we're hours into the tournament now and any fish that were in that cove have probably been either caught or spooked by the other boats. If we can't get a prizewinner here, the chances of us catching one somewhere else are low.

But Logan doesn't say it and neither do I. We ignore it just as we ignore everything that's happened in the past few days. There's too much on the line today for idle talk. And the tournament is too important to be saying negative thoughts out loud.

The next cast falls in a clearing between two clumps of weeds. From the boat, the bottom looks sandy. But no shimmer of silver catches my eye. The tip of my rod stays upright. The line remains slack.

"Just one more try," I say as the jig reaches the surface. "Last one, I promise."

"Take your time," Logan says. "I'll stay here all day if you think it's worth it."

"Maybe just a little longer. They've just got to be here. They have to. I refuse to believe I lost the only fish of the day..."

"I'm sure you didn't."

"I hope not," I say, casting again. This time I miss the weeds, casting instead in the slightly deeper water. I curse under my breath and prepare to reel it in and try again.

But when I go to reel, the rod tip bends. And the line feels heavy.

Real heavy.

"Logan, oh my God! I think I have something! Huge!"

"Really? A fish? You think it could be a bonefish?"

"I don't know! Grab the net, grab the gaff, get ready for some action. We're not losing this one. No matter what!"

I open up the reel's barrel and let out a little line. Then I close the barrel and fight the fish like I did the last one, lifting the rod tip up, then reeling in the slack line as I lower it.

My arms shake. My breath is hot and shallow. I scream to Logan for water. He pours half a bottle in my mouth, and the other half on the reel to cool it down.

"This...fish...feels...massive," I say, reeling in the slack line. This time, I try not to think about exact weights or size. Or what that all could mean. Instead I focus on lifting rod, then reeling the line. Tiring out the fish. Before he can tire me out.

But my arms are really stinging now, and on the skiff there's no fighting chair where you can sit down and really dig in your feet. So instead I keep walking back and forth, bending my knees and reeling and grunting and praying that this is it.

The fish fights too. Every single reel. He jumps once, showing off his silver scales and a thick, gray head.

"Oh wow, Piper, this is it! You've got a bonefish!"

"Yes! We're going to get this one!" I reel harder, faster, worrying less about lifting the tip of the rod and more about bringing the fish in.

Logan hovers over me, the gaff in his hands.

I give the reel one last turn, then back away from the side. "He's right by the boat, ready for you to gaff him."

"This sucker's all mine." Logan swoops down with

the metal hook and gets him on the first try. He gaffs him right through the gills and lifts him into the skiff. Just like a professional.

"Jesus! Look at him, he's huge, Logan, huge! It's the biggest bonefish I've ever seen!" I'm crying now and not even trying to stop the tears gushing out of my eyes. I bend down to the fish and remove the hook. The rod free, I throw it toward the bow, never taking my eyes off the fish.

"Should...should we get him into the fish well?" asks Logan.

"Uh, yeah, let's do that," I say, "But let's weigh him first."

Logan runs to the stern and grabs the scale. We hook it through the fish's gills like a gaff and lift it up. The scale chirps, then registers the maximum weight. 15 pounds.

"Oh my God," I say, "This baby could be the winner! 15 pounds for a bonefish is crazy! It's massive! We did it, Logan, we did it!"

"Hey, I didn't do anything. I'm nothing but a spectator."

Then Logan kisses me, his lips firm and salty. His lips set mine on fire and I kiss him back, as all the pain and hurt from the past few days vanishes. We stay there, bound together, until the fish beats his tail against the boat.

"We better get him in the fish well. Don't want to

lose him," I say, breaking away.

Logan runs the gaff through its gills one more time and lifts him into the well. The fish is so long that it barely fits in the largest well on the boat. Even if there was no tournament, even if this was a normal fishing trip on a normal day, this baby would be a prize.

I run to the center console and grab my phone from its plastic bag, eager to tell Mom and Dad about the catch. Only out on Lignumvitae, the cell signal is weak. The call fails. Leaving Logan and me to celebrate in secret.

We throw down the anchor and take a quick swim, dunking and splashing each other until we wither up like prunes. Then with the sun hanging low over the water, we pull the anchor and head back to Rosalie's. Most of the boats are already back when we arrive at the docks. I tie up the skiff while Logan fills a garbage bag with our catch. Together, we jump onto the dock and climb the ramp to the weigh station.

The area surrounding the scale is buzzing. There's a huge crowd of fishermen waiting to have their catch weighed. An even larger bunch of bystanders is talking wildly. Apparently about Wyatt Jacoby. And some monster catch.

A monster? My heart sinks. Could he really have done better than us?

Through the crowd, I hear Dad's voice. "Piper!

Logan! You're back!" He pushes aside one of Wyatt Jacoby's cameramen and runs up to our side. "How'd it go guys? Catch anything big? I tried to call a few times, but you know how signal can be out there..."

"We did great," I say. "How about you guys?"

Dad smiles, turning to Mom. "We had a really good time, didn't we? Biggest fish we caught was 10 pounds. I thought we might have a chance with that one too, only it seems that Wyatt Jacoby once again has outdone us. He's got a fish up there that's over 17 pounds! Can you believe it? That's close to world record size!"

My stomach turns. "Seventeen pounds? Crap!" I wipe my eyes and look away, trying to stop myself from crying.

Mom reaches out to pat my back. "Oh honey, it's okay. No one would ever expect you to catch a 17-pounder. That's insane, there's only a few bonefish in the ocean that are even that big. And besides, with all those cameramen and publicists and fishing buddies that guy has out there with him all the time, I wouldn't be surprised if he's doing something to cheat."

"But, Mom... you don't understand," I say, between sniffles. "We were so close. The scale in the boat maxed out at 15."

Mom gasps as Dad takes a step back. "Wait. Are you telling me you have a 15-pound fish in there?"

Logan opens the bag just wide enough for Dad to

stick in his head. "Jesus, Piper, why are you crying honey? Your scale only goes to 15 pounds. That means this fish could be bigger! You might've won! On a world-record size fish!" Dad's dancing now, flapping his hands like a pelican, whistling like a parakeet.

Before we can discuss it further, it's our turn on the scale. Logan grabs my baby by the gills and pulls him out of the bag.

"Here's Piper's prize," he says, handing it to the judges.

"Whoa, this is a beauty," one of them says. "This fish is massive. I think it might be longer than Wyatt's!"

"But is it as heavy?" yells out someone from the audience.

I bite my lip as the judges secure my fish on the scale. The digital numbers start flickering on the display. My head feels light. Dizzy. My forehead is throbbing. I grab onto Logan's shirt as the crowd erupts into cheers.

"Seventeen point two pounds!" yell the judges.

For a moment, everything goes black. Then Logan is shaking me and screaming and Dad's jumping up and down like a kid. "We have to get your mother! This is insane," he's yelling. There are tears in his eyes, too, and also in Logan's. I think of the $25,000 and three-minute interview the winner gets with ESPN and I almost faint again. We did it. Me and Logan. And Dad, of course. I scan the crowd, looking for Benny. But before I can really look, one of Wyatt Jacoby's crew members comes running. Holding Wyatt's fish.

"Here he is," he says, handing it over to the judges.

"Great, thanks," says the judge. Then he turns to the crowd. "Now since we have two fish that are basically the same size, we are going to weigh Wyatt's one more time. Whichever fish weighs more will be the winner!"

A chill runs down my spine as Wyatt's fish is placed on the scale. I look away from the crowd. Out at the harbor. At my skiff. Whatever happens, doesn't matter, I tell myself. I caught an awesome fish. With Logan. And that memory will always be mine. But even as I chant the words over and over in my head, they fall flat. Because right now I want to win. More than anything.

Wyatt's fish dangles for a moment while the digital scale settles on a number. As the scale stops moving, the crowd goes quiet. Even the pelicans stop honking.

"Seventeen point six pounds." The judge mumbles the words, sounding disappointed.

I bury my head in Logan's t-shirt and cry, big wet sloppy tears. My face is on fire. My knees shaking. All I want to do is go home. We've come in second place. They'll be no $25,000. No ESPN interview. Just a trophy. And a $500 gift certificate to the Bass Pro

Shop. Enough to get a couple rods. Maybe a new GPS. But not a boat.

Only right now, the crowd doesn't seem to care that my fish weighed four tenths less than Wyatt's. And Mom and Dad aren't even trying to console me. Because right now, everyone is cheering. No, they're screaming, actually. For me. And Dad's too busy running down to the boat for an extra Wesley's Charters t-shirt to care about second place.

The news crew descends on us just as Dad gets me the t-shirt. "Do I look okay?" I ask Logan as I throw it over my head.

"Gorgeous," he says. "Now no more crying. Right now you're the star."

The *Key West Citizen* gets to me first. They ask me how long I've been fishing. Where I caught today's monster. Why I thought to try Lignumvitae, an island known more for its botany than fishing. I give the truth – well, most of it – leaving out the parts about my reconnaissance, but talking freely about my love of the ocean. How I've spent years learning the behaviors, and quirks, of the bonefish.

Keys Weekly asks me about the t-shirt and Dad's charter business. I talk about my time helping out around the docks, and how I know the waters better than I know the land. They ask if I have any advice for other young aspiring fisherwomen and I say just to work smart. And go with your gut. Sometimes you just have to trust your instincts, even if you think it could be wrong. I turn to Logan and smile on this, thankful that he's here. That he camped out on the Whaler. And that we got a second chance.

My hands shake through the first two interviews, then start to relax just as a paper from Miami approaches. I smile, excited to talk to them. But out of the corner of my eye, I see something. Or someone, moving toward us. Now my knees begin to shake as his face comes into focus. Because it's Benny, with a big smile on his face. Ready to congratulate me.

CHAPTER TWENTY-FOUR

"Benny!" I yell across the crowd.

He waves. Jogs over. Looking nervous, but moving like nothing's wrong. And it's in that moment, as he dusts off his shorts and takes off his sunglasses that I know we'll be okay.

Maybe not the same as before. But better.

"Hey," he says, catching up with me as I dodge another reporter. "I've been trying to get to you guys ever since you came in, but you've been swarmed."

"Yeah, I know," I say.

"Well congratulations," Benny says, turning to Logan. "Were, you, uh there today?"

Logan nods. "Lucky for me Piper let me come

along."

"Yeah, we talked this morning. Worked a few things out."

Benny nods, then looks down and for a moment my throat runs dry as I think of how me and Benny still have so much to figure out.

"Well I always knew you could do it, Pipes," Benny says, still looking away.

"Hey, you're still a part of this victory, too. I mean, you did put in a lot of practice," I say, trying to bring him back.

"You mean a lot of time complaining about the weeds."

"Something like that."

Benny smiles, then shoves his hands in his pockets and looks away.

"Hey, you okay, man?" Logan asks.

"Yeah, I'm fine."

"You know, you haven't been permanently replaced," I say, reading Benny's eyes as they scan the horizon. "The old skiff we fixed up, it's big enough for three people. Even during tournaments."

Again Benny smiles, but his eyes still look sad. "Thanks Pipes, that means a lot. Though I think my days of fishing are over, at least for a while anyway. You and Logan, you're a good team. No sense in disrupting that."

"Well if you ever change your mind, we can always

use another boat handler."

"Or someone who knows how to work a net," says Logan. "I still don't know how you always get them on the first try. It usually takes me closer to ten."

"Believe me, after one off season with Piper, you'll never miss again."

"Uh-oh, it's that bad?" Logan asks.

"Let's just say Piper likes to win," Benny says, "and she doesn't let you forget it."

"Hey, I'm not that bad," I say, bringing my hands to my hips.

And we all laugh, deep belly laughs that cause us all to double over in pain. But it's good pain. As if with each heave of my stomach, I'm healing myself. Scarring over old wounds. Becoming just a little bit stronger.

I reach for Logan's hand just as Benny backs away, ready to say his goodbyes and continue back on to Oswardo's to help his parents with the dinner rush. It's the first I've heard of him clocking any real time with Mrs. Benitez in months, and I have to say I'm glad to hear it, even if I do know he'll be missing quite the party.

Benny heads off toward the parking lot as the clouds above swirl orange and purple overhead. We follow him to the small footbridge before pausing to look for the stingray that once got stuck.

"He must have made it out," I say to Logan, "and

learned not to come back."

He laughs. "Guess he was smart. This island is nothing but trouble."

I giggle back, just as Mom and Dad break from the crowd, their faces glistening with sweat and excitement.

"Anything in the ditch?" Dad asks, already peering down at the water.

"Not today," I say.

"Then I guess everything is where it should be," Mom says, wrapping her arm around my shoulders.

I smile and hug her back, just as the band starts counts down to its first song.

"Should we go join the crowd?" Dad asks, already tapping his foot to the beat. "We've already scoped out a table."

"Sounds like a plan," I say.

I turn back toward Rosalie's just as Logan taps my back.

"Wait a sec, is that Sardi? Running through the parking lot? In heels?"

I spin around to find Sardi running on her toes, her six inch heels perched just centimeters from the ground, with Travis following a good ten feet behind.

"Piper, hey, wait! Don't leave!" she yells.

"Hey, what's going on?" My stomach starts twisting, afraid to confront another disaster.

"It's your turtles!" Sardi yells between breaths.

"They're hatching! We just came from Becco. There's a whole crew of people there to help too."

My mouth falls open as I turn to Logan. "Did you hear that? The turtles are alive!"

"Of course they are, I knew they'd be okay," he says, but from his tone I can tell he's just as surprised as I am.

"Dad, can we go? I know we're supposed to go to Rosalie's, but we've been taking care of these turtles all summer and it's the first nest we've seen in years..."

He cuts me off before I can finish. "Everyone to the truck, there's no way we're missing this!"

We start running before the words finish leaving Dad's mouth, reaching the truck in seconds, only to find the car filled with tackle boxes, coolers and a cache of fishing rods.

"Looks like we'll need to use the bed," Mom says as she inches into the driver's seat. "There's barely room for me in here."

"No worries, we're fine," I say, already anticipating another shriek from Sardi.

And sure enough, the idea of riding in back excites Sardi so much that she starts squealing, and climbing and begging Travis for help just as Dad runs over to join us.

With everyone secure, Mom takes off toward the Becco Lodge. The air feels cool and dewy as we pick up speed and my hair starts flying in all directions.

Sardi starts educating me on the importance of hair elastics, then stops long enough to congratulate me on my finish. "Second place! Wow, I heard there are fishermen who fish their whole lives and don't get that. The fish you caught must have been huge! Just huge! It's such a shame though you lost to Wyatt Jacoby. But then again, you know he is the best..."

She continues talking rapid fire, her high-pitched voice roaring at full speed.

"So you won't even believe the scene at Becco right now," she says, her hands a flutter, "It's just nuts there, just nuts. Right Travis? Isn't it nuts?"

Travis nods. "Uh yeah, there's a lot of people, from this turtle group. Turtle Save?"

"You mean Turtle Watch," I say.

"Yeah, that's it!" Sardi says. "How'd you know? They're all wearing these Turtle Watch t-shirts and according to Marina, they've been there all day. They're staying at Becco too. The hotel is packed. Completely full! It hasn't been this crazy there in months! Maybe years!"

"Wow, that's great," I say, folding my arms over and over in my lap, hoping that she doesn't ask more questions about how I knew the group was Turtle Watch. Or figure out that I called them. Not that it should be a secret. Calling in the group was really necessary, for the turtles. But at the same time, I don't want Sardi figuring out that part of the reason for calling was about Marina. And bringing some attention to Becco.

Luckily, Sardi is so lost in her own conversation, that she's already forgotten the name of the rescue group by the time Dad interrupts her. Sardi might not be too perceptive, but Dad is.

"I'm glad someone got the professionals down to help," he says, staring at me. "They should do a good job making sure the turtles make it to the water. I wonder if they'll tag them, too, so we'll know if any of them come back."

"Oh yeah, they talked about tagging," says Sardi. "They are so excited, you should see it! They said this is the first nest on the island in five years! Can you believe it, it's been five years of no turtles!"

The truck slows as we turn into the main drive of Becco Lodge. Cars line the narrow road, parked all along the side. Mom inches forward into the main lot. It's overflowing. Not a free space in sight. She double parks behind a Becco Lodge van as we start pouring out.

"This way!" Sardi yells, pointing toward my hidden beach. A flood of emotion overtakes me as I remember all the time I've spent here over the past three months. Marina's bonfire. My first kiss. When Benny first bailed on me.

Logan grabs my hand and starts running before I

can dig any further.

"Slow down," I say, "I can't keep up."

"Come on! We don't want to miss it," he says.

The grasses hiding the beach have been mowed back when we arrive, giving way to caked sand and a plastic orange barrier that's been put up by Turtle Watch. Two workers are guarding the entrance, leading to the beach.

"Sorry, no one beyond this point. You can watch from the edge of the beach," says one. He points to a crowd that's gathered near the ocean. Marina and Benny are there, and Sardi and Travis are just joining them. There's a bunch of reporters, too, and what looks like the camera crew from Wyatt Jacoby's show. I start to walk toward them just as Dad taps my shoulder.

"Excuse me, but this is my daughter, Piper Wesley. She and Logan here, they're the ones that found the nest and called it in. They've been monitoring it all summer."

"Oh geez, I'm sorry, I had no idea. You two have done a great job, this nest is pristine! No animal tracks near it or anything. And you called just in time. We called one of our field workers to take a look this morning, and there were already signs of hatching. We got our crew down just in time."

I kick my feet through the sand, stopping when my toe hits a rock. "Yeah, I'm sorry we didn't call sooner."

"Nonsense, we're just happy you called at all. A lot of people might not have understood the significance. Imagine, the first Loggerhead nest in five years. Maybe the island is recovering after all."

"Yeah, maybe," I say.

The worker moves aside the orange fencing and lets me, Logan and Dad into the restricted area. "Just stay to the side and don't touch any of the turtles, okay?"

"Of course," Dad says as we line up next to the fence.

And then, time stands still. As the camera crews shoot and the field workers run to and fro tagging the baby turtles, we just stare. At the leathery hatchlings pushing themselves out of the sandy nest. At those a few minutes older, already inching towards the cresting waves. And then finally, the first hatchlings, those disappearing into the frothy water, ready to fight against the insurmountable odds that lie between this moment and their return. Only one or two of these turtles will live long enough to make it back. Only the surviving females ever will. But that doesn't stop these babies from trying. From dodging the sea gulls that the field workers can't scare away. From taking each tiny step farther, fighting against the sinking sand and strands of dried seaweed without any knowledge of what lies ahead. Only the determination to go on and fight. To survive.

As the waves fill with tiny turtles, I turn back to the nest, where the number of new hatchlings is slowing. There I see one just breaking free of the sand, his legs still covered with the remnants of his egg.

He raises his flipper-like legs and pushes back against the sand, reaching for the top of the nest. He pushes again and again until he lands on the summit.

There he stops, takes in the view. Lifts his little head to view the world. And then he's gone.

As if sensing the danger of the hovering bird above, he descends off the mounded nest quickly, his flippers moving even faster than before. Within seconds, he reaches a cluster of his siblings. He's safe. For now.

Without showing a single sign of panic or exhaustion, he moves forward with them, then bathes himself in the warm water of the ocean as a wave takes him up over the shoreline and into the great unknown. A tear falls down my cheek as I follow him, over one wave and then the next, until he drifts out of sight, his small green shell nothing more than a dot in the dark, inky water.

"I hope he makes it," I say to Logan.

He grabs my hand and squeezes. "I guarantee you that one will. He'll do exactly what he's meant to, I'm sure of it."

The field workers take down the orange fence as the last of the babies reach the water. We file back to the crowd, where Mom and Nick and the others are waiting.

Benny reaches us first, already apologizing for how hard he was on me about the turtles. I smile and tell him it's okay, happy that with each word, he's sounding a little more like my friend. Mom and Dad let us talk for a while, but before Benny finishes, they're telling me it's time to go. It's been a long day. And a long night. And we still haven't even had dinner. So I start to say goodbye to Logan, who grabs my arm before I can go.

"Can I come with you?" he asks. "You know, so we can fill your parents in on all the tournament details?"

I smile. "Sure, let's go," I say, then we wave to the group and start walking, past the bonfire and small guest cottage and the smells and sights of summer.

Marina catches up to us in the parking lot. I hadn't even noticed before now, but she was definitely not talking to Benny. Maybe they really did break up. Maybe he was just here to be nice. Or maybe because of me. More likely it was to tell her about the fishing tournament, and tell her how me and Logan almost won. So as she opens her mouth, I'm prepared, ready to thank her for her congratulations. But like usual, Marina takes me by surprise.

She grabs my arm and squeezes. "Thank you," she says. "For everything. The hotel is full, and the team here is staying for a week. They're making plans to come back again soon, too, to look for more nests. Looks like we're finally on the map."

"You're welcome," I mouth, before jumping into the truck and waving goodbye.

"See you next week at school," she says, as we pass by.

EPILOGUE

"Did you see Benny today in Gym? He looked pretty banged up, guess that football's taking a lot out of him," says Logan, grinning as we walk down the side of the road. It's October now, but the sun is just as strong. It beats down on our backpack-covered shoulders, weighed down by the books and binders nestled inside.

I place my thumbs between the straps and give my back a rest. Only two more blocks to home. "Yeah, that black eye did look pretty nasty. Are you sure you don't miss it?" I tease.

"Oh yeah. Black eyes were the best," he says. "Truth is I think Nick misses it more than I do. He used to really like going to the games. But once I told him I was using this year to get ready for next year's bonefish tournaments, and that there were more than twenty five we could enter, well that shut him up. Football was great, but fishing has prize money."

I laugh. "Exactly. I'm so glad he and your mom decided to stay down here, even after his assignment ended."

"You and me both," he says, grinning, "I think your dad had a lot to do with it, the way he was so nice after what he did to him. But then, he also claims he's got some new venture down here with Expedition in the works, so who knows what's up."

"Very true, though this time, you better not be involved," I say, not wanting to think about any more of Nick's ventures.

As we reach my house, I open the gate, letting me and Logan inside. Liggy is waiting for us, her water bowl perpetually empty. I reach for the hose as Logan turns on the faucet.

"You really need to get her a water cooler," he says. "Who knew deer could drink so much?"

"Seriously. Ever since we started school she's been acting like she's been abandoned."

Logan laughs as I reach for the key, then push the door open with my side. It's Mom's day volunteering at Theater of the Sea, so I run into the office off the main hall and boot up the computer, ready to check for any urgent charter requests before slipping into my bathing suit and heading down to the docks with Logan. It's our new routine now that school's in session, me and Logan stopping in, then going off to practice. Usually he'll chat with Mom – who's been super busy booking appointments ever since the Scramble – and grab a snack while I change into my suit. Then we'll repeat a similar process at his house and head down to the docks.

"I think there's some Key Lime pie in the fridge," I say as the computer whirs to life, a screen of unread emails greeting me.

"Sweet, my favorite," he says. I hear the fridge door open followed by the cabinet drawers as I sift through the messages, deleting the spam and placing the charter requests into a folder for Mom to follow up with later.

"Hey, cut me a slice, will you?" I say, as the list dwindles.

"Already done." He walks into the office and slides over a plate. Grabbing the fork, I dig in.

As I take the first bite, something catches my eye. It's one of the emails toward the top of the heap. At first it looks no different than any of the other messages we receive. Only this one, its subject line is addressed to me.

"Hey Logan, check this out," I say, clicking on the message.

He walks around the desk as the message loads.

And then I see the header. From the Expedition Channel.

"Oh my God," I say. "Oh my God!"

"What is it?" Logan asks.

"It's the Expedition Channel. It's from the producer from Wyatt Jacoby's show. And look here, your dad is cc'd. He wants me to call or email him right away. They want to talk about a series idea, right down here in Islamorada. They want me to...to...be the star!"

Logan drops a forkful of Key Lime pie onto the ground.

"Holy crap," he says. "Talk about a new venture! I can't believe Nick didn't tell me about this! Are you sure it's real? What does it say?"

"Only that the special episode of Wyatt's show on the Bonefish Scramble was a huge hit. It got them the highest ratings the show's ever gotten. And that Nick thinks there's real potential for a show that follows a local. It says here they're even willing to work around my school schedule!"

I push back the chair from the desk and stand. Before I know it, I'm jumping up and down, giddy with excitement. Logan grabs my hand and joins in, each of us wailing and yelling until our throats are sore and dry. "I need to tell my parents! And Benny! We need to get down to the docks!" I say, my arms a shaking mess.

"And we need to thank Nick!"

We race out of the house without cleaning our dishes and take off toward Rosalie's.

Yet as my head starts to clear, I find myself a little nervous. A show would sure help Wesley's Charters, but what about the fish? And my reconnaissance? Could I really give all those secrets away? The ones I tried so hard to protect? And that Wyatt almost stole?

I slow my gait, turning to Logan, whose face is still one big smile.

"Hey, you all right?" he asks, brushing the hair out of my eyes.

And that's when I see it, glistening in Logan's eyes. Turtle Watch descending on the beach just in time. Logan, learning to fish and love the island just like me. And Benny, finally realizing that it's better to struggle than profit with a lie. All made possible because of secrets I didn't keep.

So I squeeze Logan's hand tight and smile back. "Yeah, everything's fine," I say.

And together, we run down the road hand in hand, overtaken with laughter. And I find myself smiling, excited by the possibility that maybe this show is what we need to really save the island. Maybe it's time to share my secrets. And hope that something good is waiting up ahead.